ISBN -13: 978-1719467971
© PJ Shann 2018

# THE 2nd HORROR SHORT STORY COLLECTION

### BY

## Jim Mullaney

*Stories Never End*

# *<u>Contents</u>*

*I kicked off my first short story collection by saying that I believed every writer of horror should have one short vampire tale in them. Well, as this is now my second story to feature bloodsuckers — and as there will quite probably be at least one more to come, perhaps in Volume 3 — it appears that I may have drastically underestimated their hold on my imagination. I don't know why I should be so surprised by this development. I have always loved vampires. So dark, so cool, so resilient to the passage of time and ever-changing literary fads... They're not called the Undead for nothing.*

A kid giving his stepmother's Pomeranian its morning drag through the sand found the fifth victim.

At first, from a distance with the sun in his eyes, the boy thought that it was a bum sleeping off a drinking jag, and then, when he got a little closer and saw the long chestnut hair, that it was maybe some party girl who'd got too wasted to know better than to spend the night on the beach.

The fresh morning breeze skimming in off the Atlantic had half-covered the body with Indian Harbour Beach's fine, white sand, but the few revealed parts of her paler-than-pale anatomy finally drew the kid closer than he might otherwise have ventured. His reward was an ample portion of shapely rear, and the side of a firm-looking, hefty breast, with just a hint of nipple.

The kid was thirteen-going-on-thirty-one and certainly wasn't averse to copping a free eyeful when he could get it. But when he got close enough to see the girl in even more detail, he began to seriously doubt the true extent of his curiosity.

For one thing, he wasn't happy with the way his stepmother's mutt was suddenly hanging back and acting so antsy, just like the time a 'gator had taken up residence in their neighbour's pool. Furthermore, the chick in the sand wasn't moving at all, not at all. He couldn't even see her breathing.

He took another couple of faltering steps toward the girl, finally saw one fixed, staring brown eye with a fine dusting of sand clinging to the dull retina, and then he knew for sure he was looking at something with all the life of a leg of lamb in a Costco chiller cabinet.

Just as he was about to turn away and look for help, the breeze changed direction like an out-going tide and the sand moved a little and revealed the girl's slender neck — her neck and the awful gouging bites that had so badly disfigured it — and then the boy panicked and started to run away, the dog at his heels, barking crazily.

Bo eased his way through the throngs of people populating South Beach's colourful nightlife, searching for that certain special someone.

She was here, close by, he could tell.

He could feel the tiniest impulses of her body and mind, as though she were a fly trapped in the web of his thoughts. All he had to do was follow the vibrating threads, and sooner rather than later, he would have his meal.

A large man dressed in hilarious vacation pastels gave him an uncommonly sharp glance as Bo slid by him on Ocean Drive, and Bo, almost without thought, sent him a small, but potent, distraction — an image of the man himself, his pockets stuffed with money, a gorgeous blonde on his arm — and his curiosity was instantly diverted by the fantasy. No more problems there, no more threat.

Some people saw more clearly than others, that was all, but they were generally easy to blindside. Simple mental suggestions usually did the trick, the more simplistic and clichéd the better.

If that didn't work... Well, if that didn't work, then there were always other, less subtle ways to turn the trick.

The Floridian night was full of music and life, full of beautiful young people at play, eating, drinking, flirting and loving in the humid heat. Bo turned a corner and saw her instantly, the one he'd been searching for. She was a blonde, tall and slim and beautiful, and he was amused to note that she bore more than a passing resemblance to the image he had used to distract the man in pastels.

Funny how precognition could still take you by surprise.

The girl was standing in a knot of other attractive, scantily-dressed girls on the sidewalk outside a packed bar, all sipping cocktails and all talking animatedly at the same time, like a flock of exotic birds sharing a telephone line.

Now that he could see her, Bo could also smell her.

He could smell her perfume and her deodorant and her cosmetics and her shampoo and toothpaste and the lemon juice she'd used to lighten her hair and the wax she'd used on her legs and her bikini-line... and under all that seductive modern-day camouflage, he could smell the essential primitive essence of her; the oil oozing from her pores and the salt-smack of her perspiration, the tidal surge of her breath sweetened by its passage through her healthy body, and the clean fresh smell of her youthful sex.

Most of all, he could smell the tantalising tang of the rich blood racing just beneath the surface of her smooth, supple skin.

Bo had a momentary flashback to the good-old/bad-old days, the grand old days of barbarism and wanton excess.

He saw his own hand moving across a young body much like the girl's, with the same beautiful, flawless skin, saw it leaving her throat, tracing the contours of her full breasts. He saw his thumbnail tracing a razor-thin red line over a tight little belly and down into a soft tangle of fragrant pubic hair, and he saw the flesh part as her torso opened up like a side of beef under a butcher's knife...

Ah, but those times were now long gone. They were ancient times, although sometimes they seemed so close.

But so much else had changed.

Tonight's victim wore a tiny gold wristwatch aligned with satellites to keep perfect time and powered by the kinetic energy generated by her own body's movement, and almost her entire understanding of the world came through social media. Yesterday's victim had told the time by the sun's position in the heavens, and believed witches rode broomsticks across moonlit skies with their cat-familiars tucked up behind them.

It was a strange kind of existence, walking through time, hand-in-hand with human ignorance.

He began to move towards the girl, and when he was halfway there he gave her a tiny suggestive psychic nudge, and she turned to look at him.

Her name was Megan.

He saw himself through her eyes for a moment, and saw a tall, handsome young man with dark brown hair and electric-blue eyes, wearing a black shirt and pants. A man with all the confidence in the world, a man who moved through that world with the self-assurance of a prince, the muscular poise of a panther.

Despite her blonde hair, the girl was naturally olive-skinned and had tanned well. He was white-skinned, and in places his flesh shone like mother of pearl. They were natural physical opposites, and opposites, she firmly believed, attracted.

Bo, still inside Megan's mind, felt her irises expand, her heart beat faster, and blood race to harden her nipples and swell the saddle of tender flesh between her legs.

This one was so ripe and ready he hardly had to press any of her buttons at all. It was her good luck that Bo had been the one to find her tonight, rather than one of the many other, more natural predators out there. Pastel man, for example.

She absently handed her drink to one of her friends, who accepted it equally absently, and stepped off the sidewalk to meet him. He was careful to make sure that not one of her companions noticed anything specific about him they would later remember.

'My hotel room?' she asked when they met, as though this were the culmination of a long, intimate conversation and not the beginning of one, and Bo simply nodded.

He couldn't smile back. She had begun to excite him and his canines were already dangerously long.

In the room, Megan turned on a lamp, kicked off her high-heel pumps, and then nervously turned to face him. Music from the tourist drag far below filtered up on the gentle ocean breeze.

She was about to explain to him that she had never done anything this impulsive before in her life, that she'd only been with a few men so far, that she believed in safe-sex, that she liked things to go nice and slow and steady, that she liked tender kisses and firm but gentle hands, and that she wasn't interested in anything weird or kinky. None of that Fifty Shades business for her, thank you.

Bo stepped forward and silenced her with a small shake of the head, and then he began to undress her.

It took only seconds, but the sure, infallible movement of his hands captivated her immediately, like hypnotism. His fingers on the straps of her silk dress, hooking them over her tawny shoulders, smoothing the sheer material down over her hips so that it whispered down her legs to the floor, and then

6

curling an arm around her waist to lift her out of the puddle of silk.

He felt her thrill at the effortless display of his strength. Her panties were also silken, matching the colour of her short dress, and they were already soaked through. Bo could have laid her down on the bed and slipped into her without a single second of foreplay, and the girl was so juicy and lush that he would have done so without hesitation.

If he had been a man. If he had been human.

Instead, he clasped her tighter to his chest, crushing her small firm breasts against the unyielding shelf of his chest, and a small moan of pleasure escaped her parted lips. She wrapped her legs around his body and began to grind against his hip, unable to resist the powerful pleasure impulses he was transmitting in an ascending wave-pattern, spiralling up and up to a soaring peak.

Megan closed her eyes, her mind a whirl of thoughts he could taste on his psychic palate like spices: *my friends will never believe this, I'll never tell my boyfriend this happened, I've never felt this way about anyone this fast, it has never felt this good with anyone else...*

Bo brought his hand up to cup the back of her head and they began to kiss, their tongues entwined and writhing with fevered passion, and whenever the girl's tongue entered his mouth, his sharp white teeth made a series of long, deep slits in her tender, vulnerable flesh.

The painkilling qualities of his inhuman saliva masked even the smallest pain, and worked to repair the damage almost instantly. But in the brief moment of time each wound was open, a tiny amount of precious, satisfying blood was seized and absorbed by his system. He could feel it at work inside him already, saturating and replenishing his cells.

It was a fractional amount of nourishment, but that was all Bo needed these days, a gentle top-up after all the great bloodlusts of the distant past.

In all, the feeding took just five or six minutes, sweet young Megan eventually thrashing against him as she reached her largely self-induced orgasm, and then losing consciousness in his arms.

He laid her carefully on her bed, licked the last few streaks of blood from her open lips, and sighed. Her blood, like the rest of her, was delicious. If he had been a greedy vampire, he might have stayed for more. If he had been a cruel vampire, he might have drained her as far as death and left her to rot. If he had been a less principled vampire, he might have ravaged her sexually... but he was what he was.

An original. One of a kind.

Lawman of the Undead.

He stayed for just a few moments longer to sooth the girl, his hand resting on her smooth brow, his thumb settled in the shallow hollow of her temple. He sent her a few choice images and sensations to augment her real memories.

She'd recall a much longer encounter, with many wonderfully erotic moments, including the tenderness she ultimately craved. When she woke up she'd have no regrets and no after-effects, aside from a deep feeling of relief that she'd been a very naughty girl and got away with it without any unpleasant repercussions.

8

This was the best way for his species to exist now, Bo reckoned — *carefully*.

Very carefully indeed, for most of the world's deeper shadows had already been vanquished by human technology, and true hiding places were scarce. This was the 21st century and the wise vampire covered his tracks well, and tried his damnedest to reduce his haemoglobin footprint as he moved through the world.

Unfortunately, not every vampire believed the same things that Bo did, and then there was trouble.

Trouble that he had to deal with.

The Black Widow lived in the White House, a large stucco and red-tile mansion which stood in its own high-walled compound and had the appearance of a foreign embassy in an action movie. As Bo approached the gates, he allowed the heels of his shoes to strike the pavement, politely forewarning the vampire guard of his presence.

As soon as he heard, the guard vanished from his post thirty paces away and reappeared only inches from Bo, forcing him to stop moving. The guard was grinning like a lunatic and his breath smelled like an abattoir.

He was Newborn, of course, and so fresh you could still smell the human on him. This was no great surprise. The Black Widow was notorious for making Newborn servants from attractive young men, and equally notorious for feasting upon them the very moment they ceased to please her eye, or no longer served her purpose.

It had always amused Bo that not one of them ever seemed to ask themselves how the Widow had come by her unsettling sobriquet before it was too late for the answer to save them.

'What...' the Newborn said, then vanished and reappeared at his original position by the gate.

'...do...'

Now he was standing atop the high stone wall that surrounded his mistress's property.

'...you...'

Now he stood directly behind Bo, his lips and bare fangs a nip away from Bo's ear.

'...want?'

Now he was back in front of Bo again, grinning, a vicious challenge in his eyes.

Bo casually glanced around, glad that the White House was situated in a quiet, supremely private section of Coral Gables, far away from the thronging bars and clubs of the Miracle Mile, and there had been nobody to see the Newborn's immature display of his powers.

Newborns always seemed to be frantic to demonstrate just how much of a vampire they were. This one had probably been only nineteen- or twenty-years-old when the Widow made him, and had maybe lived only a handful of months in his life as an undead being. He was still overwhelmed with himself.

If by some miracle he lived long enough, the guard would most likely learn better manners and hopefully a little common sense. The powers of mature vampires, the Alphas, were far, far greater than the Newborn, but they rarely used them when there was any chance they could be observed. In fact, most Alphas preferred to appear as human as possible at all times.

It saved an awful lot of trouble in the long run, and the long run was what being a successful vampire was all about.

'What...'

Bo groaned to himself. It seemed that the arrogant Newborn was about to run through his newly-mastered repertoire again, but Bo had already passed his tolerance-quota for the evening.

'I'm here to see the Widow,' he said.

'*Are* you?' the Newborn asked, with a mocking little cock of the head that made Bo want to rip it off. Instead he took a deep breath, and then began again.

'She'll want to see me.'

'*Will* she?'

'The name's Bo.'

'*Is* it?' The Newborn laughed in his face. 'Really? Bo, as in B-O? As in Body Odour?'

'That's right.'

'As in Big Orifice? As in Blood O—'

The Newborn seemed to choke on his words as he realised exactly who he was speaking to.

His face had suddenly lost its last vestiges of colour, and Bo could feel the young vampire's heart frantically pumping his stolen blood and beating like a snare drum. He was radiating fear and awe in equal measures. His fangs had entirely retracted, and he looked young and vulnerable and somehow emasculated.

Bo almost felt sorry for him.

This one wouldn't even put up a fight when the Widow came to suck him dry, Bo thought. He'd look at the Widow's seductive outer shell and see a girl not that much older than he himself had been in life, a young woman barely out of her teens. He wouldn't see the vicious, amoral, merciless butcher of thousands, the unrepentant murderer of helpless innocents, whose bloody existence had spanned centuries.

Not until she had him helpless and she *chose* to let him see, that was.

Not until it was too late.

'Take me to her now,' he commanded.

The last time Bo had been in the Widow's Florida home, a decade or more ago, it had been full of human beings, attractive young creatures much like the girl he had fed from earlier. Every six months or so the Widow threw a wild, extravagant party to which only the young and beautiful were invited, and she presided over them all like the queen she would so dearly love to be.

In life she had been pale-skinned and red-haired, a delicate beauty from the colder climes of Northern Europe, and of course she still looked that way. But her cool and remote beauty concealed a ravening, pathologically greedy monster.

He stepped down into the Widow's sunken lounge, a large airy circular room built of marble, with a domed glass ceiling high above that allowed a full, uninterrupted view of the heavens, all the constellations bright and visible. In the daytime the lounge would be a natural suntrap, saturated with golden sunlight, but of course it was a room that the house's residents would never use during the day.

Now the enormous space was lit only by a series of small flickering sconces, equidistantly spaced along the curved wall. The seating area was dominated by three huge, purpose-built crimson leather sofas, curved to match exactly the shape of the room they occupied. Light from the wall sconces lapped over the furniture like flame.

Although they were currently empty, Bo had often seen the sofas filled with intoxicated and drugged human beings. Humans having sex. Humans being bled out like cattle. Humans dying, sometimes in ecstasy, sometimes in agony, and sometimes in a terrible mixture of the two states.

The Widow had always been very fond of her entertainments. In fact, it had been her dangerous habit of parading herself before human beings that had first brought her to Bo's attention.

In the year 1911, while posing as an émigré from the music halls of London, England, the Widow had been appearing in the vaudeville theatres up and down the East Coast under the stage-name of Lilly Greenleaf. There she had quickly established a reputation as an amazingly accomplished and graceful dancer, as well as a singer of astonishing range and power, whose performances literally enchanted her audiences.

Bo, returning from a long peacekeeping tour of the Far East, had missed her in New Hampshire, New York and Delaware, but had eventually caught up to her when she moved west, to California. When he did find her and had discovered the details of her latest scheme, even he — with all his experience and his research into her bloody history under other identities — had been shocked by the scale of her ambitions.

By her appetite for attention, by her craving for visibility.

In the city of Los Angeles, she had captivated a certain human being, one of the foremost technical pioneers of the rapidly developing motion-picture industry, who had filmed almost a dozen screen-tests of the Widow after she had painstakingly painted her entire face and body, like a Roman or Greek statue, to a garish facsimile of life.

Bo had witnessed the shocking, yet fascinating results of the experiment for himself, as the filmmaker, by then a mindless slave to Bo's mesmeric will, first laced and then ran the projector.

Encapsulated within her thick shell of make-up, the Widow had paraded herself before the camera, effortlessly pantomiming sorrow, joy, surprise and fear with a perfect but heartless accuracy. She looked almost human, apart from her eyes, of course, which were invisible to the film's chemical emulsion. The grotesque hollows left behind seemed bottomless, and the black emptiness within revealed the malignant abyss inside the souls of all vampires, rendering the entire charade pointless.

The filmmaker, Bo learned from searching his mind, had been commanded to have a number of contact lenses made in an attempt to overcome this problem. But that was never going to happen.

After the impromptu premiere was over, Bo immediately slaughtered the filmmaker and burned his Inglewood home and workshop to the ground.

Then he had gone to confront the Widow in her lair, and to offer her the choice he had offered so many others throughout the centuries: either an eternity of anonymity in the shadows, or a swift and immediate destruction.

The Widow had chosen wisely: eternity.

But then she had taken his hand, and then kissed it, and Bo, alone for so many years and more desperate for companionship than he had known, had allowed her to seduce him.

He sat down now and considered the circular table at the centre of the sofas.

Dark, old wood, a table older than the Constitution of this young country, and upon it a wide circular bowl of beaten bronze, filled with fresh oranges. He picked one up, ran a thumbnail around the fruit's dappled circumference and then watched it fall neatly in two on his palms, as though halved by the keenest blade. The layer of yellow pith looked like the layer of fat that lay under human skin, and the pulp was deepest orange, streaked though with veins and clots of dark crimson.

They were blood oranges, the fruit from which his own name had been derived, and their presence here was a sure sign that his arrival in Miami had been anticipated. Anticipated and, perhaps, engineered, although to what end he couldn't as yet imagine. He let the halves tumble back into the bowl, untasted.

Bo let his mind slip back to the time he and the Widow had been on more friendly terms than they were now. *Intimate* terms. Then one evening she had fed him his favourite fruit injected with large quantities of a poison of her own creation, something adapted from a toxic potion she'd discovered in the ancient books of black magic she had patiently collected over several centuries of research.

It didn't kill him, of course, didn't even come close, but it had caused him many nights of pain of an intensity he had rarely encountered before in his life as a vampire. Later, in the face of his anger, of his outrage, the Widow had explained her actions in the simplest terms possible:

*I just wanted to see what would happen to you, that's all*, she'd said, frowning in innocent confusion, as though it were Bo's anger that was inappropriate, not her actions. *It was just an experiment, my love. I only wanted to see if I could...*

*To see if you could* what?

*To see if I could kill you...*

Even so, it wasn't the pain she had caused him that ended their close association. Physical pain, no matter how terrible, was merely a memory of what it was to be human, and memories of his own long-lost humanity had become too few and far between for Bo to be precious about how they came.

It was the betrayal that really finished their alliance. It was Bo's realisation that the affection he had begun to feel for this creature was not reciprocated in any measure, and that the Widow's only true desire was the desire to know all his secrets, to open his mind and read him like one of her dusty grimoires… and perhaps, if it were possible, to steal his powers for herself.

Since that night they had met only sporadically, and when they did they maintained a wary, uncomfortable distance, like predators forced by expediency to temporarily share the same small territory. Bo might have avoided her company altogether, if not for the suspicion that she, perhaps more than any other vampire he was aware of, would bear watching.

But now he wondered if this feeling had been mere suspicion or an actual premonition?

He looked up suddenly and saw that the Widow had silently joined him. She sat down opposite, facing him across the table and the bowl, and smiled sweetly.

'Not hungry, my love?'

Bo shook his head.

'No, you fed before coming here, didn't you? But not on fruit. I can smell her on you, just the slightest nose. A red-head, I hope?'

He eyed her artfully arranged locks, long braids like heavy, rusted chains that reached down to her fine shoulders and beyond. For a moment or two his mind insisted upon showing him a vivid image of the hair between the Widow's legs, a thick tangle of fine copper wires he could curl around his fingers, but then he shook the memory away.

'Blonde,' he replied.

The Widow sighed unhappily. 'Will you never trust me again?'

'You know the answer to that question as well as I do.'

'Then why have you come?'

'You know why.'

The Widow nodded. 'It's the killings, I suppose.'

'They need to stop immediately.'

'I agree completely.'

Bo stared at her intently, trying to pierce her mask of studied innocence. But she might have been a porcelain doll for all the expression she betrayed. Had he ever really expected anything else?

'You deny any involvement?' he asked at length.

'Emphatically. And, may I add, your suspicion wounds me deeply.'

Bo laughed shortly. 'It does nothing of the kind.'

'What gives you the right to laugh at me?' the Widow demanded.

She was still smiling, but now Bo could see the murderous rage flaring in her eyes, twin infernos generating a terrible heat. The pitch of her voice alone would have driven a human being into a gibbering wreck.

'What gives you the right to speak to me this way? To question me? Or any of us, for that matter?'

Bo ignored her questions.

'Bodies have been found drained of blood in this city,' he said calmly. 'The newspapers, the internet and television news are full of vampire stories. They have named the killer "Blood Orange". They have given the killer *my* name. This is not a coincidence.'

'Nonsense,' the Widow shrugged dismissively. 'Just some sadistic human psychopaths with a pathetic vampire fetish, that's all…'

'Or a real vampire playing games with me, trying to provoke me into a reaction.'

'And so of course you suspect me. But why would I ever do something so… so *meaningless*?'

'Because this challenge to authority is exactly the sort of thing you might do, and I'm sure it would be far from meaningless. It's the way your mind works, Widow. You can't help trying to subvert the rules for your own gain.'

'*Your* rules,' she spat. '*Your* laws…'

Bo could see the blood rising into her face, simulating a human response to stress and anger, and he knew that he wasn't the only one to have fed before this meeting. But from the depth of her blush, he knew she had stolen a good deal more than just a few drops.

Somewhere in this house there were a couple of fresh corpses awaiting their appointment with the Widow's furnace.

'I've told you many times before,' he said patiently, 'I only enforce the laws, I didn't make them.'

'Then who did?' she demanded. 'Exactly who gave you this authority? It wasn't the other Alphas, of that I'm sure. Who appointed you to your lofty position? Who made you judge, jury and executioner? Was it the Council of Elders? Or was it someone, *something*, else? Tell me!'

'You've asked these questions before.'

'And you have avoided them before…'

She smiled suddenly, changeable as the wind.

'You have so many secrets, my love. You pretend not to, naturally, but we both know you do.'

Bo sighed. 'Widow, I promise you, you do not want to know the things I know.'

'But I *do*,' she insisted. 'I always have. And I *will* know them, before you and I are done. My love.'

After leaving the White House, Bo headed across to the mainland and entered a large, noisy club on Biscayne Boulevard, not far from the Miami Shores Country Club.

At the bar he took the stool next to a woman wearing a dark, crumpled business suit and a dark, crumpled expression on her face, making her an incongruous sight in the midst of the colourfully-dressed and joyful revellers. She was drinking a dirty martini, had another on stand-by, and was quietly radiating an aura of fuck-off-and-leave-me-alone so powerful that Bo didn't require psychic abilities in order to feel it.

It was not the woman's first drink of the evening, but she wasn't even close to being drunk. That would take many, many more, Bo sensed, and he also understood that she was determined to have them. This was Detective Sara Mila's first night off in more than a month, and she felt she deserved to kick back as hard as the world had been kicking her, and that had been very hard indeed.

After a moment or two, Mila realised someone was looking at her and wearily turned her head to acknowledge the compliment. Her eyes widened a little when she saw how handsome her admirer was, but they quickly narrowed again into what was obviously a habitual, narrow regard.

'Well, you're pretty enough, I guess… Sorry, pal, nothing doing. I wouldn't be good company tonight.'

She turned back to her drink with a dogged determination, fishing the olive out of her cloudy drink and tossing it into her mouth, but Bo continued to stare at her profile until finally she turned all the way around to face him. She looked him up and down more carefully, took in the fact that he too wore a sombre business suit in a tourist club, and then she took in his short, neatly-combed, neatly-parted hair and the way the hang of his jacket betrayed a shoulder-holster.

She sighed. 'Ah fuck, what now…'

He placed a slim leather card case in her hand.

When she flipped it open, she saw photo ID identifying Bo as Elijah Fredericks, an FBI special agent out of New Orleans. Bo calmly watched her give the ID the closest scrutiny. He wasn't concerned about her finding a flaw, because the ID was entirely genuine.

The photograph was *not* genuine, of course, but Bo knew a talented vampire artist in Berlin who specialised in the production of photo-realist portraits, and this was an example of his very finest work.

Mila handed back his card case. 'You're a long way from home, Elijah.'

'I'm on vacation. Next stop, Seaworld.'

'Yeah, sure you are. What can I do for you?'

'Well, you could let me buy you another drink… or I suppose you could offer me a little professional courtesy and satisfy my curiosity about one of your cases.'

'And which case might that be?' she asked with heavy irony. 'Gee, let me *think*…'

'It's the Blood Orange Case.'

'No shit, Sherlock.' She gave him a look far more unfriendly than any other he'd seen for a long while, and that included the Widow's parting glance, which had blazed like one of her wall sconces. 'You guys trying to take over my investigation?'

Bo shook his head. 'That's not the plan.'

'So why would you be interested?'

Bo leaned a little closer to her. 'Confidentially, we have a number of unsolved cases in our files which could be connected.'

'Unsolved cases involving suspected vampire killings? Seriously?'

Bo shrugged. 'Unexplained cases in general.'

Mila laughed without much humour. 'You know, I used to watch the re-runs of that show all the time when I was a kid. Never thought I'd end up living in a fucking episode.'

'I need to know everything, Detective. Then maybe I can help you.'

Mila stared at him levelly, and Bo let her do it.

He knew she was thinking about how her investigation had been floundering in a sea of unbelievable, inexplicable evidence from the very first, and about how the Brass were continually on her back because the politicos were always on theirs, and how the whole city was running scared of ruining the steady flow of tourist dollars.

*It's like* Jaws, he caught her thinking. *It's just like* Jaws, *but with vampires instead of sharks…*

At last, she said, 'Okay, I guess I'd be open to a little help.'

As they left the club a few moments later and exited the parking lot, Bo sent his mind back to the club's general manager, who was sitting in his office with glazed eyes and drool running from the corner of his mouth, and suggested that the security system might now successfully reboot itself if he were to switch it back on.

Mila drove them to the Medical Examiner's building on NW10th Avenue, and, against all her expectations, found the Morgue Bureau nightshift staff both extremely cooperative and completely incurious about their wish to view the bodies of the Blood Orange victims at this late hour.

At no point did anyone ask to see proof of their identification or their authority to do so.

'I know this suits us tonight,' she whispered to Bo as they walked down a long, grey corridor, 'but it's kind of worrying, too. I mean, who else do they let in without making a record or checking their badges?'

Bo, who had skilfully manipulated the ease of their passage through the system, smiled to himself.

'I believe you're overlooking your own notoriety, Detective Mila,' he said. 'I'm sure they know very well who you are. As for me, they've probably seen enough FBI to recognise it when they see it. Plus, as this is something of an unconventional case, maybe they feel that different rules apply.'

They reached the end of the corridor and paused outside the double doors into the morgue. Mila was eyeing Bo closely again, and he saw that the narrow, distrustful look had returned.

'What do you mean by "notoriety",' she asked shortly.

Bo briefly considered deflecting her suspicion psychically, as he had with pastel man earlier and with the mortuary-staff just now, or even completely taking her over, as he had with the girl he had fed from. But he sensed that any one of these alternatives would be entirely the wrong move.

He was slowly coming to understand that Mila was a highly intuitive woman, and perhaps even had her own small twist of psychic ability, which probably enhanced her abilities as a police officer — she would be a detective of many good hunches, he imagined.

He knew that her mind would be difficult to penetrate without leaving a trace. If he were to force his will upon her, she may not know exactly what was happening at the time, or have any chance of resisting him, but she would still understand that *something* was wrong.

Afterward, it would play on her mind, and play and play, and might one day come back to haunt him.

The long run, he reminded himself.

'Hey, take it easy,' he said mildly, 'I just meant that you're an officer with a certain reputation.'

'Meaning?'

Bo quickly summarised what he had discovered about the detective from the more vulnerable minds of her peers: 'Meaning that you don't suffer fools gladly. And you have a short temper. And you never forget. Or forgive. In other words, you're kind of a pain in the ass.'

Mila stared at him impassively for a few more seconds, and then shrugged. 'Oh, *that* kind of notoriety. Okay.'

They pushed through the double doors and approached the steel wall of cold chambers.

'You want to see the most recent first?'

'The freshest, yes.'

Mila gruntcd. 'Nice way to look at it.'

She slid open the drawer.

'Meet Sandy,' she said. 'At least, that's what the crime-scene boys called her when she was just a Jane Doe they picked up from the beach. She was finally identified just before I signed out tonight. Real name's Veronica Metz, twenty-four-years-old. A dental nurse, originally from Kissimmee. Went missing two days ago, never reported.'

In life, Veronica Metz would have been universally considered as beautiful, a quality she had unfortunately been unable to carry with her through the portal into death.

'Hope she's fresh enough for you, Agent Fredericks. Autopsy's due to take place first thing in the morning.'

'So I see.' Bo stepped closer to the open drawer.

Veronica's naked body clearly showed the vivid marks of her killer's activities. Her arms, shoulders, hips and legs were heavily marked with bruising that appeared to take the shape of very large hands. There were puncture wounds consistent with canine teeth all over her body, including her genital area, although her neck was clearly the major point of interest, the jugular and carotid arteries being badly mangled. The open wounds were still peppered with sand.

'Not going to win a beauty pageant anytime soon, is she?' Mila asked.

Bo shook his head thoughtfully. 'Tell me, how did the killer come to be called Blood Orange?'

'That was another bit of crime-scene shorthand that unfortunately leaked to the press, although they haven't found out *why* we call the perp that, thank God. It came about because each victim was found with an orange jammed into their mouths, pushed in all the way behind the teeth — some of them, we had to dislocate their jaws to get them out. Turned out they were blood oranges. We took Veronica's out earlier today, just to be sure it was the same.'

'Which it was?'

'Sure it was. With the first one, we thought it was some kind of S&M thing, you know, like the rubber balls those guys strap in their mouths when they're getting it on? Or maybe as a gag, to keep the victim from screaming when things turned extra-nasty? But then the others cropped up, and we realised it was a kind of signature.'

Bo looked closely at the enormous hand-print bruises on Veronica Metz's shoulders, on her ankles, thighs and hips, the long blue-black finger marks that in another century, on another continent, could quite easily have been his own.

'All this is the work of a single individual?'

'We think so. The hand-spread is absolutely identical…' Mila grunted. 'For God's sake, don't go around telling people there might be a whole bunch of these evil fuckers on the loose. Every tourist in the state would take the first flight home.'

Bo held up his hands. 'I'm saying nothing, believe me.'

'You know, the guys here take x-rays of the victims before they start the autopsies,' Mila said. 'I've seen them for myself, and those marks aren't just bruises. This perp's grip is so powerful it actually *crushes* the bones underneath. They estimate it'd take

26

a PSI of around 400 to do that kind of damage to human bones, which is about the same as the jaws of a wolf.'

Bo had moved on to the badly gouged neck.

'All the bodies were pretty much completely drained of blood,' Mila continued, 'which, as you must know, is highly unusual in itself. All the wounds were caused by bites — in the other victims they found microscopic traces of enamel, and saliva around the wounds. Funny thing is, the enamel isn't human enamel and the saliva isn't human saliva. They also don't appear to belong to any animal on record. Nobody seems to know what the fuck they are.'

'That's incredible,' Bo said.

'Gets worse,' she replied. 'All the bodies have been dumped in crazy public places, but there have been no witnesses, not a one, as though the goddam perp's invisible. Also, we have no rational explanation for *how* they got dumped in the places they did — unless they got dropped from the air, maybe. For example, Veronica here was left in the middle of a beach, and the only footprints anywhere near her belonged to the kid who dropped the dime and his fucking mutt.'

'Odd.'

'Yeah, odd about covers it, I guess. So maybe now you can see why we're quietly running around in circles on this.'

For the first time, Mila's mask of hardened professional glibness slipped a notch.

'I mean, what the fuck?' she whispered. 'My mother was a big believer in this kind of garbage.

Man, she believed in everything; ghosts, voodoo, werewolves, witches, Bigfoot, and the Loch Ness fucking monster. But not me. *Not me*,' she repeated, as though she were desperate to convince herself just as much as Bo. 'You got anything in your Monster-of-the-Week files about this kind of shit?'

Bo did not reply. Instead, he placed one hand on Veronica's forehead, the other on her thigh, and leaned close to the body, eyes closed, his pale face hovering just millimetres above the dead flesh of her breast.

Even if people had a faith, even if they believed in an afterlife, they still mostly imagined that once life was extinct in a human organism the body was nothing but decaying flesh. People believed this largely because science had taught them to believe it.

But science had also taught them to believe that the vampire was a myth which couldn't possibly exist.

Bo had known that the human brain was a computer long before the scientists, and he also knew that as long as it remained physically intact — until natural decay reached an advanced stage, say, or until it was removed for an autopsy — all its software files were still accessible, if only one had the right program to retrieve them.

He reached out to Veronica's residual memories now, and patiently began to search and filter.

Images began to appear before his eyes.

Images, and then sounds, sensations, locations, personalities…

Soon, a rush of detailed information washed through him, and he sighed in dismay.

*Betrayal*, he thought. *Betrayal upon betrayal.*

He stood up again and opened his eyes to find Mila regarding him with both confusion and suspicion.

'What the hell was *that*, Fredericks?'

'Thank you for your time and cooperation, Detective,' he said crisply. 'I'll be in touch very soon.'

Mila caught his arm as he stepped around her, and as impatient as Bo suddenly was to go, he allowed himself to be prevented from leaving.

'What the fuck are you talking about, you'll be in touch? You think you can walk in here for some one-on-one with my girl and then just walk out again, without giving me anything in return?'

Bo gave Mila his eyes. Quietly but firmly, he said: 'Mila, go back to your precinct, assemble your team and wait for an anonymous phone-call.'

'What are you saying?' she asked incredulously, taking a firmer grip. 'You know who did this? Just like that? You do your laying-on-of-hands shit and suddenly the case is busted wide open? Just who the *hell* are—'

'What I'm saying, Detective — *all* I'm saying — is that I was never here. Do you understand? You never heard my name in your life. You never saw me.'

He gently removed Mila's hand from his arm, very conscious that he was currently so furious that one tiny error of judgement on his part might mean the detective's fingers and wrist being badly broken, leaving injuries much like those Veronica Metz had suffered.

'Hey, Fredericks!' Mila angrily called after Bo as he walked away. 'Remember that "you-don't-forget-you-don't-forgive" gag you made about me earlier? Well, that was right on the money, mister — this isn't over!'

'You're so right, Detective,' Bo said to himself, pushing through the double doors and escaping into the corridor. 'This is only the beginning.'

Outside, the night called to him, and he became one with it.

Situated in the approximate centre of the large industrial park, Unit 13 looked just like its neighbours; smart, modern façades of washed river stone and heavily tinted glass, behind which all manner of small business enterprises and light-industries plied their various and largely innocent trades.

Although at this time of night the Unit appeared to be as dark and unoccupied as the others, a large black van, its engine still ticking as it cooled, was backed up close to the main entrance. Signwritten on the side of the van in large ornate gothic lettering were the words, *The Dark Arts*, and below them, in a simpler, more business-like font, were the address of an online domain and the street address of a gallery somewhere over in the city's arty Wynwood District.

Of course, Bo didn't need the cooling van to alert him to the presence of human beings within the large industrial unit. All he had to do was concentrate, and then he could hear them breathing and the meaty thud of their heartbeats from where he stood on the roof. There were two of them, one male, the other female.

They were enormously excited, both sexually and mentally, their conjoined mind-set literally buzzing with malignancy.

When he listened just a little harder, he found that there was another, much calmer heartbeat, too, hidden beneath the couple's excitement, and a soft, slow respiration, both much subdued by artificial means. This third human being had been heavily drugged only a short while earlier.

This was the next victim.

Bo soundlessly dropped the seventy feet to the ground and then slipped into the building through a fire door at its rear, operating the locking mechanism with his mind. He left the door carefully ajar behind him, and then stealthily moved through a series of dark corridors and doorways, every surface clad in thick soundproofing materials, until he reached the unit's heart.

Then he paused, silent and watchful.

In the centre of a huge, otherwise empty space almost as high as the building itself, an unconscious young woman with long black hair lay spread-eagled and naked upon a gleaming autopsy table. Her whole body was a canvas of body-art, her creamy skin liberally tattooed with a legion of demons, wraiths, and deaths-heads. The tentacles of a giant octopus uncoiled from her inner thighs and across her shaven pudenda, and points of light reflected from multiple piercings in her ears, nose, nipples, and labia.

Constructed around her body, looming over her like a giant spider, was the framework of some kind of complex, elegant sculpture — a *machine* — made primarily of steel.

Parts of the sculpture, Bo saw, were designed to move and were fully articulated, all operated by small but powerful hydraulic pumps. Some of these parts took the form of large metal hands, at least seven pairs, each sheathed in gloves of a fine, pale leather. Other parts of the device had been fashioned to resemble human jaws, each with their own sets of long canine teeth, which could be positioned to 'bite' at many different parts of a body at the same time. Evidently the teeth had been drilled hollow, and long coils of plastic tubing ran from them into waiting plastic drums.

The device's artificial hands, Bo saw, had been carefully applied to the unconscious woman's body, at her shoulders, her forearms, her hips, thighs and ankles — at precisely those places, in fact, where the hand-shaped bruises had been placed on Veronica Metz's body — and then their grip hydraulically tightened just enough in order to subdue the victim once she regained consciousness.

Then, Bo imagined, the crushing pressure would gradually be increased in a number of agonising stages, each indicated by her torturer's levels of arousal, and all the while, the other moving parts, the jaws and teeth — the *fangs* — would stand ready, awaiting their moment.

When he had first begun to recover the jumbled nightmare images from Veronica Metz's slowly decaying mind, Bo hadn't been sure if he could entirely believe the story they appeared to be telling him.

But he believed it now.

Incredible as it seemed, Bo was looking at the modern-day equivalent of a fabled device from vampire legend and myth — here, now, tonight, in the city of Miami — not at a time-faded illustration on a crumbling Vellum scroll, but the device itself, created with modern technology.

This was a version of the *Apparatus Martyris*. The so-called Martyr Machine.

He shook his head. This could not be. This *should* not be.

For the first time, Bo turned his focus to the killers who dared to call themselves the Blood Orange, and despite the amount of trouble they had caused him, and the greater problem their folly only made plainer, he almost laughed aloud.

The pair were dressed like movie vampires, albeit from separate eras; the woman was kitted out in skin-tight dominatrix gear, and the man was actually wearing a red-lined cloak, a tuxedo, and patent-leather shoes with spats. His thinning dyed hair was gelled back from his forehead in a sharp widow's peak. Both of them were white-faced with make-up and be-fanged with plastic teeth.

He recalled the Widow's curt dismissal of the people responsible for the murders as "sadistic human psychopaths with a pathetic vampire fetish", and of course she had been correct... but Bo now knew for sure that she had been correct only because she herself was their sponsor in this madness.

Clearly she had attempted to wipe their minds clean of any trace of her involvement, but for Bo it was the work of a moment to core down into the deepest parts of their minds where the truth lay hidden. Later, in the custody of the police, they would claim sole responsibility for their crimes, and they would genuinely believe that their lies were the truth. So would the police, for that matter, because the lies were far easier to deal with than the truth.

But Bo saw all.

He saw the couple, formerly completely legitimate members of the Miami art community, attending one of the Widow's infamous parties. He saw how quickly she had divined their potential for her schemes, and how she deliberately set out to dazzle them. He saw how flattered they were when she visited their Wynwood gallery, exclaiming over the dark paintings the woman had produced by her method of mixing pigments with animal blood from a local slaughterhouse, and professing admiration for the macabre mechanical installations the man had designed and engineered.

He saw the way the Widow had gone to work on them both, steadily, slowly guiding their minds and their imaginations down darker and darker roads and sidetracks until they eventually reached her intended destination.

The construction of the *Apparatus Martyris*, and ritualistic, fetishistic murder.

Bo abruptly stepped out of the shadows and snapped his fingers loudly, and as the man and woman began to turn in surprise, he transmitted a powerful silent command that froze their perception of time and place.

He moved closer to the *Apparatus* and studied it in more detail.

He understood at once that the Widow had sacrificed many of her Newborn to this enterprise, and had harvested from their bodies to provide the artists with the raw materials for her commission; vampire fangs wrenched for the hydraulic jaws, and vampire flesh flayed to glove the articulated mechanical hands.

Vampire saliva, too, which the killers pragmatically kept in an oilcan on the floor at the foot of the device and applied to the victims' wounds following their agonising death. This explained why the inhuman saliva discovered on the victims' bodies had not repaired the injuries the jaws and teeth had inflicted — it had been collected from the mouths of slaughtered vampires.

The Widow had also ordered her Newborn to supply the couple with their victims — save for this last one, the tattooed girl who had been chosen, foolishly and self-destructively, from among their own social circle — and had then commanded still other Newborn to dispose of the bodies in very public places.

Places that would generate maximum publicity. Publicity that she knew would inevitably draw Bo's urgent attention.

Then he moved even deeper into the killers' minds and saw something that took his breath away, and then he understood that this infernal machine — which had been adapted to simulate the marks of a predatory vampire purely as a lure to draw Bo into the Widow's web of intent — was nothing more than a prototype.

Bo took his mobile phone from his pocket and keyed in a number. The call was answered on the second ring. 'Mila?' he asked.

'Yes, who am I speaking to?'

'Nobody you know.'

He gave her the address of the Unit, and then suggested she get there as soon as possible, if she didn't want another Blood Orange victim on her hands, or on her conscience.

'Tell me your name,' Mila said, playing her role just as he'd hoped.

Bo hung up on her and tucked his phone away, retreating into the shadows to wait. He didn't have to wait long.

There were no sirens, but he heard them coming all the same. Mila must have taken him at his word and had her team standing by to move immediately. They came in through the fire door he had left open for them at the back of the building, and then moved past him blindly, weapons drawn and cocked, less than a quarter-hour after his call.

Mila was in the lead, naturally. She was focused, intent and, to Bo's hypersensitive vision, seemed almost incandescent with purpose and bravery.

At the last second, he released his psychic hold on the two killers and they finally completed their interrupted turn, just in time to face the officers' weapons.

'Got you, you fuckers,' Mila said. 'Facedown on the floor, now! Now!'

Bo vanished.

He stood with his back to a large palm surrounded by lush vegetation, feeling his body reacting to his mind's warning that conflict was close at hand. The great wars of his kind predated human history by several millennia, but still every cell in his body was clamouring to answer the battle cry. Already his clothes felt too small and restrictive, his teeth crowding his mouth in overlapping profusion.

Bo was just a mile away from the Widow's property. He had already sent out his senses like a nest of snakes and been through her entire house, exploring every nook and cranny even to the smallest detail. He could feel her mind seething as she impatiently waited for him to arrive, both she and the hordes of Newborn foot-soldiers she had created to help her restrain and defeat him.

And he had discovered the large chamber she'd had constructed deep beneath her house, built specially for just this purpose, for this exact moment in time.

Housed within this chamber was the new device he had seen in the killers' minds just before he'd called Mila, and now he had seen it again through the eyes of the ignorant Newborn who stood guard by its side. Unlike the machine currently in the hands of the human police, the second device was entirely faithful to the original ancient design.

This was the real *Apparatus Martyris*, and it was meant for Bo alone.

In place of the mechanical hands, there were great clamps made of solid silver from which Bo would be unable to break free. In place of the stolen fangs, there were long, hooked razor-sharp silver blades around which his flesh, once penetrated, would be unable to heal. His lifeblood, the blood of countless centuries, of untold feedings, would pour out of his wounds in a seemingly unending flood and cascade into the collection well that had been dug beneath the device.

At some point as Bo struggled and suffered and bellowed his agony, the Widow would step forward and read powerful incantations from the text of a dusty grimoire. Then she would wait in breathless anticipation to see if this mythical ceremony, the ritual sacrifice of an Elder vampire, would work as the legends promised, and call into her presence one of the Ancients — those vampires said to have been born as the Earth itself was born, and who were now believed to exist in an eternal realm of fire.

Bo had no idea whether this ceremony would work or not, but he knew that even if it did, the Widow would not receive the dark bounty of knowledge and power she believed Bo possessed and she craved so badly. As far as Bo was aware, he himself was the only vampire still in existence to have any personal experience of the Ancients, and he knew that their summoning was the very last thing any creature, mortal or immortal, should ever desire. The world might not survive such an event as their coming.

Bo kicked off his shoes and began to remove his clothes.

Initially, he had been taken by surprise by the intensity of his own hunger for the coming battle. But now he almost felt that he owed the Widow a debt of gratitude for the unexpected opportunity. For this one night he could pretend that the old days had come again, the glory days, where a skirmish might last a decade, a war a thousand years. Where bloodshed was not shameful and secretive. Where carnage was simply the way a mark was made upon the world, the way a line was drawn.

The Blood Orange would draw that line, here and now.

There was much of pride and glory in battle, he knew, and fierce joy, and there was a rare intoxication in feasting upon one's own kind, through whose veins ran the sweetest, richest blood of all.

Bo could feel every molecule of him shrieking out in its own anticipation. His body began to swell, to grow. His canine teeth had fully extended, now more like tusks than teeth. At the centre of his body a roaring void howled and screamed, an unstable vacuum that longed to be once more filled with massacre, with savagery, and most of all with thick, hot blood.

'Widow,' he said aloud, speaking directly into her mind. 'Widow, I have indulged you too long and forgiven you too much. But now your judgement is finally at hand...'

He raised his arms to salute the night, and then he flew.

There were more than thirty Newborn laying in wait for him outside the Widow's compound walls. The majority of them were dead before they even knew he had arrived in their midst, their heads torn from their bodies by the ferocity of his passage, like red wheat felled by the reaper's scythe.

The handful that remained attempted to engage him in combat, but they were as hatchlings attempting to contend with an eagle. Bo ripped them all to quivering shreds in a matter of seconds and bathed himself in their blood, which instantly vanished into the pores of his flesh as his system absorbed their lives and strength.

Bo leapt to the top of the high wall and saw a swarm of Newborn surging through the grounds toward him from the direction of the house, and he smiled before pouncing down into the heart of them.

He let them surround him, allowed them to clamber up onto his back and shoulders, and to cling to his legs and arms, but they weren't strong enough to hold him still, and even the sheer weight of their numbers was unable to pull him down to the ground. They tried to bite him as they bit their human victims, to drain the majority of his strength so they would be able to drag him down into the Martyr Chamber as their mistress had commanded them, but their Newborn fangs could not penetrate his Elder's flesh.

The Widow had clearly never told them how powerful Bo was. But then, how could she, when she hadn't the slightest notion herself? She had been entirely correct in her assumption that the Blood Orange had his secrets, but even she could not have guessed what they were, or how they contributed to his enormous power.

Bo gave the Newborn army a few moments more to mass around him, and then he gave himself fully to the battle.

The world became blood, and nothing but blood. And blood. And blood.

Bo slowly descended into the Martyr Chamber, a huge, echoing manmade cave carved out of the bedrock and which took the shape of a colossal upturned bowl. At its centre stood the *Apparatus Martyris*, so like the one used by the Widow's human puppets, but on a much larger scale.

The Widow herself stood passively beside the device, one hand resting upon one of the silver blades she would have been delighted to thrust deep into Bo's throat, had she had the chance. Merely touching the silver must have been causing her considerable pain, but her face betrayed not a single twitch of discomfort, nor of the fear she must have been experiencing as the conqueror of her forces approached, the creature she had attempted to shackle and sacrifice.

Her poise was admirable, and she was very beautiful. Her colour had risen as she had felt the psychic impact of his slaughter of her Newborn, excited despite herself by his display of power and his savage appetite.

Normally Bo stood only a head higher than the Widow, but now he towered over her by as much as three feet. He stopped before her and she reached out to touch his larger, battle-ready body, fully engorged with blood, to trace the swollen veins that patterned his naked chest and arms. Her own chest, he saw, was heaving with excitement.

'I have longed to see you like this for than a century, my love,' she whispered. 'I have dreamed of seeing you as the courageous, merciless warrior you should be, and not that weak and tedious upholder of foolish laws…'

Bo could not reply. He had gone too far. He was beyond speech, almost beyond thought, running on instinct, lost in the bloodlust.

'Would it really have worked?' the Widow asked suddenly. 'Would it—'

Bo's arm lashed out like a whip and he caught her about the shoulder, crushing it as her puppets' victims had had their bones crushed, and then he drew her slowly, inexorably toward him, and she was no longer able to control her terror. She was crying tears of blood, pissing torrents of blood, turning the ground beneath her feet to crimson mud.

'Are you an Ancient?' she asked, even as Bo raised his free hand to grip her head and began to crush her skull, even as his thumb punched through bone and buried itself deep into the meat of her brain. 'Are you…'

Bo closed his jaws on her throat and tore off her head.

He had returned to his palm tree and dressed in careful, languorous silence, once more calm and composed, and completely satiated in the afterglow of battle. Now he stood watching the Widow's house burning, a vast funeral pyre that soon would be nothing but ash, and that itself would in short order be carried away on the rising wind and out across the ocean, from which there could be no return.

From the distance, Bo heard multiple sirens wailing as the Fire Department began to make the frantic journey from the old Cutler Road station.

He wished the Fire Officers luck. They would discover soon enough that it wouldn't matter how quickly they arrived at the scene or how much water they pumped on to this fire, it would continue to burn until the burning was done. Vampire bodies were uniquely combustible, and he had piled close to a hundred of them in and around the *Apparatus Martyris* before setting them ablaze.

Even if the chamber beneath the Widow's house did not collapse in on itself, as Bo fully expected it to, all that would be left of the device would be an unidentifiable mess of molten silver and steel that could have been anything, and certainly would never be connected to the bizarre instrument of torture used by the Blood Orange killers.

In any case, now that the police had their killers in custody, Bo believed that most of the curiosity regarding the unidentifiable biological samples they had collected during the course of the investigation would die down quickly, as new live cases began to occupy their minds, man-hours and budgets.

Even Detective Sara Mila would eventually have to put her doubts and suspicions away and get on with her life, although he suspected they would never entirely leave her.

Sometime soon there would be a small fire in the place where the samples of vampire trace evidence were stored, or perhaps a simple filing mistake would result in them being permanently misplaced. These kinds of unfortunate accidents and mistakes happened all the time in a red-tape bound, bureaucratic system such as law-enforcement. It truly was the curse of the modern world.

Bo suddenly heard the scrape of a boot-heel behind him, and he smiled. He'd known another vampire had been close for some time, and he'd been wondering when the survivor would announce his presence.

He turned around and saw with no surprise that his visitor was the Newborn guard who had challenged him at the Widow's gates during his first visit tonight. The Newborn had sunk to his knees before him, his head meekly lowered, all trace of his former arrogance burned away.

'My Lord, I am Gareth,' he said quietly, trembling. 'Yours to command.'

Bo had no use for servants, Newborn or otherwise. But now that the bloodlust had left him, he had no more taste for killing, either. Furthermore, this one had displayed bravery by making his cautious approach, and the boot-scrape, the sound he'd deliberately made to forewarn Bo of his presence, was a nice touch, a perfect echo of the way Bo himself had revealed his arrival outside the Widow's house earlier.

Here, it seemed, was a Newborn capable of learning from his mistakes. Always a welcome discovery.

It was possible that this one might actually be worth saving.

'On your feet, Gareth,' he said.

The Newborn rose to his feet and summoned up the nerve to look Bo in the eye.

'Go,' Bo told him gently. 'Go make a place in the world for yourself. Do no harm. Leave no trace.'

'My Lord.' Gareth bowed low and began to back away slowly, as though he feared Bo might change his mind. Finally, he bowed once more, then vanished.

'Don't make me come this way again,' Bo whispered, and he knew that he had been heard.

Dawn was fast approaching and Bo knew that soon he'd have to retreat to the temporary sanctuary he had established nearby. Still he lingered, watching the blazing fire turn the firefighters' jets of water into vast clouds of steam, but at the same time as he lived in this moment his mind was far, far away.

*Betrayal*, he had thought the instant he had seen the device imprinted upon Veronica Metz's dead memories.

*Betrayal upon betrayal*, he had thought, because he knew that the Widow could not have come upon the design of the *Apparatus Martyris* by accident, nor the specifics of the ceremony meant to accompany it.

These things had been given to her, as gifts from an admirer.

He'd seen as much in her memories, just before he crushed her brain to a pulp. He'd even seen the image of a male figure shrouded in a dark grey robe, a vampire with a mind like Bo's, a mind the Widow had been unable to touch.

As far as Bo knew the designs the Widow had worked from only existed in three places in the whole world, hidden away in secret subterranean vampire libraries scattered across the globe, and all three were in the care of fellow Elders he would, before this moment, have trusted unto his own destruction.

But now that trust would have to be called into question, because one of them was not what he seemed. One of them was playing deadly games with forces he did not understand, and he had to be stopped.

Bo nodded to himself, the decision made.

When he awoke at dusk, he would begin making the arrangement to travel to Europe. He would travel first to Rome.

A visit to his oldest friend was long overdue.

*The idea of the hunter becoming the hunted is a pretty well worn trope in the tale of terror, almost a sub-genre in its own right, in fact. But that doesn't make it any less satisfying when you read about some thoroughly nasty piece of work getting their well-deserved comeuppance. Somehow, though, it seems to make it all the sweeter when it happens as a consequence of true love.*

Alan slipped his arm around the woman's narrow shoulders as they walked through the pitch-black alleyway, and the way she quivered in alarm at his touch brought a happy smile to his lips. The smile stayed and even widened when the bitch didn't attempt to remove his arm, or shrug him off, despite her obvious discomfort at his touch.

She *wanted* him to touch her, that was the truth of it, but she was scared because she was totally inexperienced with men. He knew this for a fact, because she'd already admitted as much back in the nightclub, during the section of the hooking-up ritual Alan liked to call *Storytime*.

As far as Alan was concerned, *Storytime* was simply a boring necessity of the seduction process, and it was boring largely because every bitch he'd ever chatted up basically told the same banal story, with only a few small details thrown in to personalise them.

The stories were tedious beyond belief, completely self-serving, and utterly maddening. But it seemed that listening to the self-obsessed bitches babbling on that way was the price he had to pay for his small pleasures, and so he did it without resentment.

Well, without any *apparent* show of resentment.

But deep inside, it was at this point that his large pot of rage, always simmering over a low heat, steadily began to boil.

He hadn't found the woman tonight, she'd found him, which was something of a first.

He'd been basking in one of the few pools of darkness the busy nightclub offered, checking out the talent on show and gauging it against his own personal scale of desirability. It was looking to be a bad night, with not even one girl displaying all the characteristics that might pull his inner trigger.

Then, just as if she'd materialised in front of him, suddenly there she was — some little waif of a girl in painfully old-fashioned going-out clothes, a dreadful no-style hairstyle that showed off a fine collection of split ends, and a stammering, hesitant voice that sounded like a mouse-fart even when she was shouting to be heard over the music.

'Hi, I'm Annie,' she'd said.

A spray of light from a rotating spotlight fanned its way across her face and he saw that she was actually a woman, not a girl — nowhere near as young as the bitches he usually preyed upon, but not

**48**

actually decrepit either. Slim heading for scrawny, and in her early thirties somewhere, he thought, with a pretty but careworn face, all its finer edges frayed by a complete lack of self-knowledge and a crippling lack of ego.

He recognised her immediately as a woman with all the confidence and composure of a mongrel dog that had been kicked into whining submission every single day of its miserable life. Desperate for attention, desperate for affection, desperate for love, or some second-rate facsimile of same.

Exactly Alan's kind of woman, in fact.

'Hi to you, Annie,' Alan had smiled back at her. 'I'm John.'

He'd bought her a drink and led her to a booth at the back of thc room, below a conveniently broken lamp, and then expertly coaxed her towards *Storytime* (not that the bitches needed too much coaxing to prattle their poisonous little hearts out), and tried not to yawn too obviously.

Annie was closer to forty than thirty, it turned out, but she was a genuine innocent. She'd never even been in a nightclub before, nor a pub, and she'd never had a boyfriend, nor been out on a single date. She'd been the main carer for her two disabled parents ever since she was a teenager, but slightly less than a year ago they had both suddenly died within a week or so of each other, and now she was all alone in the world.

Most of that not-quite-a-year had been taken up with a candid re-evaluation of her life, she said, facing up to the sad fact that her parents, no matter how much she had loved them and how much they had loved her, had taken advantage of her. They had kept her in a state of servitude for their own benefit, and in doing so had stolen her youth.

Annie said that she had passed through the inevitable wasteland of bitterness and resentment that followed this realisation, and had come out the other side whole again.

Now, she'd further explained, she was trying to strike out on her own, trying to make friends, to carve out some kind social life before it really was too late for her. She lived locally and had been walking past this nightclub, in all its previous incarnations, for most of her life, and she'd always wondered what it would be like to venture inside.

Then, only this morning, carrying back a single carrier-bag from the supermarket with the few pathetic items for her lonely evening meal, she had passed it once more, and on the spur of the moment decided that she would make it the launching pad of her new life.

Alan did the nodding-with-thoughtfully-kind-eyes thing throughout, only half his mind following the story, which was, admittedly, slightly less tedious than most... but only *slightly*. If it hadn't been selfish parents, it would have been something else — violent ex-boyfriends, or sexist pigs in the workplace, or some other bitch-like shit.

The rest of his mind was busy making comparisons with his past conquests.

He'd picked up six girls since Donna had blown him out, and all of them had been sweet little mice just like Annie, which was exactly what Donna had been when they'd first met. This was long before she'd started making friends behind his back, going to women's groups, and getting empowered or emancipated, or whatever it was those evil werebitches called it when they brainwashed their new recruits to turn on their men, turning them into werebitches as well.

He'd screwed them senseless, all six of the little mice, and hurt them a little into the bargain, too, and then left them crying into their pillows, never to be seen again. It had felt so *good*. He wanted to call it closure, but it was probably closer to revenge. A revenge that never brought closure. Alan was big enough to admit that to himself.

Look at me, he thought, the new man.

He looked at the Annie-bitch again as she droned on and on, his interest only sparking as she reached the conclusion of her colourless, pathetic tale, and the truth finally came out — the truth he'd known before she ever opened her mouth. She wanted a man, but she had not a clue what to do with one if she found one.

She'd read that the first time for a woman could be a terrible experience. She needed a man of the world, a sensitive man, to treat her right and to teach her how.

'Then look no further,' Alan smiled, taking her small hand across the table. 'I mean, I'm no Casanova, but I'm pretty experienced with the fairer sex, and I've been told that I'm a gentle lover. I could teach you a lot. I'd be tender, and I'd make it good. If that's what you'd like...?'

Annie dropped her eyes from his as her face flushed dark with colour, but her grip on his fingers grew almost painfully tight.

'I would like that,' she said. 'I really would.'

A moment or two later she'd excused herself to go to the Ladies and Alan sat back and finished his drink with a great deal of self-satisfaction. The first and most difficult stage of the mission had been accomplished, and from now on it was all jam.

But at the same time, he issued himself a stern warning — keep a grip this time, old son.

With the first couple of Donna-clones, it had been easy enough to do that, just a little bit of rough sex, with little regard for their pleasure, just satisfying his own lust and decanting a small measure of the enormous well of anger held over from the way Donna had treated him.

But then with the next few girls, it had gone a few steps beyond that, hadn't it?

*Oh yes...*

He'd slapped those pumping little arses a little harder than mere passion and the heat of the moment could account for, and sometimes he'd bitten instead of licking, and he'd left bruises, he'd split lips.

*Oh yes...*

And with the last one, almost a month ago now, he'd choked her almost unconscious.

When he'd managed to prise his own fingers from around her throat and knelt there beside her on the bed, murmuring calming apologies and stroking her thigh as she coughed and spluttered and gasped in air, he hadn't felt anything like remorse — no, not a bit of it, he'd actually felt *cheated*.

Cheated that he hadn't been able to finish her properly.

It had taken a long time to smooth it over with the girl, but he'd eventually managed to do so. Nevertheless, he'd spent the next week or two in a sweaty funk waiting for the police to call on him, which thankfully hadn't happened.

Alan looked at his watch.

Almost fifteen minutes had passed and Annie hadn't returned from the Ladies yet. He stood up and conned the nightclub, but was unable to see her coming toward him through the anonymous crowds. He made his way to the corridor leading to the toilets and watched the Ladies door for ten minutes as a parade of pissy stuck-up bitches came and went. When he was sure that it would be empty of everyone but his scared little mouse of a date, he crept in to check.

All the stalls were empty. She was gone.

With blood now pulsing uncomfortably in his temples, he went back out into the main body of the nightclub and double-checked the places where she might be. The dance-floor, the bar, the booth where they'd been sitting, the other small pools of darkness, and the walls this shy little flower may have decided to return to. But she wasn't anywhere.

Alan headed for the exit, hoping to find her picking up her coat from the cloakroom.

No joy.

He pushed his way out onto the street and stood for a while glancing up and down, looking for the merest sight of her. He didn't realise that he was panting as though he'd been sprinting, and muttering under his breath, until one of the bouncers asked him if he was all right.

He faked a smile. 'No problem, I just thought I'd seen a mate of mine heading out.'

The bouncer told him that the only person to come out in the last few minutes had been a woman in a hurry. Was that his mate?

'No, 'fraid not. My mate's a rugby player. Six-three, built like a brick shithouse...'

Alan went back inside and attempted to shake off the disappointment and pick up where he'd left off, trying to snaffle another cripple from the back of the herd, but it was no good. Not only were the pickings too thin tonight, but the lust and bitterness and bile and anger he had been hoping to purge on the mousy bitch was all trapped inside him, so thick and foul that it was almost choking him.

You *bitch*, he kept thinking. You fucking cock-teasing evil *werebitch*...

After half an hour of this torture and humiliation, he'd had enough, and he left the nightclub encapsulated in his own tiny bubble of venom. He smiled a quick, insincere goodnight to the doorman as he went by, telling him that he hadn't found his friend inside, that he must have been mistaken in the first place.

It never hurt to cover your tracks, he had learned, and by now it was becoming an instinctive trait.

Out on the main road, the taxi-rank was already twenty people long and Alan was too wound up and jittery to wait in line, especially as the majority were female. He started to walk home, but he was no sooner out of sight of both the nightclub and the taxi-rank than he heard someone calling out to him, using his fake name.

It was the werebitch's voice.

'John!' she whispered urgently. 'John!'

He turned and saw her beckoning to him from the shadows of a narrow alleyway. He hesitated for just one moment and then walked toward her, with his heart racing in his chest and his mind working a mile a minute.

'I'm so sorry I ran off like that, John,' Annie said when he reached her, her hands working at each other nervously beneath her small breasts. 'I like you so much, but I got cold feet all of a sudden, and I had to get out of there and get some fresh air. I wanted to come back immediately, but I didn't know how to. I didn't know what to say. I didn't know if you'd forgive me. I've never done anything like this in my life before and I was scared. Please, please, forgive me.'

Alan was staring, absolutely fascinated, at the tears and the desperate sense of hope he could see forming in her eyes.

He was also fascinated by the possibilities he was beginning see forming in his own mind's eye, and by the growing conviction that somehow this was all meant to be.

'I don't live far from here,' Annie said, stammering. 'You could come back with me now. You could teach me...'

'Teach you a lesson?'

'Yes.' She ducked her head shyly. 'You could teach me all the lessons you wanted...'

'This is it?' he asked, standing before a tall, solidly constructed Edwardian terraced house.

'Yes, this is my home,' Annie whispered.

All the other houses in the row were dark and silent at two o'clock in the morning, and the single light showing in the house before them only dimly illuminated the decorative fanlight above the dark, peeling front door.

Alan couldn't exactly say why, but just the sight of the house gave him a chill.

Nevertheless, when the woman walked toward it, rummaging in her small clutch-bag for her keys, he quickly followed. He didn't want to give her the chance to get cold feet again, not now that he was so close. Now that he had the most marvellous gift almost within his grasp.

He was finally going to be able to let go completely, to unburden himself of all the savagery that lurked within his soul.

It was amazing, he thought, how opportunities like this came at you by accident. Astonishing, how a weird, totally unexpected intersection of circumstances could open your mind to the most extreme possibilities.

If Annie hadn't made him feel like so much dogshit by running out on him tonight, a feeling so like the one Donna had put him through...

If he hadn't left the club alone, completely unconnected to Annie by any witness, running on instinct alone by automatically completing his performance for the doorman's benefit...

If Annie hadn't led him to her empty house, through dark back-streets that were themselves entirely deserted...

If he hadn't already experienced the bitter dissatisfaction of going only so far along the road to true self-discovery, and then having to stop short of an incredible climax...

If any of those things hadn't happened, then he wouldn't even be contemplating the course of action he had now absolutely decided upon. The Annie-bitch would be his seventh little mouse since Donna, and seven had always been his lucky number.

It would begin as it always did, he imagined. Kissing the two-faced little werebitch as they sat side by side on a sofa, followed by the touching and undressing rigmarole, all peeling and fumbling and tugging, before getting down to the real business.

First he'd introduce her to old One-Eyed Jack, and let the old fella tickle her tonsils for a while. Then, once they were well underway, he was really going to go to town on the bitch, fucking her up and down again, fucking her every which way.

When he'd satisfied that basic, physical part of his need, he was going to strangle the bitch to death. No stopping this time, because there was no need to stop, absolutely no need at all.

And after she was dead?

Well, the fun didn't have to stop there, did it? The possibilities of the hours ahead were making him dizzy.

Just ahead of him, Annie slipped her key into the lock, but then hesitated short of opening the door. Alan reached out and gently stroked her hair and asked her if there was anything wrong.

She looked back over her shoulder at him, and he saw that there was definitely fear in her sheep's eyes.

He smiled warmly to reassure her, imagining his cock buried deep inside her torn and bleeding snatch, while his thumbs came together over the white skin of her throat to crush her windpipe.

'No,' she whispered. 'Nothing wrong at all. Come on in, before any of the neighbours see us.'

'Good idea,' he whispered back, and felt like bellowing out mad laughter.

They slipped inside the house and Annie locked the door behind them.

Alan had intended this moment to be the first of a number of escalating game-changers. This was where he meant to take the bitch in his arms and kiss her for the first time, a big romantic moment intended to make her legs go bandy. But even before he'd had time to adjust to the grubby, gloomy depths of the hallway, the smell hit him like a slap in the face.

His hand had risen to cover his nose before he could control himself.

'What the hell...'

'Sorry, I meant to warn you about that,' Annie said mournfully. 'My parents were really very ill for the last few years of their lives. I'm afraid they were incontinent most of the time...'

But they died a *year* ago, for fuck's sake, Alan almost said aloud. Why does it still smell this way?

'I've cleaned and cleaned and cleaned, but it never seems to get any better. I think I might have to clear the house eventually. Tear up the carpets and throw out the furniture. Redecorate.'

'I might be able to help you with some of that,' Alan said, recovering his poise. 'But let's not talk about that right now. There's something much more pleasurable we could be doing...'

He finally leaned in toward her and brushed her lips lightly with his, his hands coming to rest on her hips. After a moment of resistance, she allowed herself to be drawn even closer, and then he slipped his tongue into her mouth. One hand dropped to fondle her buttocks, the other rose to cup a breast.

He gave her a few more moments of this softening-up treatment, and then he withdrew and smiled at her again. He took her hand and kissed it.

'Where can we go?' he asked.

She stared back into his eyes. He could see no fear in her now, just the first dawning of wild excitement, of awakening. But the fear would return soon, and in far greater measure.

He guaranteed it.

'Come with me,' Annie said, and began to lead him down the hallway toward the door at its end.

Alan noticed that there were three heavy bolts on the outside of the door, but all of them were undrawn, and he assumed that along with whatever physical ailments the werebitch's rancid parents had been suffering from, they had also probably developed a touch of dementia, and maybe had to be corralled from time to time for their own safety.

She opened the door and Alan suddenly found himself half-blinded by light.

The large room beyond the door was high enough to have a chandelier, and the chandelier held eight unshaded high-intensity bulbs that illuminated the place like floodlights at a football match. Despite being mostly empty, the room was an ungodly mess.

There was a large discoloured rug at the centre, covered in the most appalling stains, a large old leather sofa pushed back against the side wall, and a small dark wooden sideboard in the corner, its dusty top covered with tarnished silver-framed photographs and a record player that looked like a time-traveller from the 1970s.

The rest of the floor around the rancid rug was dark-stained floorboards, covered with scratches and gouges, and mounds of unidentifiable litter that looked like, but surely couldn't be, smeared animal droppings. The smell in the room was even worse than it had been in the hallway.

If he didn't know better, Alan would have said that the smell was fresh. And it wasn't just the smell of shit, either, although it was mostly that. There was something else in it, something that was musky and animal-like and, at the same time, something that was unlike anything else he'd ever smelled in his life.

It was wild.

It was *wrong*.

At the other side of the room was another closed door which also had a series of heavy bolts set top and bottom, although these were still drawn and the door therefore sealed. Beyond the old-fashioned heavy curtains he saw that thick sheets of marine ply had been nailed over the windows.

This, Alan was beginning to think, was some strange shit going on here. Had the werebitch barricaded her crazy old parents in here 24/7, like the inmates of some ancient lunatic asylum? What kind of life must that have been for a young woman?

He almost felt sorry for her.

*Almost.*

'Those are my parents over there, in the frame,' Annie said.

Despite the acute discomfort he was beginning to feel about the house, Alan still expected to go through with his plan, and if it took him dredging up a few kind words to say about the werebitch's dead parents, he was quite prepared to do it.

He drifted over to the sideboard, sensing the woman following close behind. He picked up the photograph from beside the old record player and wiped away a film of dust and grime to take a closer look. The werebitch's hand settled in the small of his back and timidly caressed him, and he repressed the urge — for the moment — to turn around and break her wrist.

The script now called for him to say something positive — they look like *such* lovely people, some kind of old pony like that. But seeing the photograph close up made him ask a different and entirely honest question.

'Who's the young man?' he asked.

The two older people, who actually *did* look like lovely people, were flanking a third person, a dark-haired smiling man either in his late teens or his early twenties. The photograph had obviously been around for a long time, taken long before her parents went loopy.

'Oh,' Annie said. 'Yes, that's Rick.'

'Rick,' he echoed. A flare of alarm went up in Alan's mind. Was Rick her brother? Did he live here, too, and was he on the premises right now? 'Who's Rick?'

'Rick's my husband.'

Alan began to turn to her in surprise. 'He's your *what*?'

Before he could complete his turn, something struck him on the side of the head with a devastating force. The pain was huge but short-lived, and the darkness into which he sank seemed deep and never-ending.

But it wasn't. Not yet.

Alan regained consciousness, not by incremental stages, but suddenly and all at once, and his body tried to jumpstart into fight-or-flight mode before his brain could even catch up. But the attempt failed, and once he understood why, he began to realise the depth of trouble he was in.

His arms were bound tightly behind his back, his legs similarly bound at the knees and ankles. It wasn't rope, it was tape, many layers of wide brown packing tape that would be next to impossible to break free from without a knife. The same tape had been wound around and around his lower jaw, effectively sealing his mouth and silencing his voice.

The sound of his own anxious breath seething and whistling in and out of his nostrils seemed deafening.

He told himself not to panic, and tried to clamp down on a wave of nausea that was threatening to make him puke behind the tape. If he did, he would probably end up either suffocating or choking on his own vomit.

He closed his eyes for a moment, trying to calm himself, and then reopened his eyes.

The first thing he saw was the Annie-bitch sitting on the musty sofa. She wasn't looking back at him, didn't even seem to be aware of him at all. In her lap, she was holding the silver-framed photograph which was the last thing he'd seen before... before what?

Before she coshed you, he answered his own question. She clobbered you while your back was turned, but why?

She surely couldn't have guessed his intentions. Maybe she was more afraid of this new experience than he'd ever imagined and she panicked, just like she'd panicked back in the nightclub... but, no.

No.

It wasn't that, and he knew it wasn't.

The werebitch was crazy, genuinely crazy. The bolts on the doors, the boards over the windows, and the stench of the house should have alerted him earlier, and probably would have if he hadn't been so distracted by his own overwhelming desires. But now there was no doubt, no doubt at all.

The younger man in the photograph was her husband, she'd said. Which must mean that all that crap about her being innocent and virginal had been a lie. How many lies had the evil, crazy little werebitch told him, and why?

What the hell was she going to do to him?

He quietly tried to sit up, but only managed to raise his head about six inches from the floor before something around his neck stopped him. It wasn't tape this time. It was a chain, a good thick one. He could hear its rattle and clink and feel the fat greasy links locking on the skin of his throat, pinching his flesh sharply.

By twisting his head as far to the right as he could, Alan saw that the chain was padlocked to a heavy iron cleat that had been screwed into the floorboards. The rancid rug that had hidden the cleat had been thrown aside into a corner.

'Awake, are you?' Annie said, breaking the silence.

When he looked at her again, he saw that she was back with him now. She had been somewhere else for a while, the place where the picture had been taken, perhaps, and with the people posing in it.

She leaned forward a little, to examine his head.

'I didn't break the skin, that's good. Once he smells fresh blood, there's no controlling him, light or no light...'

Alan began to make small, questioning noises behind his gag of tape, turning on his side to hold out his taped wrists and shrugging his shoulders, as if to ask what the fuck was going on, what was she talking about?

Annie got it right away.

'Okay, John,' she nodded, sitting back. 'This is the part of the evening that I've come to think of as *Storytime*.'

If she saw the surprise in Alan's eyes as they opened wide at this use of his own phrase, she gave no indication.

'*Storytime* is where I try to give my unfortunate victims an explanation of why they're in this terrible situation — if they're in a state to listen, that is. Not all of them are, unfortunately, but I always make a point of trying, because I believe that an explanation is usually the very least they deserve. I generally apologise to them, too, and thank them with all my heart for the sacrifice they're making for me... well, for *us*.'

She shrugged.

'You know, they weren't bad people, most of the men I've brought back here. They were just normal guys looking to have a good time. I suppose the worst that could be said of them is that they were trying to take advantage of another person's naivety, and haven't we all been guilty of that at some point in our lives?'

She stared into his eyes.

'But you're a slightly different case, aren't you? Something's making me think that you don't deserve *anything*, John. Not an explanation, an apology, or a single word of thanks. There's something about you that just isn't right, you know? I get feelings about people sometimes. It's pure instinct. It's like I can smell badness on them, and I can smell an awful lot of badness on you.'

She shook her head slowly, turning her suspicions over in her mind.

'I'm assuming that your name isn't really *John*, but this goes so much deeper than simple deception, doesn't it? It's not just your identity you're trying to hide, it's not just *who* you are, it's *what* you are. You're different. You're so much worse than the others... and actually, that's *good*. It means I don't have to feel so badly about this.'

Alan did his best to try to convey with his eyes the impression that he didn't have a clue what the werebitch was talking about, that he was as innocent as the day was long, but he could see it was a lost cause. She'd obviously picked up on some of his rage and hatred somehow — and who knows, maybe she *had* smelled it on him — but that wasn't why he was here now, trussed up and held captive.

He could have been the gentlest man in the world, a saint in human form, but somehow he thought he'd still be in the same unfortunate position, helpless, waiting to learn what it was she wanted from him.

Even if she were to take the tape from around his mouth and allow him to speak, to work his magic, he doubted he could convince her to release him. How did you bargain or reason with a lunatic?

And he had no doubt at all that she was a lunatic. She had used the word, *victims*.

Then she had said something even stranger — *once he smells fresh blood, there's no controlling him, light or no light...*

What was that about?

He saw the werebitch's eyes sliding back to the photograph in her lap, drawn there, fixed and brooding, building herself up to speak again. Alan thought he was going to get some kind of explanation, after all, despite her suspicions and denials, but he didn't believe it was out of any consideration for him as a human being.

He thought it was because the Annie-bitch was genuinely afraid of taking the next step, whatever that may be, and wanted to delay taking it for as long as possible.

In fact, he actually found this the most disturbing thought of all — that as crazy as she was, she might actually fear her own future actions.

'They weren't my parents, if it matters to you,' she said, tracing the three figures' outlines with a short fingernail. 'They were Rick's parents, and they weren't sick at all. They were both fit and healthy, in the prime of their lives, when he killed them...'

Alan had been glancing around on the floor, looking for anything sharp that he might be able to use to saw away at his bonds, but now he froze in place.

'Yes, he killed them,' the bitch said quietly. 'But he wasn't *responsible* for their deaths, not really. You see, my husband was, and is, terribly ill. He has this... this *thing*... inside him. I don't know what you'd call it. Demon, spirit, creature, or whatever, it doesn't matter. Names aren't important.'

She put the photograph away from her abruptly, at the other end of the sofa, as if she could no longer bear to look at it.

'Every so often, this thing, this parasite, comes to live inside my husband and it takes him over — which sounds completely insane, I know, but it's true. It started a few years ago, and we had no idea what it really was. In the beginning, before it really took hold of him, Rick was just a little bit strange, acting out of character, saying things that made no sense at all. But I could smell the badness growing inside him, although I couldn't accept it at first. Not in my own beloved husband. Then one time, I woke up in the middle of the night and found him crawling around on the ceiling like some kind of giant spider...'

Alan's eyes widened.

'He was staring down at me, and his eyes were like embers from a fire. The day after, I came home to

**67**

find both his parents dead. They'd come to visit him because I'd told them he was ill. He'd slaughtered them, and eaten parts of their bodies. Once the thing inside him had fed, it vanished. My poor darling Rick was himself again, and we were left to pick up the pieces of our ruined lives.'

She looked at Alan, who was now staring back at her in disbelief, and went on with her tale.

'Of course, we had to construct some elaborate fantasy for the authorities to explain his parents' disappearance, which was difficult and dangerous and all-consuming, and all the while, we — poor Rick especially — had to live with the guilt and the horror of what he had done while he was inhabited by this creature. But we did it somehow, we survived, and we kept our liberty. We had each other, and our great love, and we were strong. We thought that was finally the end of the nightmare, but of course, it wasn't. Three months later, it came back.'

She glanced at her wristwatch for a moment, and when she resumed speaking it was at a faster, less reflective pace, her tone now brisk and disturbingly business-like.

'We think now that what this thing does is swim around in the ether of whatever world it inhabits, and from time to time it finds special people, like Rick, human beings who are like fishing holes where these creatures can come to feed. Of course, the trouble is that it *remembers* where its fishing holes are, and whenever it grows hungry again, back it swims...'

She got up from the sofa and took the photograph back over to the sideboard, putting it back in the precise spot it had been before.

'There have been six men who have gone through this before you, John — or whoever you really are. All of them were lured here in exactly the same fashion.' She turned again, and deliberately fixed him with her eyes, as though in accusation. 'I am not proud of what I have done, but I can assure you that it was done out of necessity, desperation and love, not anger, not hatred, and certainly not cruelty.'

Alan felt his face burning.

'We discovered quite by accident that the longer the delay between the thing's initial possession of my husband and its eventual feeding, the longer the period before its subsequent return. That was when we realised that we might be able to *train* it — to wean it off using Rick as a source of nourishment. So now, each time it comes, we starve it for a while. Each time we make it wait longer and longer for its meal, and consequently the period between its visits are also growing longer and longer. With number six, we managed to make it wait sixteen days — over two whole hellish weeks with it living in Rick's body, forcing me to imprison him here to nest in his own filth, like a mad animal...

'But it was worth it. After it fed that time, it didn't return for over a year and a half. This time around, we've made it wait two *months* for its meal, and I'm hoping for at least five years of remission. With luck, maybe more. Perhaps it will even be permanent, and we'll never have to go through this horror ever, ever again. If all goes well, John, you could be my lucky seven. What do you think of that?'

Alan didn't know what to think, but he knew that lucky number seven had turned its back on him.

The werebitch stood up. She looked tired and afraid and sick to her stomach, but there was a cold distant light in her eye that Alan recognised from his own reflection when he looked in a mirror. This, whatever it was, really was going to happen. There was no stopping it now.

She stepped over him and went to the door sealed with heavy bolts, and one by one, carefully drew them, trying to make as little noise as possible.

Oh my God, Alan thought. Suddenly, he thought he knew what it was.

She had some kind of *dog* hidden in there, some poor American Pit bull or Rottweiler that she'd abused and starved and infected with her own strain of craziness, training it to savage her victims. He began to struggle against his bonds, even though he knew escape was impossible.

Annie drew the last bolt, turned the door handle, and gently threw the door open.

Rigid with terror now, Alan stared past her into the new room, which was dark beyond all understanding, like a deep pool of black ink. The powerful light from the chandelier should have shone into the farthest depths of that room, no matter how large it was, like a searchlight.

But the light seemed to simply stop about three or four feet beyond the threshold, a division between light and dark so sharp and defined it might have been painted on the floorboards.

The werebitch slowly backed away from the doorway, never taking her eyes from the darkness of the room she had revealed.

She stepped over Alan without looking down and backed all the way over to the sideboard, and then risked turning to quickly turn on the old record player. Some ancient classical music started up, some slow drone of brass and woodwind instruments. Then she moved toward the room's other door, the one which Alan had entered God alone knew how long ago, with no idea of what awaited him.

She opened the door and then stood poised in the doorway as the music began to build.

'This is from Mendelssohn's incidental music for *A Midsummer Night's Dream*,' she said, her eyes fixed unwavering on the dark doorway at the other side of the room.

Tears were running down her cheeks now, but he saw that they were tears of anticipatory joy.

'Rick grew up listening to music like this. It's always been a part of his life, but he had to teach me about it. This is his favourite piece, the *Nocturne*. This is the music that accompanies the sleeping lovers as they dream, you see, and that's what I like to think that *we* are — lovers, temporarily trapped in a terrible dream. I've taken to playing it whenever the thing is about to be fed, because somewhere deep inside the madness and chaos of that other world, I know that Rick's waiting and listening. When he hears the echoes of this music, he'll know that his time in the darkness is almost over.'

Alan watched her reach for something that hung by the door, a piece of dangling nylon cord, and then he realised that the bright chandelier overhead was controlled by this single light-pull. He watched the werebitch hook the string over the top of the door and then carefully pull the door closed behind her. Then he heard the heavy bolts being shot into place.

The next few seconds of waiting seemed like an eternity, and then he saw the light-pull cord jerk taut, and heard the switch snap, and the bright lights of the chandelier went out. Alan immediately swung his head in the direction of the open doorway, but in the new pitch-blackness, he couldn't locate it.

He waited and waited, all his senses straining out into the darkness. For the longest time there was nothing, except for an increase in the stench.

But then he began to hear noises, first a stealthy shuffling that set his skin crawling, and then the sound of a heavy chain, just like the one around his neck but longer, slowly unravelling, link by link by link.

The smell, already foul beyond his experience, steadily grew worse and worse, making his gorge rise behind his muzzle of tape. The sounds of what were maybe claws scraping on floorboards grew closer and sharper, but still he could see nothing, even though he was straining his eyes into the black nothing where he imagined the doorway to be.

Then he belatedly realised that the scratching sounds were not coming from floor-level.

He recalled with a thrill of terror what the werebitch had said about waking up to discover her husband crawling around on the ceiling like a giant spider.

He rolled his head and looked up into darkness above, and finally did see something, the merest suggestion of shape and movement, a shadow within a shadow. And abruptly, at the centre of this greater darkness, two eyes snapped open, red eyes, as the werebitch had promised, like coals tumbled from the heart of an intense fire. They were entirely human in shape, but something impossibly inhuman was looking out through them.

Looking at *him*.

It paused for the briefest of moments, fixing him with its fiery glare, and then it dropped on him. Behind the tape, Alan tried to scream as it bit the first large gobbet of flesh from his scalp, cheek and ear, and then shifted around with grotesque alacrity to bore in for the soft, succulent meat of his belly.

He struggled and fought for survival as best he could within his limited means, but not for long.

Then there was only the sound of tearing, chewing, and gnawing, and above it all the sombre bassoons of Mendelssohn's *Nocturne*, calling Annie's beloved back home, perhaps this time for good.

*In this story I was trying to capture something of the atmosphere of those nightmares where you have committed some crime, or have performed some act so terrible and appallingly final, that in those few seconds of confusion between sleep and wakening, you actually believe it was real, and you have absolutely no idea why you did what you did, or why you ever imagined that it would make things better instead of so much worse.*

We were up on the Hill when it happened… although, now that I come to think of it, that's really something of a redundant statement. It happened on the Hill because it couldn't have happened anywhere else. Not on that night, and likely not on any other night in the future, no matter where in the world we were.

I think about that sometimes. During the long, lonely months and years that are my penance, and with the benefit of hindsight, I think about how easily it could all have been avoided, and about how different things could and should have been. Sometimes I think about those things a lot.

But I find that there are gaps in my memory, even now.

In fact, there are a great number of very *significant* gaps, some of them deep but narrow crevices I have been able to step over with relative ease, but others are great, bottomless chasms, which I've had to cross in a series of careful, imaginative and, I hope, intuitive leaps.

These efforts eventually resolved themselves into a fictional narrative, a neatly streamlined version of events that is probably as close to the truth as I, or anyone else, will ever be able to get. And while I understand that this will not be good enough for some people — Mike's bereft widow and his poor, broken-hearted children, for example — unfortunately I believe that it's the best I will ever have to offer.

I have tried so many times, you see, but I simply cannot seem to explain myself or my actions in any other way. This short and terribly bitter story is all I have. The eyes I use to look back into my own past are still full of a blinding, alien light, and I find it all but impossible to see anything else with genuine clarity.

There are shadows, sometimes, yes. Shadows, misshapen and dreadful. Fearful silhouettes, sharply framed against the stars.

But I suspect that they are all of my own making.

Still... I'll tell you what I know, shall I? I'll tell you what I *recall*, at any rate. What I *think* happened that night. What I felt *then*, and what I feel *now*. I'll tell you what I actually *believe*. Perhaps then you can be the judge as to whether my imagination and intuition have spoken truly, or whether the blood on my hands is a mark of pure evil.

The mark of Cain, you might say.

I remember Mike disgustedly shaking his head at the thick blanket of cloud-cover that had gathered to obscure the night sky from horizon to horizon, and I remember him muttering under his breath as he cursed his bad luck. He was something of an amateur astronomer and had spent most of the day prior to us setting up camp telling me — in a little more detail than I really cared to know — about the many wonders of the planet Venus.

Apparently that had been the night when the planet reached an astronomical position known as the 'inferior conjunction', which Mike said was the closest it ever came to Earth. However, he'd also admitted that this wasn't exactly a rare event. In point of fact, it happened every 584 days. But it had never before coincided with one of our campouts, and that's what made it a special occasion for him.

'Venus is our closest neighbour,' he'd told me with his usual enthusiasm as we loaded up the car with our gear earlier that afternoon. 'It's named for the Roman goddess of love and beauty, of course, but it's also known as the Morning Star or the Evening Star, depending on its orbit relative to the Earth.'

Later, as we drove to the Hill, he told me that Venus was easy to pick out with the naked eye, because apart from the moon it was always the biggest and brightest natural object in the night sky.

'And as there'll no moon at all tonight,' he'd added, with the satisfaction of a gambler laying down a winning hand, 'we'll be able to see it perfectly, with nothing to distract us…'

But as the afternoon wore on it started to look as though he was going to be wrong about that.

Not that he was wrong about the planet's position in the heavens, Mike really knew his stuff, but there was nothing he could do about the capricious nature of the British weather.

Even though it was the middle of August and the forecast had been good, promising an almost perfect night for stargazing, as the afternoon steadily became the evening, the sky had begun to fill with dark, opaque clouds that soaked up the daylight like colossal sponges.

By the time we had the tent erected and our little campfire merrily flickering away, there had been virtually nothing at all left of the clear, starry night he had so hoped for, and Mike didn't even bother unpacking the telescope he had brought along in its own padded carry-case.

To be honest, being aware of just how keenly Mike had been looking forward to this event, I'd expected him to be a little more upset at the missed opportunity than he was. But — initial dark mutterings aside — he'd actually seemed resigned to making the best of it, and appeared to be doing his level best to shrug off the disappointment.

As he'd told me after we'd eaten our fill, as we opened another couple of beers and clinked our bottles together in the shifting firelight, he was quite sure that there'd be another chance for us to witness the phenomenon properly at some later date.

*It'll come around for us again*, he'd sighed. *It's not the end of the world, is it?*

And I, trying to make a joke of it, had replied: *You don't know that...*

The things that come back to haunt you.

Mike and I first started our Saturday night campout tradition when we were still in our early teens.

Actually, we may even have been a year or so younger than that. Eleven or twelve? We were innocent, at any rate, just a couple of ordinary boys, still only children, and no meanness at all in either of us.

To begin with we camped in the unused and overgrown paddock that lay directly behind my parents' small detached cottage, or sometimes under the shelter of the apple trees at the end of his Aunt Charlotte's back garden on the very outskirts of our village. There we indulged ourselves with midnight feasts of crisps and chocolate, and Heinz baked beans or spaghetti hoops eaten cold from the can, and gallon upon gassy gallon of coke, lemonade, and ginger beer.

Then we would spend the rest of each night giggling about those things which only small, overtired boys can giggle about, and holding epic farting competitions until we were both utterly exhausted and partially asphyxiated, and then we would finally fall asleep.

Two or three years later we discovered the secluded privacy to be found on the summit of Gooseberry Hill, which rose to a lofty elevation out of a patchwork of wheat fields and looked across at our tiny village from about a mile away, and we immediately adopted it as our own sovereign territory.

I would like to be able to say that we had moved our base of operations to this remote eyrie because we enjoyed the slightly otherworldly feeling of being cut off from the rest of society, and of being at one with nature… but mostly that would be a self-serving lie.

We *did* like both those things, of course, but pretty much the sole purpose of the relocation was to escape the watchful eyes of interfering adults and to accommodate what we believed to be the increasing sophistication of our tastes, which by that time ran to dog-eared copies of top-shelf magazines and large bottles of very strong cider.

These two forbidden luxury items were regularly sold to us at a very generous discount by the delightfully irresponsible proprietor of the local newsagent shop, for whom we both worked weekday paper rounds.

Mike and I loved Mr Prasad, who was funny and kind and irreverent and mischievous, and who seemed to understand boys so very well, even though he and his wife had only managed to produce a series of five almost identical daughters.

Mike's full name was Michael Philip Ellory. He was my best friend in the whole wide world, and now I find that I can't actually remember a time when I *didn't* know him, when he *wasn't* already my best friend. Mike had been raised entirely by his maternal aunt, because his parents had died in a car crash when he was only a baby, but this terrible stroke of bad luck had never seemed to darken his character in any way that I could see — and we were so close that if there had been anything to see, I would certainly have seen it.

Practically from day one Mike and I had been like peas in a pod. We were like brothers, like twins bonded for life, and we were completely inseparable. Mike was my ever-present shadow, my clear-eyed reflection, and I know that I was his.

I think we must have gone through just about every childhood development and adolescent trauma together in almost perfect synchronicity, losing our front teeth at the same time, catching colds, coughs, and even measles at the same time, and then, when the time came, surging through puberty together, our voices actually breaking in exactly the same hour of exactly the same day.

Then, of course, the long years passed, as they do, and the world changed in a thousand different ways we could never have foreseen.

Who could have guessed that Mike would have become an industrial chemist, or that I, one of the least organised creatures ever to have walked the Earth, would end up making a living as the operations manager of a large logistics company. Who could have guessed that we — both of us only-children — would go on to raise large families of our own?

Not us, that's for sure.

Having said all this, perhaps our own world hadn't changed as greatly as it might have done had we been slightly different people, or if our childhoods had been any less idyllic than they were.

Some thirty years on we had both still lived within easy reach of the same small village we had grown up in, and we'd still known most of the same people we had grown up with and around. And even though real life had certainly encroached upon our close friendship, it had never even come close to breaking it.

In spite of the ever-increasing calls on our time and energy made by the combination of relationships, families, kids, and careers, our tradition of summer campouts on Gooseberry Hill had continued pretty much without interruption... although, it is certainly true that the *frequency* of our campouts had steadily dwindled to the point where Mike and I had only been able to get together just once or twice each year.

Just a couple of nights every summer, instead of what in the good old days might have been a dozen or more. Sometimes the restriction seemed a little unfair.

But you know what? In a strange sort of way, even this limitation seemed to work quite well for both of us. It allowed us the freedom to periodically escape from our happy but fairly humdrum lives, if only for a short while, and to abscond from all our cares and responsibilities and duties. Those campouts became our lives' pressure valve.

Up on Gooseberry Hill we didn't have to be husbands or fathers, wage-slaves or care-givers, or anything else for that matter. We didn't even have to behave like *adults* if we didn't want to. We could simply chill out and reconnect with the innocent, carefree boys we had once been. We could plug back into that easy-going fraternal relationship, slip effortlessly back into character, and just...

I don't know... just *be...*

Of course, the days of cold baked beans and fizzy drinks were long behind us, as were the dirty magazines and economy-sized bottles of White Lightning.

In those later years our food supplies usually came courtesy of the supermarket deli' counter, and consisted of platters of continental meats and truckles of obscure cheeses, of dips, stuffed olives, tapas selections, and artisan breads.

Likewise, our tastes in liquid refreshment had evolved in a very similar fashion, and we tended to take along either a selection of subtle micro-brewery ales or a number of really good bottles of wine, or both if the mood happened to be upon us.

Also, and completely without fail, we always held in reserve a spectacular single malt to see us through the wee small hours, before we finally retired, a little the worse for wear, to our airbeds.

Some years, if the weather wasn't so great, we had actually been known to stay tucked up inside the tent all night long, guzzling and gorging ourselves stupid under canvas, and maybe watching a couple of brainless action movies on my iPad. But if it were at all possible, we preferred not to submit to this weakness.

If we could, we liked to spend most of our time out under the stars, because when darkness at last fell on Gooseberry Hill, and if the weather actually deigned to cooperate, something truly magical happened.

After what seemed like a long, lingering dusk, an even greater sense of peace always seemed to descend upon us as the last of the light bled from the sky, a sense of an almost holy blessedness that I for one had never felt anywhere else in the world — or in anyone else's company, for that matter.

Once the dozen or so streetlights down in the village went out at around midnight, there was absolutely no trace of light-pollution whatsoever in any direction, not even over the farthest horizon. There were so many visible stars that at times it felt like we had somehow passed through the cloudy membrane of our planet's atmosphere and were actually travelling through space.

We would lie on our backs, feel the motion of the earth as it hurtled and spun through the cosmos, and just enjoy the show.

That had always been enough for me, just looking up at the witchy light of the stars, drinking them in through a comforting alcoholic haze.

But it wasn't enough for Mike.

From practically our very first night on Gooseberry Hill he'd wanted so much more. Mike had wanted to know what he was looking at, he'd wanted to be able to name the constellations, and when Mike set his mind to do something, drunk or not, he invariably did it. It wasn't too long before he'd begun taking books on astronomy up there every weekend, as well as a large notebook for making his own primitive star charts.

Pretty soon he'd been gassing on about Ursa Minor, Ursa Major, The Plough, and Orion's Belt, and then increasingly about nebulae, galaxies, and light-years, and so many other bits and pieces of astronomical jargon that I often fell asleep to the comforting rhythm of his rambling, inebriated, enraptured voice.

From our little camp on the Hill we had watched the moon wax and wane a hundred times, we had seen a handful of partial eclipses and one stunning complete eclipse, as well as Orionid and Perseid meteor showers by the dozen, and I had listened with half a drunken ear as Mike babbled endlessly about the legacy of the Big Bang, and the scientific wonder that was Hubble, and the possibilities of a still-expanding universe.

But on that night — on *that* night — there had been nothing to see above our heads but the swollen underbellies of the dark clouds, and Mike had seemed disinclined to begin one of his meandering, amiable lectures.

Instead we had taken the unexpected opportunity to discuss our lives, just like real grown-ups.

We'd talked about our children, our wives, and our sex lives, and then we'd talked jobs, politics, world news, and sport, before moving on to movies, books, and music, and in the process we had managed to consume all the beer and make significant inroads into our supplies of wine. The night had flown, and dawn was only an hour or so away.

I will not deny that we were intoxicated when it happened. I *didn't* deny it later on, when I was interviewed by the police.

In fact, I actually went further, and admitted that the pair of us had been completely rat-arsed, pissed out of our tiny skulls. But there again, we'd often been in the same lamentable condition, and probably in conditions a great deal worse, many, many times before while camping on the Hill, all of which had passed off entirely without incident.

The alcohol in our systems, I told them, had played no part in what happened, none at all.

I did what I did, I said, because at the time it seemed that there was simply no reason *not* to.

I told them that at somewhere around three or three-thirty in the morning, I heard Mike saying, 'Hey, look!'

I didn't immediately respond, being somewhat preoccupied with trying to read the label on our final bottle of wine by the light of the small campfire, which by that late hour had been only ashes and a few glowing embers. By squinting I managed to make out a few words, but they soon began to double and treble, and I gave it up as a bad job.

I unscrewed the cap and took a drink direct from the bottle. It was warm, it was wet, and it was red…so it was probably the claret.

'Hey, Pete,' Mike called again. 'Pete, you've really got to see this…'

Some distance behind mc, Mike had been making use of the Grand Ceremonial Pissing Stone, a unique feature of our campsite that was also occasionally known to us as the Rugged Rock of Relief. This was a very large lozenge-shaped rock which overhung the edge of Gooseberry Hill by a good three feet.

If there had been a nice deep lake at the bottom of the Hill, the Pissing Stone would have been a natural diving platform, but as there was only a long steep slope composed of dirt, rocks, scree, and a lot of old woody gooseberry bushes too mean and ugly to die, it had always served us as an *al fresco* urinal. I had already used the facilities myself a little earlier, achieving, I firmly believed, a record distance.

'Hey, Pete, seriously, you've got to look….'

Mike's voice was perfectly clear. I recall being envious of the way he could drink so much and yet sound so sober. A couple of drinks in, I always sounded like a dentist had injected about a litre of novocaine into my tongue. By comparison, Mike just sounded like a slightly giddy BBC newsreader.

'What is it?' I slurred back at him. 'And don't try to tell me you've set a new record, because I won't believe you.'

'You *won't* believe it.' I realised that Mike's voice was suddenly full of the old enthusiasm again. 'There's a gap in the clouds now,' he said urgently, 'honestly, there's a really big gap, it just opened up out of nowhere. It looks like we're actually going to be able to…'

Mike's voice seemed to fade somehow away then, as though he had fallen into a trance.

Finally curious enough to bother looking, I twisted around and saw him standing perched atop the Pissing Rock, his shorts and pants still pushed halfway down his thighs. He was standing staring up into the sky.

When I followed the direction of his gaze, I saw that he was right. Sometime over the last half hour or so, as we'd drunkenly been putting the world to rights, a huge wedge-shaped cloud-gate had opened directly above us. A field of bright stars twinkled down through it.

Then I looked just a little higher into the firmament, and I saw Venus.

I saw Venus.

And suddenly nothing else mattered.

*Nothing*.

All the time Mike had been chattering about the planet, both earlier in the day and on so many other nights in the past, I'd imagined that I had succeeded in filtering most of it out, the same way Mike must have filtered out my voice when I began to waffle on about the films of the 1970s, which were my own personal obsession. But without my being aware of it, my subconscious must have been taking a lot more notice than I ever imagined.

I knew *so many* things.

Venus was sometimes called Earth's 'sister planet', being of both similar size and similar proximity to the Sun. There was some suggestion that billions of years ago it must have had its own supplies of water, oceans and seas and rivers, and therefore quite probably its own organic life.

But not anymore.

As the planet's molten core had cooled, Venus had lost its magnetic field, which had then allowed the solar winds to sweep its oceans away into interplanetary space. Everything that may once have lived there, flora, fauna, bacteria, vertebrate, invertebrate, or even sentient being, would have instantly perished. The atmospheric pressure was now ninety-three times that of Earth, and the temperature of the planet's surface, a mixture of arid, lifeless desert and vast, glassy volcanic plains, was the hottest in the solar system — hotter even than Mercury, which was probably as much as ten million miles closer to the sun.

For one moment it was as though I were *there*, somehow standing there, watching the never-ending Venusian winds swirl the soupy clouds of sulphuric acid in which the planet was perpetually wreathed, watching the heat haze rising in the vast empty distances, and feeling the deathly intensity of the strongest greenhouse effect in the entire solar system.

This sister planet of ours, a planet once so like our own, now possessed nothing less than the very landscape of hell. And, I thought, what could happen to *one* sister could very easily happen to the other, and probably would.

It suddenly became very clear to me that this would be the future of our own planet, and as far as I was concerned that was just as good as saying there was *no such thing* as the future. I understood that everything the human race had accomplished and all that it might accomplish would all be for nothing, because eventually everything would be destroyed, and nothing could be saved.

Civilizations would fragment and crumble and cities would fall. The encyclopaedia of human knowledge would calcify and turn to dust. All life would perish. Human history would cease to have meaning. Human concepts like Good and Evil, Pity and Mercy would cease to have meaning… but then I began to understand that in a way these terms *already* had no meaning.

After all, nothing has value if it cannot endure, and nothing could endure in this hell.

Nothing but demons.

Our world would meet its end like Venus, and it wouldn't matter what one individual person did or did not do. People around the world worshipped their gods and served their charities and fed their poor… but why did they bother? In the end, it would make no difference. How could it?

In a billion years' time, when the Earth and all its inhabitants, every man, woman and child, every creature, every fish and fowl, every leaf and every bud, were dead and gone, after the oceans had fled and the sky was a whirlpool of acid, what would it matter if I had lived a good life, or if anyone had *ever* lived a good life?

Would it matter if instead of indulging his paperboys like the sons he was incapable of fathering, Mr Prasad took them one by one into his stockroom and forced himself upon them? Or if I did the same thing to my own children once my wife was firmly asleep? Or if she actually *helped* me satisfy my perversity? What if Mike took his knowledge of chemistry from the industrial laboratories where he worked and poisoned the water supply of a whole city, hundreds and thousands of men, women and children dying in agony?

What if *nothing* mattered? Not pogroms, ethnic cleansings, or final solutions. Puppy dogs, poppies, or love songs. Torturers, serial killers, or teenage suicide bombers. What if all of these things amounted to exactly the same in the end, and not a single one of them mattered?

I blinked and immediately found myself back on Gooseberry Hill.

I felt as though I had been gone from this world for decades, for centuries. The fire still possessed its glowing embers, the rent in the cloud cover was still there, and Mike was still staring up at Venus, transfixed.

The only thing that seemed to have changed was my own position.

Somehow, during the moments that I had left my body and travelled to that other world, I had risen to my feet and walked over to where Mike stood. I had mounted the Grand Ceremonial Pissing Stone and placed both my hands on Mike's back.

I could feel his muscles quivering under my fingertips, but he did not flinch from my touch. Not at all.

No, I understood that he had been *expecting* it. Mike and I — so very close for so many long years — had looked upon Venus and seen the same terrible truths. Our minds, our thoughts and beliefs, were one and the same. We were brothers, twins to match the sister planets. And like the sister planets, the only meaningful difference between us now was simply a matter of position.

I looked up. The gap in the clouds was slowly closing again, but for the moment Venus was still perfectly visible. I felt the waves of its despair washing over me, washing through me, bathing my face, sinking into my pores, drowning me in that alien light. I was waiting for something. Some kind of instruction. Some order. Some final, irrevocable message.

Then it came. I heard it, I *felt* it.

So did Mike.

'Do it,' he whispered.

Without a fraction of hesitation, I pushed him.

He dropped silently, without a single murmur or cry, but a few seconds later I heard his body strike the ground heavily, and then his tumbling progress all the way to the bottom of the Hill. I thought of the rocks he must have landed upon breaking his bones, the thorns of the old gooseberry bushes ripping his flesh like the talons of some alien beast. He would have been shattered, torn open.

When all the sounds of his descent had ended, I listened carefully to the silence, waiting for a groan of pain, a whimper, a sob, but there was nothing. I lingered a few more minutes, looking at my hands and marvelling at how incredibly steady they were, and then I climbed down from the Pissing Stone.

I slowly retraced our steps from much earlier that day and unhurriedly trekked down to the base of the Hill, where we had left Mike's estate car parked, and then in utter darkness found my way around the foot of the Hill, clambering over rocks and ghosting through thick clumps of gooseberry bush with a nerveless, sure-footed ease.

When I reached the place one hundred feet directly below the Pissing Stone I could see nothing, but I began to hear a faint laboured breathing, and I edged further forward. Then suddenly I could smell shit and blood and sour piss, and I realised that I had found Mike.

I squatted down into the dying stink of him.

Although the darkness there was absolute, I never once doubted that he was at least partially conscious, and that he knew I was there in his last few moments. I reached out and touched him, found his shoulder, his shirt torn and damp with blood. His painful breathing hitched for a moment, and then continued, slower and slower at first, and then faster and faster and faster as the end approached.

He might have said something in that instant, and so might I, but neither of us did. There was no need. We both understood.

When it was over, I left my hand where it was for another few minutes. Actually, to tell the truth, I forgot it was there, I forgot what I was touching and why. Because that was the first moment when I began to think about what might happen next, when I actually began to consider the consequences of my actions.

I imagined myself returning to our camp and taking my mobile phone from my backpack and turning it on to make calls to the emergency services. They would send an ambulance. They would send the police. Then I would try to decide what to tell them when they came, the truth or lies.

Mike was an unhappy man, I could say...

Every time we came back to the Hill, he was a little worse, a little unhappier in his career and a lot more dissatisfied with his family life. He told me how much he hated his wife and detested his children, how he wished he could finally be rid of them and find some kind of peace. I could explain how he jumped up on the Pissing Stone, sobbing that he couldn't bear it any more, that he wanted to die, that he'd *rather* be dead... and then before I could move, officer, he simply *jumped*.

We were having a great time, I could say...

We'd been talking about how lucky we both were, about how life was so sweet, and had just finished discussing how we were going to club together and take our two families on holiday the following year, hire a huge RV and tour North

America for a month. And then Mike jumped up on to the Pissing Stone, drunkenly talking about how he was looking forward to standing with his children on the rim of the Grand Canyon, and how his wife, so nervous of heights, would be hanging back and getting her leg pulled for her timidity… and then, in his drunken excitement, officer, he just *slipped*.

When it first got dark, I could say, another couple of guys turned up out of nowhere, perhaps drawn by our firelight...

They said they had planned to camp on the Hill too, but suspiciously they had no tents or gear of any kind. At first we tried to accept them at face value, and even gave them some of our food and drink, but things soon turned unpleasant. We argued, and they left, threatening retribution. Much later on, when we were too drunk to defend ourselves, they came back and started pushing us around. Things got out of hand… and before I knew what was happening, officer, one of the men *pushed* Mike over the edge.

These were just some of the thoughts that ran through my head at the time, and to me each idea seemed just as good as the last.

I realised that the police likely wouldn't be convinced by any one of them for long, but that didn't matter, of course, because *nothing* mattered. So I resolved that I was going to tell them the absolute unvarnished truth as I saw it, because the truth was surely just as meaningless as any lie or fabrication of the truth that I might devise.

They would probably disbelieve me at first, perhaps. But then, as I continued to talk, as I continued to explain to them all I had seen and felt, they would slowly begin to understand, and then their stupid, ignorant faces would grow long with horror.

They would have me sectioned for mental health tests, I knew.

They would begin their forensic examination of the Hill, interview everyone who had ever known me, everyone who had known Mike. Our wives, our children. The tabloid headlines would be lurid. My family would be driven from our home, my wife spat on in the supermarket, my children hounded out of their schools by vicious bullying. Mike's wife would seek solace in the bottle, and their children would go feral, the rest of their lives ruined, haunted by the ghost of their murdered father. And while I was on remand, prior to my trial, another prisoner would try to slash my throat with a knife his sweet little pensioner mother had smuggled in for him.

I knew all of this. But it didn't matter. Nothing did.

At long last I'd stood up, wiping Mike's cold sticky blood off my hands and on to my jeans with no more emotion than if it had been strawberry jam…but then, in the very next instant, it seemed as though a long needle of ice had suddenly slid into my gut, a terrible feeling that almost doubled me over with agony.

I suddenly became aware of exactly what it *was* I had just wiped off my hands, that it was nothing less than my friend's lifeblood. I knew that Mike — my friend, my brother — was dead at my feet, and that I had killed him.

It was at that moment that the veil truly lifted, and the sheer enormity of what I had done fell on me like an anvil. I finally understood the awful finality of the crime I had perpetrated, and I understood that it could not be undone, it could not be taken back.

I began to cry, to sob uncontrollably. My heart broke, and my mind cried out for answers they would never receive. The unnatural clarity of thought that had stolen my reason and directed my actions had evaporated like treacherous morning mist. The twisted sense of rightness, of complete assurance, of rock-solid logic, that had made Mike's murder seem not only inevitable but also completely insignificant had vanished.

In absolute desperation, I looked back up into the night sky, searching again for Venus. I felt that if I could gaze upon its alien face for just a few more moments the mere sight would rekindle my earlier conviction, and re-establish the beliefs which had seized me so powerfully and the temporary madness that had used me so coldly.

But high above Gooseberry Hill, the cloud-gate had closed up once more, and there was nothing to see but darkness.

*This is one of those stories that have been floating around at the back of my mind for a couple of years without ever coming completely into focus — until now, that is. It began with a single image. Just an ordinary man sitting on a bench, looking for a house, a very, very old house, that only he seemed to be able to see. A simple set-up, of course, but it posed so many questions I felt I needed to know the answers to. All I had to do in order to satisfy my curiosity was go to the house and open the door.*

Morgan sat on the wooden bench and stretched out his long legs, crossing them at the ankles, and then casually draped both arms along the backrest. He was trying his very best to appear as relaxed as possible… or perhaps he was really only trying to convince *himself* that he was feeling relaxed. But whichever one of them it was, it wasn't working too well. In actual fact, he was tense and nervous, and slightly nauseous, and he suspected that just about everyone who passed him by could probably sense it.

Luckily for him this was central London, which meant that even at seven o'clock in the morning nobody had either the time or the inclination to wonder exactly what a well-dressed, middle-aged man occupying a public bench might have to be so nervous about. This was an arrangement which suited Morgan right down to the ground.

After all, he thought, it wasn't every day a man attempted to steal a building that might eventually be worth three or maybe even four million pounds.

No, I'm not *stealing* it, he quickly corrected himself, stealing would be a different thing entirely. I'm *appropriating* it, that's what I'm doing. I'm taking *possession* of it, I'm assuming *ownership*.

In any case, surely it was impossible to steal something that appeared to belong to no one? Wasn't that just called *discovering*? People the world over had been turning that little trick for millennia, and in fact whole empires had been founded on the same basic principle - a] find someplace you like the look of, b] stick your little coloured flag in it, and c] put your feet up and make yourself at home.

All you really needed was the balls to stake your claim in the first place, and nobody had ever accused Danny Morgan of not having balls.

'Finders keepers, losers weepers,' he whispered to himself, and remembered standing with his nose practically squashed up against the thick glass of a departure lounge window, watching as a colossal Cathay Pacific Airbus slowly taxied away from the terminal to begin its sixteen-hour journey to Bangkok's Don Mueang International Airport.

He'd waved until the plane had taken off. Then he had continued to wave until it vanished into the low cloud-cover and was completely out of sight, because he'd promised that he would. When it came to Nok and Noi, the most important people in his life, he had always kept his promises. Always.

All but the very last, of course.

'I'll see you very soon,' he'd told his wife and daughter as he kissed them goodbye. But he'd never seen them again. Not alive.

Not whole.

It was a beautiful, clear-skied spring morning, a Wednesday, and the small enclosed park to Morgan's back emitted the pleasant fragrances of recently mown lawns and early blossom, which at this tender hour of the day were still strong enough to overcome the carbon monoxide fumes that he knew would later predominate and eventually smother them.

He was on the south side of Templar Square, in the very heart of the capital, and he was sitting in the exact spot that had once been his favourite resting place during the long-gone and unlamented days when he had lived on the streets, when he had been one of this vast city's vast legion of homeless waifs and strays.

That was twenty-five years in the past now, a quarter of a century almost to the very day — practically a whole lifetime ago.

Back then he'd dropped by Templar Square most afternoons, largely to escape the hustle-bustle of the tube stations and street corners where he peddled his armfuls of the Big Issue, but also to chill out on his bench and covertly smoke a little weed. Then he would finally snooze in the shade of the trees, dreaming of a better future, all the while quietly convinced that for him a dream was all it could ever be.

He had yet to learn that dreams sometimes came true... also, that a whole decade of such dreams could turn into an inescapable nightmare in less than a single hour.

It wasn't the *same* bench, of course, not after twenty-five years. But it was in precisely the same location as its predecessor, and that was the really important thing. This was the very spot from which he had first seen the house he hoped to make his own today, the same place almost to the inch, and if he ever hoped to be able to find it again, he knew that this was where he would have to be.

He understood that the house he sought was not a normal house; that much was perfectly clear, even if nothing else was. It was a mystery, an enigmatic rune, a secret written in code, and it was almost wilfully difficult to see, which was how Morgan imagined it had managed to evade ownership for so long.

The first time he'd seen the house, Morgan had assumed that he was either still dreaming or having some kind of drug-induced hallucination.

He'd been smoking a lot more than usual at the time, and, in addition, popping some anonymous but thoroughly kicking pills that had lately fallen into his possession. It had seemed perfectly reasonable to him that either one or both of these substances might have helped him achieve some kind of altered state, or opened up the doors of perception, or whatever it was they called such lunatic visions.

In any case, one moment there had been the familiar unbroken terraced row of tall Georgian town houses standing before him, all mostly redeveloped into offices for solicitors and advertising agencies and film production companies, nothing unexpected or out of place… but then an unknown something had caught in the corner of his eye like a granule of broken glass, and in the next moment he had seen the mouth of an alleyway.

A narrow little alleyway tucked in between two of the buildings, an alleyway he had never noticed in all the months he'd been coming to the Square and sitting on a bench directly opposite it.

And he'd wondered, how was that possible?

Morgan had risen uncertainly from his seat on the bench, still not quite sure if he was in the real world or not, and stumbled across the road, heedless of the traffic, somehow drawn to this architectural anomaly.

He'd heard blaring horns, the squeal of hastily-applied brakes, and a loud, rough voice growling expletives out of a cab window. He remembered reaching the pavement and then just standing there for the longest time, his mouth agape, actual drool shining on his chin, like he was some kind of village idiot at his wit's end faced with the wonders of the big bad city.

He remembered looking through the long, narrow cobblestone alley to the cobblestone courtyard at its end and the house that presided over it, a gracious house that seemed much older than those in the Square, a house that was both wide and grand, four generous floors high.

The image had seemed to waver in front of his eyes, like a mirage floating in the air above a desert floor. And then...

What then?

Well, *then* there had been the old lady and her granddaughter.

Or maybe it was the old lady's *great-*granddaughter, because this was probably the oldest old lady Morgan had ever seen in his entire life, then or since. Absolutely — almost unbelievably — ancient, she had been painfully emaciated and bent almost double, her face and her toothless mouth a twisted mess of deep wrinkles, her fine white hair thinning almost to baldness across her crown. Nevertheless, she had immediately attacked him, using her walking stick to beat him about the head and shoulders.

The blows she rained down on him weren't actually all that painful — she was too old, too weak, and too crippled by her arthritis to be able to really hurt him, even if that had been her real intention — but they were certainly enough to distract him from his vision of the house.

Morgan was forced to take a step or two back as the old lady advanced upon him, ineffectually swiping and jabbing with her cane, and the alleyway, the courtyard, the house, everything, had instantly disappeared, vanished, slipped out of sight with a jarring abruptness that made it hard to believe it had ever been there at all.

A second later a gorgeous-looking blonde girl of around Morgan's age had arrived at the scene, either the granddaughter or the great-granddaughter, and she'd gently restrained the old lady. It didn't look like too difficult a task, for the old lady seemed to have thoroughly exhausted herself with her efforts. The girl was almost supporting her entire weight, at least until she managed to get the cane under her again.

Once the old lady was a little steadier, the girl looked directly at Morgan for the first time, with eyes exactly the same piercing shade of electric blue as the old lady's, and, it seemed, with exactly the same degree of animosity.

In a low, cold, and somehow deadly voice, she had commanded him to leave the Square immediately.

'We've seen you hanging around, you know, taking your filthy drugs,' the girl said, her voice beginning to shake. 'You get away from here, and don't ever come back, or we'll call the police on you.'

Then the old lady had begun to bellow again, that hoarse, incomprehensible, gummy voice ranting away nineteen to the dozen, and not one single solitary word of it recognisable as English. The meaning, however, was perfectly clear.

Get away, stay away.

The old lady was terrified of him. They both were.

So Morgan had fled the Square. But he had come back the next day, and the next day, too, and the day after that, each time hoping to get a better, closer look at the fabulous house of which he had caught such a brief but tantalising glimpse. A house that very obviously did not *want* to be seen, but which drew him nevertheless, making him feel something like the needle of a compass, powerless to resist the inexorable forces steadily drawing it north.

And each day he had arrived in the Square to find the old lady and the girl waiting for him, now actually occupying his favourite bench, just as if they knew what he had come back for. The very instant the old lady saw him, she was up on her doddery old legs again, shaking her cane at him and shouting in that weird, gummy-nonsense language, and the granddaughter or great-granddaughter would be carefully holding her back and staring daggers at him all the while.

On the fourth day he tried coming much earlier in the morning, many hours before his usual time, but even that tactic didn't work.

Even worse, that time they'd had company, in the form of a uniformed policeman, who immediately arrested Morgan for possession of Class B drugs with the intent to supply. The girl had clearly accused him of trying to sell her weed or pills. It wasn't true, of course, but when the copper made him turn out the pockets of his filthy cargo pants on the bench and there was a small baggie of skunk in amongst his other few meagre possessions, not to mention the remains of his pill stash, it had been case closed.

He didn't know how many times over the following few months he had cursed those two women and all he felt they represented; the class-ridden unfairness of British society, the prejudice against the poor and the homeless and the disenfranchised, the inequalities of a system that allowed people like them to have people like him hounded and harassed and eventually extracted from their perfect little worlds just because the sight of him disturbed them...

He didn't know, but what he understood *now* was that it had actually been the making of him.

If it *hadn't* happened, he knew he wouldn't be sitting here on this bench today wearing a bespoke suit that cost him almost two thousand quid and a pair of handmade shoes that cost even more. He wouldn't have a Rolex on his wrist, a Jag', a Merc', and a Landrover in his garage, a handsome portfolio of stocks and shares, three villas in Spain, another couple on Cyprus, and fifteen full-time employees on the books of his rental properties company.

'Boss! Oi, Boss! Where'd you want me?'

Morgan realised that a white van had materialised on the road in front of the bench and that one of his oldest and most-trusted employees, Jack Fallon, was hailing him from it.

'Park anywhere,' he said.

Jack peered out the windscreen dubiously. 'I'll get nicked. It's all fucking yellers or permits round here.'

'Just park somewhere close, I'll pay any fines. You brought everything I asked for?'

'Yeah, sure. What're we up to today?'

'You'll find out.'

Jack rolled his eyes. 'As usual, a man of fucking mystery...'

Morgan watched the van slowly move off as Jack searched for somewhere to park, and he once again tried to focus his attention on the row of houses across the street. He couldn't see the alley yet, but he somehow knew that he eventually would. He knew that this was *meant* to be. It seemed to him now that there was a direct line that ran through his life from the day he was arrested to this moment right now.

Twenty-five years ago the judge had given him a suspended sentence — even back then possession only warranted a slap on the wrist — but he had also been offered a place in a work program out of town, all the way down in Croydon, which at the time had seemed like the other side of the world to him. It was just about the last thing he'd ever imagined doing, and he had surprised himself by accepting the offer. More, he'd actually *clutched* at the opportunity, like a drowning man fighting for his life.

Who knows, he speculated now, maybe that's actually what I *was* doing. He wondered if his subconscious mind had known exactly where his escalating drug use was heading, and had slapped the emergency self-preservation button before it was too late.

In Croydon, he and a small crew of other indifferent, mostly court-ordered ne'er-do-wells worked for the local authority as a part of a larger team maintaining council properties, and when the program ended six months later, Morgan had quickly found himself a similar job with a contractor in the private sector and started to work his way up.

It wasn't long before he was scraping together every penny he could find to invest in his own first property, a shabby little fixer-upper he immediately let out to students while he himself slept on a selection of mates' sofas and floors to maximise his profits. That first house was the seed of his own company, soon to flourish and quickly bear fruit.

It was also where he had met the young woman who would go on to become his wife and the mother of his child.

Her name was Unchallee Wimsawit, one of his tenants, but he had soon learned to use the affectionate nickname by which she was known to her family back home in Thailand — Nok. It meant 'bird', and it suited her perfectly, for the delicacy of her bone structure, the lightness of her movements, and the brightness in her eye.

When Nok's studies came to an end, she had stayed in England and married Morgan. Within a year their daughter was born, a month-and-a-half premature, and weighing only slightly more than 4lbs. They named her Noi, which meant 'small'. They had been very happy together for a long time.

But then time had stopped.

'Where are we, Boss?'

Morgan stood up at the sound of Jack's voice calling from the other side of the road, but he didn't so much as glance in his odd-job man's direction. Instead he began to cross the road without looking right or left, pretty much the same way he had crossed the road twenty-five years earlier, and the result was much the same, too, a small screech of tyres, and curses both thrown and ignored.

He reached the other pavement just as Jack strolled up, pulling his rolling tool-chest behind him.

'You sure you've brought the new locks and handles?'

'Yeah, no sweat, just tell me where to put them.'

'We're going down this alley here.'

Jack followed the direction of Morgan's nod, then frowned. 'Here where? There ain't no fucking alley.'

'Oh *ain't* there?' Morgan said, imitating Jack's accent. 'Look again.'

Morgan suddenly took a bright red and gold headscarf out of his jacket's inner pocket, shook it out, stepped past his workman, and tied it tightly around the top of one of the black railings.

Jack took a surprised step back and nearly tripped over his own tool chest. The gap between buildings had appeared to widen before his eyes.

'Fuck me, where'd that come from? Why didn't I see it before?'

'Don't worry, it's just an optical illusion.'

'I'll fucking say it is. How'd you manage to—'

'How about we save storytime till later, Jack?' Morgan snapped. 'I want to get this done as quickly as possible.'

'Time's money,' Jack nodded without resentment.

'You'd better believe it. Especially today. Now come on...'

Morgan began to stride off along the alleyway, his leather soles whispering and scraping over the cobblestone pathway, totally focussed on the house ahead, unblinking, as though even now he was afraid it could vanish in front of him. There had been a part of him that had been afraid that Jack would be unable to see it, that it had, after all, been some kind of drug-flashback, and had only ever existed in his head. At least now *that* option had been closed off, although his heart was still beating so hard he could feel it kicking at the wall of his ribs.

He knew a little more now about architectural eras than he had as a teenager, so he knew that he'd been right all those years ago; the house *was* older than the Georgian houses on the Square, a great deal older. As they got closer, he could hear Jack struggling to keep up while dragging his tool-chest's wheels over the old, uneven cobblestones, but he couldn't bring himself to slow down and offer to help.

As the house began to loom over him, Morgan remembered the way the aircraft hanger in Kent had done exactly the same thing, and the chill he had felt to the depths of his soul as he was engulfed by its shadow. Then he'd been inside the huge, echoing structure that was as cold as a walk-in meat locker, and a good thing too, because that was exactly what it had become.

There had been no aircraft inside the hanger anymore, just an enormous grid of dead bodies, row after row after row of them, mangled, dismantled, and burnt, all carefully set out on the concrete floor, each neatly covered by a white sheet.

He remembered being led through the seemingly endless rows by an Air Accident Investigation Branch official with a face like an undertaker, until the man halted, double-checked his clipboard, and then gestured down at two of the sheets. Print-outs bearing his wife and daughter's seat numbers had been taped to the floor at the foot of the sheets.

Morgan remembered the AAIB official's hand settling on his shoulder, the professionally modulated voice asking him if he'd mind trying to identify the remains.

If he'd *mind*?

He remembered shaking his head, remembered thinking that the bodies under the sheets seemed far too small to be his wife and daughter, even smaller than they had been in life, and remembered also how he'd felt a tiny bubble of hope float loose from the wreckage of his dreams; maybe it *wasn't* them, after all, maybe someone had made a silly mistake.

Oh maybe, maybe, maybe.

Then he'd reached down to the first of the sheets and begun to pull it back….

…and he consciously pulled himself away from the thought of what he had seen next.

He preferred not to dwell upon those terrible memories, and had tried his utmost to cast them from his mind. Now, whenever he called up images of his family, he only envisioned his wife and daughter at the party they had thrown for Noi's seventh birthday, her last, with both of his beautiful girls dressed in their favourite colours, Nok in a slim-fitting red dress that made her look like a model, and Noi in the gorgeously foolish gold tutu that had been her favourite gift that year.

These two colours were replicated in Nok's old headscarf, which he had lately taken to carrying with him wherever he went. For luck.

'Thank Christ for that,' Jack sighed, bumping and trundling his way across the cobbled courtyard to join Morgan facing the house's doorway, and then looked at his employer curiously. 'You okay, boss?'

Morgan nodded shortly. 'You?'

'Dunno, those cobbles are a right bastard. Might want to get the whole lot resurfaced if you're planning to do a lot of work up here.' He looked up at the house and grimaced, as though he had felt something cold and uncomfortable materialise in his stomach. 'Boss, you sure we should be here at all?'

'Why do you ask?'

'Dunno, it seems… seems like private property, like.'

'Well, it *is* private property now — mine.' Morgan gestured towards the door. 'Go on then, open her up.'

Jack hesitated for a moment, but then, feeling his employer's eyes on him, he moved forward again. He knelt down on the top of the three steps leading up to the door and peered closely at the handle and the keyhole.

'Well?' Morgan asked impatiently.

'It's a bloody antique, this. Be a shame to ruin it by trying to force it or drilling it out.'

'Can't you pick it?'

'I can try.'

Jack turned back to open one of the drawers in his tool chest, and Morgan saw just how pale the man had gone in the few seconds he had been close to the house. Sweat had gathered on his face and forehead like the glaze on a ceramic vase, and he looked on the verge of fainting. Nevertheless, he fished out the small roll of dark fabric that held his collection of picks, and then took a deep breath before turning back to the door with what was now very obviously reluctance.

Then Morgan had a moment of inspiration. 'Wait a minute, Jack.'

He noticed the way the other man pulled back from the door immediately, as though he had only been waiting for the command. Had been *hoping* for it, perhaps.

'Changed your mind, boss?'

Morgan could hear the relief in his voice, but he didn't understand it.

'Not at all, I want to try something first, just in case...'

He stepped around the tool chest and eased past Jack, and then placed his hand on the door handle, paused for a moment, and then turned it. The door swung open smoothly under the slightest pressure. It hadn't even been locked. All these years, he thought, and never locked.

'Well, what do you know,' he smiled. 'Just like it was meant to be...'

Morgan stepped into the doorway and looked at the house's interior with something like wonder.

Although he had been thinking about this moment for so many years, he still hadn't been able to imagine what the house's interior would look like. Would it still have the last tenants' furniture and possessions crowding the rooms, like a life-size dollhouse? Would the elements have got in through a damaged roof and had their way with the ceiling and the walls, would the floorboards be rotten, would the whole place smell of rot and mildew, and centuries of mouse droppings?

It seemed that the answer to all those questions was a cautious, but gratified, *no*.

The front door opened on to a wide, deep entrance hallway, and faced a huge set of double doors that stood ajar at the back of the enormous space. A wide curving staircase climbed the wall to the right, curling around into a kind of minstrel's gallery looking down on the entrance. To Morgan's left was another set of those enormous double-doors, which were also half open.

He took another step forward and peered through these doors, and saw what might have been a gigantic sitting room beyond. There was no abandoned furniture, and not a scrap of décor, but neither did there appear to be any damage to the structure of the house. The walls were smooth, the plaster unblemished and dry, and the ceilings, replete with their original mouldings, appeared to be immaculate.

The air smelled of absolutely nothing at all, the olfactory equivalent of a mouthful of boiled water at room temperature.

'Dust,' Jack said behind him, his voice low and thoughtful.

'What?' Morgan asked. He felt as though he'd just been woken from a dream.

'Look at the dust on the floor, it's thick as snow.'

Morgan dutifully looked down at the floorboards and saw that Jack was right. The few steps he had taken so far had left clearly defined footprints, including the tread of his sole.

'Nobody's been in here for years and years.'

'*Someone* has,' Jack said. 'Take a look over there.'

Morgan followed the direction of Jack's pointing finger and saw, to his right and almost in the exact centre of the entrance hall, an area where the layer of dust had clearly been disturbed. He saw immediately what his handyman meant. This section of dust looked like footsteps in snow that the wind had partially re-covered.

He walked over for a closer look, but couldn't make out any real detail. Then, a little distance away, a little deeper into the house, he spotted something else and began to move towards it.

'Where are you going, boss?' Jack asked.

Morgan glanced back with a frown at the note of panic he heard in the other man's voice. Jack had been nervy ever since they'd arrived, and it was clear that something about the house was upsetting him. He was still standing outside on the steps, and showed no sign of wanting to come any further.

'Relax, Jack,' Morgan replied. 'I just spotted something that might make both our lives a little bit easier.'

He bent down to brush away at a small mound of dust for a moment and then stood back up again, shaking a bunch of heavy old iron keys.

'What about that, then?'

Morgan walked back to the door, selected the largest key from among the half-dozen, and slotted it into the front door keyhole. It fitted perfectly, and when he turned the key, the lock's tongue stuck out smartly without making the slightest sound. The ancient mechanism might have been oiled only yesterday.

'Looks like you won't be needing me, after all,' Jack said.

'Maybe not, but do me a favour and just hang around for a minute or two, will you? I want to take a quick look around at the back, see what's out there. Okay?'

Jack nodded, but he didn't look happy about it.

'You coming with me?' Morgan grinned.

**113**

This time Jack shook his head. 'I don't think so.'
'Suit yourself.'

Morgan strode through the dust to the double doors at the rear of the entrance hall and pushed them open wider. The heavy wooden doors swung open easily and the hinges didn't creak even a little.

He found himself in another large room that he thought might once have been a dining room. Through a door at the other side of the room was a corridor that was probably once the domain of the domestic staff, and there were three or four other small rooms off the corridor that might once have been used as bedrooms by maids and footmen, although, like the other, far grander rooms, they were entirely unfurnished.

At the end of the corridor was a large kitchen with an equally large adjoining cold pantry. One entire side of the kitchen was given over to a gigantic cast-iron wood-fired range. Under the windows were cracked wooden draining boards and deep, tarnished copper sinks.

Morgan took all these details in, but wasn't able to focus on any one of them for more than a second or two. What he could see through the kitchen windows was claiming the majority of his attention.

He moved quickly toward the single door that led outside and found that it opened for him as easily as the house's front door had. He stepped out and then just stared in disbelief. He might have hoped for something like this in a dream, he supposed, but never in reality. Never in a *million* years, let alone twenty-five.

At the rear of the house was a walled garden approximately the size of a football pitch. The walls at the other three sides, left, right, and straight ahead, were really the backs of neighbouring buildings that rose to the height of three of four storeys, but were unbroken by a single window. The walled garden was a completely overlooked and utterly private open-air space in the centre of one of the most crowded cities in the world.

Morgan thought that this discovery may have just doubled his estimation of how much the house might be worth.

Like a man in a trance, he wandered off into the overgrown garden.

Although he was genuinely awed by this place, his property-developer's mind was busy-busy-busy, automatically picking off details, identifying problems, and swiftly providing solutions. Weeds and tall grasses he'd never seen before had grown up between the rough paving slabs, but he imagined that a few buckets of weed-killer would take care of them in fairly short order, unfamiliar or not. A pattern of raised flower beds, all wildly overgrown, were arranged in a circular pattern, and would have to be cut back and dug over, but he reckoned a good team of landscapers, if properly motivated, could sort that out over a single weekend... a long weekend, probably.

At the centre of the garden, what he had first taken for a stunted tree was really part of a circular fountain with a statue at its centre, all currently half-smothered in a kind of creeping vine. Closer up, the statue looked to be the absolute double of Eros at

Piccadilly Circus, and might even have been born from the same cast. He looked at this for a long time, unable to look away.

Then, just when Morgan thought there couldn't be anything else to discover, he discovered something else.

At the other side of the fountain, the paving ended in a series of semi-circular steps that went down maybe twelve or fourteen feet and ended in a cobblestone courtyard identical to the one at the front of the house. At the other side of this second courtyard was the dark entrance to a broad tunnel that was actually built into the wall opposite the house and sealed off with heavy wrought-iron gates.

Morgan trotted down the steps, jogged across to the gates, and peered through them.

Far off, maybe two or three hundred yards away, he could see the other end of the tunnel, which was also sealed with wrought-iron gates. He saw flickering sunlight as pedestrians and road traffic passed by, but could hear neither.

Although the distance between the two gates was mostly darkness, Morgan could see far enough into his end that he was able to make out that the tunnel was broken at either side by a succession of wide bays or chambers, which was presumably where the house's original owners had kept their horses and carriages, and God knew what else besides.

After a few moments, he realised that he was holding on to the gates so tightly his knuckles had gone white, but he felt if he were to let go at this moment he would probably collapse to the ground, because he didn't think he had any strength left in his legs at all.

The thing was, he thought he knew where those gates were, where they pretty much *had* to be, considering the house's location just off Templar Square.

If his calculations were correct, he realised that he must have passed them by a hundred times in his early life without ever paying them any real attention, perhaps because they were so clearly unused, and he had probably assumed they were merely an artefact of the city's ancient infrastructure, a relic of either the railway or the sewer system, perhaps. But what it actually seemed to be was the private entrance to this incredibly substantial residential property. It also had parking space for a probably a hundred or more cars.

The footprint of the property was *huge*. And if he was right about where the other end of the tunnel emerged, on a busy city thoroughfare, the house hadn't just doubled in value, it had trebled. Maybe even *quadrupled*.

Morgan slowly made his way back into the house on legs that seemed to have all the flexibility of wooden stilts, his mind awhirl with the possibilities which now seemed close enough to touch.

As he entered the kitchen he could hear Jack calling his name, and the panic he had heard in the man's voice earlier was no longer just a single note, now it was a whole symphony.

'Boss? Boss! For fuck's sake, where have you been?'

The relief Morgan saw on the other man's face was bemusing, and touching in a weird sort of way.

**117**

'I've just been looking around a little, and you wouldn't believe what I found…'

'Don't tell me,' Jack said gruffly. 'Don't tell me, I don't want to know. Come on out of there now, let's both get the fuck out of here.'

Morgan stood still and stared at him. He felt like the other man had doused him with a bucket of cold water. 'Jack, what's wrong with you? You've been acting strange since the minute you saw the house.'

'No, it was before then — ever since I saw you magic that alleyway up out of nowhere.'

'Well, yes, now that you…'

'And do you know *why* I'm acting strange? Because *this* is strange. Everything *about* it's strange… and the strangest thing of all is that you seem to think this makes fucking *sense*. We're in the middle of London, a stone's throw from fucking Oxford Street, and I can't even hear the traffic, not one engine! How is that fucking possible?'

Jack made a visible effort to get himself back under control.

'Boss… *Danny*… Look, how long have we known each other, twenty-odd years, right? You ever seen me like this before? Ever? About anything?'

Morgan shook his head, speechless.

'That's why you should listen to me. I'm telling you this straight and to your face, I can't stay here no more. I don't want to, and I'm not going to. I'm leaving right now, and when I go, I ain't never coming back... and you should come with me. I don't know what you think you're gonna do with this place, but I'm telling you now, it ain't happening, cos nothing *can* be done with it. This ain't the sort of

**118**

place you can do things to, it's the sort of place that does things to *you*, if you give it a chance. You can sack me if you want, but that's where I stand on the matter.'

Morgan watched Jack almost hyperventilating once he'd finished his speech. And he was right about one thing, Morgan had never seen the man so emotional, or so scared.

That was what confused him so much, why Jack seemed to be so bloody *scared.*

'Jack, it's okay,' he said, pitching his voice low and speaking calmly. 'I don't understand what's got you so worked up, but you can take me at my word — nobody's getting sacked, and you don't ever have to come here again if you don't want to. There's more than enough work to keep you busy clsewhere.'

He shrugged, at a loss to explain Jack's behaviour, but feeling a need to explain his own.

'Jack, to tell you the truth, this place has been flickering away at the back of my mind ever since I first saw it, twenty-five years ago. You could even say it's *haunted* me, in a way. It just always seemed like the greatest opportunity I'd ever seen, like an adventure nobody had ever taken. It was almost like *this* was my first house, not the student place in Croydon. But now, having been inside and explored a bit, I can see just how small my dreams of it actually were. This place...'

He shrugged helplessly.

'Jack, you really have no idea, it's just incredible. Really incredible. But at the end of the day, you know, it's just a *house*. Just bricks and mortar. It's a cash cow. There's nothing more to it than that.'

Jack had listened intently to Morgan speak, but then he shook his head.

'You don't know what you're talking about, boss,' he whispered. 'You're either lying to me or you're lying to yourself, or both. I'd come in and drag you out by your ears, but I am not crossing this threshold. I'm not taking that chance. But even if I did, you'd just shrug me off and go back in again, wouldn't you? Because this isn't just a house. It's already got you in its web.'

Jack grabbed the handle of his tool chest and dragged it a few steps away.

'I want you to remember I told you that, later. If there is a later.'

'Jack, I…'

'Goodbye, Boss.'

Before Morgan could say another word, Jack turned around and moved away, hurrying across the courtyard and then down the alleyway, his rolling tool chest jumping and bumping along behind him. In a matter of seconds, he had zipped back along the alleyway, and now appeared to Morgan as a figure seen through the wrong end of a telescope.

'Jack! Jack!'

A couple of moments later, he was gone.

Morgan was more than puzzled. A part of him was even angry. He'd finally achieved an ambition he'd held for twenty-five years, and now he had to enjoy the moment entirely on his own.

He grabbed the front door and was about to slam it shut, when he abruptly checked himself. It wasn't really Jack's departure that he was so upset about, it was that the people he would truly have wished to share this moment of triumph with were no longer among the living.

For some reason his wife and daughter were very strong in his heart and mind today, and he was missing them more than ever. Time was supposed to heal all things, he had been told, and he supposed that could be the truth, in most circumstances.

But grief was an elusive thing. It hid, it lurked in the most unexpected of places. It was mostly invisible... like a house that couldn't be found unless all the circumstances were correct.

Instead of slamming the door, Morgan merely pushed it to, but left it ajar just in case Jack changed his mind and came back.

He turned about and looked up at the staircase, and he felt the excitement begin to rise in him once more; not even Jack's weird turn had been able to keep it down for long. He couldn't wait to see what the next three floors were like.

And after the upstairs, there were always the cellars to explore. He had seen another door off the kitchen that opened on to a stone stairwell, and, bearing in mind the rest of the property, he couldn't begin to imagine how far those cellars might extend beneath the house's mammoth footprint.

He moved towards the staircase and began to slowly climb the stairs, looking down at his feet as they disturbed the thick carpet of dust. He realised that he was following those earlier footsteps, the ones that the new layers of dust had almost erased like windblown snow. He found himself wondering who had been here last, and how long ago it might have been. He couldn't make out any real details, save that the footprints seemed rather small, maybe a woman's.

Then he stopped abruptly, because the other footprints had stopped.

He was halfway up the staircase. He peered closer at the blurred footprints, and identified that the other person had paused here indecisively, shuffling around, before finally turning around and backtracking. Looking over the bannister, with the vantage-point of height, he could clearly see their progress. Or, he supposed, their retreat.

Once they reached the entrance hallway, they had crossed it at speed, and just before they had exited via the front door, they had thrown down the set of keys he had picked up himself, an unknown number of years later.

He shrugged to himself in what was almost wonder. How could somebody make this kind of discovery, how could they see just this much of the house's secrets, and then turn back? He knew that he couldn't. He looked back up the stairs, smiled in anticipation, and began to climb again.

Behind and below him, the front door slowly and silently closed itself.

It was when Morgan reached the first floor that he first became aware of the dreamlike strangeness of the situation.

The stairs ended in a broad landing which gave on to a staircase to the next floor. Extending left and right from this landing were corridors that seemed almost unfeasibly long, the grey plaster walls broken by as many as half a dozen doors at wide-spaced intervals, as if the rooms the doors opened on to were themselves vast. It didn't seem quite possible, even to Morgan, who was ready to believe almost anything about the house, but those long corridors should surely have intruded into the properties either side.

The dust on this floor was even thicker than it was below, and his movement must have caused a disturbance, because he saw that a fine layer of dust seemed to be swirling through the otherwise still air, diffusing the light, softening edges. Against his will, Morgan found himself reluctant to explore the rooms on this floor. For some reason the idea of opening all those closed doors made his guts clench up.

Go to the top, then, he thought, go to the very top, then work your way down.

It took him a moment to get his feet moving again, but once he had he felt his confidence return. Jack's obvious dislike and fear of the house had obviously affected him more than he had admitted to himself, that was all. He almost trotted up the second staircase, but upon gaining the second landing, he stopped again, and the cramp in his belly seemed to tighten.

The second floor was a replica of the first, the landing giving way to the third staircase, the dust even thicker, but this time the corridors at either side appeared to stretch off into *infinity*.

And this time, all the doors were open.

A thread of unease stitched its way up his spine. His expectations of what this house might be had always been wildly unrealistic, he supposed, and yet at each step it had exceeded them. But now the things he was seeing had to be impossible.

He took a few steps toward the third staircase and looked up the stairwell to the next floor. Up there the dust looked like a physical presence, hanging in the air, and Morgan suddenly recalled watching some programme on television and learning that a large proportion of dust was actually peoples' dead skin cells.

But this was a house where nobody lived, where perhaps nobody had *ever* lived for hundreds of years, and where maybe only one person before him had ever visited, and they had only ventured halfway up the first staircase before turning and… not retreating, but *fleeing*, that was the word.

Fleeing, as if from great danger.

Suddenly, from behind him, Morgan heard the high sweet laughter of a young child. He spun around, his eyes wide as he stared down the length of the corridor.

At first he could see nothing, but then he noticed the small cloud of knee-high dust hanging in the air, spanning the corridor between two of the open doors, as though someone had moved at speed between the two rooms. He took two steps forward, away from the landing, and saw small footprints, small bare footprints, in the dust leading from the right-hand doorway.

More laughter now erupted from the room on the left to which the footprints led.

Morgan *knew* that laughter. He heard it in his dreams. He heard it in his nightmares.

'Noi?' he whispered, his throat felt choked with dust or emotion or both.

His daughter's laughter rang out again, louder this time, sharper and more focussed. Before Morgan could take another step forward, a figure stepped out of the doorway to his right. But instead of passing on, following the other footsteps, this figure noticed Morgan and halted.

It turned to him, and it smiled a rapturous smile. It was Morgan's wife.

'Nok!'

His eyes were instantly filled with tears. This was yet another impossibility, and yet he *did* believe it, wanted with all his heart to believe it. It was Nok down to the smallest detail, although it was the Nok he had met that first day she had come to rent a room in his house, that young foreign student with her enormous backpack and her t-shirt and shorts and sandals.

A tiny but penetrating noise intruded into his sense of astonishment.

*...tap, tap, tap...*

Morgan glanced over his shoulder and immediately saw the source of the sound. Somehow a small scarlet bird had managed to find its way into the house, and it seemed to have used its wings to clear the dust from the newel post upon which it now perched.

As he watched, it rapidly dipped its beak again, pecking at the wood.

*...tap, tap, tap...*

And then the bird looked up at him brightly, its plump chest pushed out in a display of its plumage, in which Morgan noticed a band of golden feathers neatly arranged within the scarlet.

'Danny…'

He turned back to Nok, and saw that she had now become the Nok he had known on their wedding night, in the privacy of their honeymoon hotel room. She was naked, her face flushed with passion, her slender arms held out to him, her tiny hands beckoning.

'Come to me,' she said. 'Come be my husband…'

*…tap, tap-tap, tap…*

The scarlet bird pecked at the newel post again, and this time when he glanced back the bird's colours seemed even brighter, standing out vividly in the white and grey dustiness of the house like blood spilled on snow. While he was looking, it pecked twice more, each time in a flurry of little blows that seemed to convey its distress and sense of urgency.

*…tap, tap-tap-tap, tap-tap-tap-tap…*

While it was still pecking, Morgan turned back to his wife and recoiled from what he saw.

It wasn't the way her body, beautiful or not, now seemed devoid of colour, especially in comparison to the bird, the way her body now seemed to mirror the house's palette of off-whites and greys. It was the *look* he saw just for a split second in her eyes. It was a look of unreasoning, insane anger that Nok's eyes could never have displayed.

That look quickly vanished, slipped under an expression of innocence like a spider scuttling under a rock, but Morgan had seen it all the same. He understood that this was Nok, but he knew now that it wasn't *his* Nok.

*…tap-tap-tap-tap-tap-tap-tap…*

He took a step back and looked at the bird again. He saw it lift off the newel post like a hummingbird and settle again halfway down the bannister, its scarlet and gold wings raising a tiny cloud of dust. Once it had landed, it pecked again, then turned its bright-eyed gaze back upon him. It hopped down another inch or two, then pecked again. Hopped and pecked, hopped and pecked.

The message was clear. It wanted him to follow it down the stairs.

'Daddy?'

He turned back and almost fell to his knees. In the opposite doorway stood his daughter, Noi. She was wrapped in a fluffy white bath-sheet that dwarfed her, as though she had just stepped out of her evening bath. He blinked and then she was dressed in the clothes she had worn on the last day of her life, in her hand the small transparent case that was her carry-on luggage. He could see everything inside. Her books, her bear.

She was crying.

'Daddy, you said you'd see us soon! Why did you lie, Daddy?'

'Yes, Danny, why did you lie?'

Nok was also dressed now, wearing her travelling outfit, but her clothes were torn and discoloured with dirt and smoke. She was also much closer to him than she had been even a moment ago, as though she had taken the opportunity to creep up on him while his attention had been on the bird.

*...tap-tap-tap, tap-tap-tap-tap...*

The bird was pecking more urgently now.

Morgan could feel its anxiety, could imagine its tiny heart beating in its chest. He didn't need to look back to confirm that it had fluttered another few feet down the bannister, he knew it, but in any case, he didn't dare turn away to look. He remembered the menacing and silent advance Nok had taken while he wasn't looking.

He had an idea that they would be unable to move as long as he remained looking at them.

Almost as if she had heard the thought in his mind, and had deliberately chosen to prove him wrong, Nok took a long step toward him. Now Morgan couldn't see anything in her eyes, because she didn't have eyes anymore, just nuggets of spoiled flesh that had cooked in their sockets.

'Husband,' she said. It wasn't Nok's voice anymore. It wasn't Nok at all. The smile that followed it was hideous, a rictus grin filled with needle-like teeth.

*...tap-tap-tap...*

Behind the thing that wasn't Nok, the thing that wasn't Noi bared her own needle-teeth and hissed at him, and took two steps forward. They were only tiny little steps, but they were very, very fast.

*...tap-tap-tap-tap-tap-tap...*

Morgan's momentary paralysis broke, and he turned and launched himself down the staircase, the scarlet and gold bird fluttering before him, leading him on. He spared one glance behind him and saw that the apparitions didn't appear to be following him down. His relief was short-lived, however, for when he reached the first floor, he found them already waiting for him.

This time it was Nok and Noi as he had last seen them, in the aircraft hanger, burnt and mutilated lumps of flesh, only recognisable by the eye of love. They were crawling along the first floor corridor toward him, and they had left twin trails through the thick dust that seemed equal parts of blood and water, both filled with flakes of black ash.

...*tap-tap-tap*...

Morgan vaulted over a blackened, outstretched hand and stumbled all the way down the last flight of stairs to the entrance hall. The small scarlet and gold bird clung to the ornate door handle, pecking at the door.

...*tap-tap-tap-tap-tap*...

Morgan realised he was still holding the heavy bunch of house keys and he tossed them away from him. They fell into the dust in approximately the same place where he had found them.

From up above came the sound of something beginning to slither down the stairs, and he ran for the door. The bird had vanished, and Morgan was afraid that in its absence his resolve to leave would falter. Either his wife's or his daughter's voice would speak in the dusty silence and charm him back into compliance, or the house itself would hold him prisoner, the door handle refusing to turn for him.

He looked back and saw his wife's blackened, partial remains crawling down the staircase. Her ruined eyes seemed blindly fixed upon him. High above the entrance hall, his daughter's body was floating in the air, burning like a candle as it descended, and leaving a slipstream of greasy black smoke behind it.

*...tap-tap, tap-tap-tap...*

This time the sound came from *outside*, from the other side of the door. How had the bird got out there?

Morgan grabbed the handle and found that despite his fears it turned easily, and the door swung open immediately.

Just as he stepped out, something struck him in the face and he stumbled and fell down the the three steps to the courtyard cobbles. Behind him he heard the door slam shut with the finality of a gunshot. Then he realised that someone was standing in front of him, female feet clad in a pair of sandals.

He looked up and saw a middle-aged woman staring down at him with an expression he had only ever seen once before in his life, a curious mixture of horror, sympathy, and despair. The last time he had seen it was on the face of the nameless official when the bodies of his wife and daughter had been revealed to him in the hanger.

The woman was holding an open purse in one hand, and a number of coins in the other, and he realised that it had been a coin that had struck him in the face before he fell. She had been throwing them at the door.

When he looked down, he saw that the cobblestones were covered with more coins, silver and copper, mostly, and a number of one- and two-pound coins.

'It was all I could think to do,' she said.

Morgan sat back in the armchair with his eyes closed. He felt utterly exhausted, totally drained.

When the woman had first helped him into her home and deposited him in the armchair, she had covered him up with a couple of thick throws, tucking them well in around his legs. He had thought it a strange thing to do at first, it being the height of summer, but he found he was glad of the blankets now. He was shivering badly, although whether it was a chill he had picked up or a delayed reaction to what he'd been through, he wasn't sure.

The woman was in the kitchen, and had raised her voice to reach him over the sound of a kettle beginning to boil.

'I was on my way back from the shop, and just outside the Square I saw some kind of tradesman getting into his van. I saw his face, and I *knew* that look, that look of terror, of... of stunned unbelief. When I turned into the Square, the very second I turned the corner, I saw that scarf tied to the railings, and I knew what was happening. I dropped my shopping and just ran...'

She must have caught sight of Jack just after he left the house, Morgan thought, and somehow connected Jack to Nok's scarf, and then connected Nok's scarf to the danger he himself was facing inside the house. She had stood outside, either unable or unwilling to enter, and to attract his attention she had begun to throw coins at the door.

'The only thing I had was my purse,' she said. 'Thank God I had so much change. I certainly couldn't have *knocked* on the door. I didn't dare touch it...'

Morgan could imagine her scrabbling in her purse for the coins, throwing them at the door in small handfuls, then squatting to scoop them up to throw again.

*...tap-tap-tap...*

He could only think that his subconscious mind must have created the small scarlet bird to explain away the sounds that it had known all along were coming from the front door.

The part of his mind not captivated by the house's spectres had wanted to live, and it had seized upon these sounds from the real world and clothed them in details that would make an impact on him. It had put together the English translations of his wife's and his daughter's names, Noi for *small* and Nok for *bird*, to create the little bird, and then it had feathered the bird in red and gold, their favourite colours.

Or, he wondered suddenly, could it possibly be that his mind had done *none* of the work? Maybe the spirits of the real Nok and Noi had sensed the danger Morgan was in and had come to his rescue, alerting him to the noise the woman was making in an effort to break his trance.

This was an explanation he much preferred.

The boiling kettle in the kitchen began to whistle, and Morgan tiredly forced his eyes open again, wondering who on earth still had those kind of kettles. Perhaps, he thought, it had been the old lady's.

He looked to his left and saw a small selection of framed pictures on the side table, all of the same two beautiful blonde girls who were too alike to be anything but sisters.

The older of the two was the same young woman who twenty-five years before, in the company of her grandmother or great-grandmother, had had Morgan arrested and removed from the Square. He had recognised her immediately outside the house, despite his own confusion and weakness. She was still beautiful, even though her blonde hair had mostly gone silver-grey, and her eyes were the same piercing blue.

He glanced around the rest of the sitting room, but if the kettle was a remnant of the woman's aged relative there were no others to be seen. The décor and furnishings were modern, and there was certainly no invalid smell to the place.

But of course there wouldn't be, he thought, the lady in question had been so very old that she must have passed on twenty years or more ago. There were no photographs of the old lady on display, but Morgan thought he could understand that.

After Nok and Noi had been taken from him, he had gone through a long period where he had been unable to bear the sight of their photographs, their possessions, or anything that reminded him they were gone. This was a phobia that existed to this day, and the scarf he had taken to carrying around with him was the only exception.

He thought again that maybe this had been another helping hand his wife and daughter had given him from some other world, so that their colours would be fresh in his mind at the time he most needed them.

He looked up toward the kitchen doorway as the woman emerged, carrying a tea tray. She brought it over and set it down carefully on the small table that stood between the armchair and the small two-seater sofa facing it. Then she sat down herself, and began to pour the tea into two china cups.

She stirred the tea for a long time, and then stood again to help Morgan take a few sips from his cup — his hands were still shaking too much to hold a full cup.

'Careful,' she said, 'it's a little hot still, and there's a drop of brandy in it.' When Morgan coughed at the first mouthful, she smiled a little. 'Well, *two* drops, maybe.'

The tea was sweet as well as hot, and Morgan immediately felt the brandy hit him. When she was sure he could handle the cup on his own, the woman returned to the sofa, and then sat looking at him. There was that face again. He saw, horror, sympathy, empathy...

In his present emotional state, the kindness he saw there was too much to bear, so he looked down to escape it and noticed for the first time that the throw the woman had covered him with was covered in grey cat hairs. He was surprised that it hadn't set off his allergies.

'I'd like to thank you,' he said thickly. 'But I don't even know your name.'

'It's Miriam.'

'I'm Danny.'

She nodded, and then sipped her own tea for a moment or two. Then she said, 'Well, at least now you know why we tried so hard to chase you away all those years ago…'

So she she had recognised him, too.

'I'm so sorry, Danny,' she said. 'I'd hoped I'd saved you back then, but I was never quite sure. Then the years went by and you never showed up, and I suppose I started to forget how far that bloody awful house can reach when it feels that it has an opportunity. What brought you back now? Was it a bereavement? It was, wasn't it? You lost someone, didn't you?'

'Yes. More than a year ago now. My wife, and my daughter.'

Miriam nodded. 'That's how it gets you. Once you've seen it, and, more importantly, once it's seen you, once it's marked you, it waits for you to weaken. It watches and it waits, and then when it senses the time has come, it uses your grief to summon you, and it drains you, if it can. Damn house is a vampire.'

She smiled again and tears leaked from the corners of her eyes.

'That's how it got Margaret, you see. Our mother died when we were both very young. I was three and a half years old at the time, and poor Margaret less than two. She didn't even have any proper *memories* of our mother, but that's what the house used to summon her.'

So she had lost her younger sister to the house, that was how she knew so much about it. Morgan glanced at the photographs on the side table, and saw how happy the two girls had been together. That must have been a dreadful loss to bear.

'Now it uses *her* memory to try to summon *me*,' Miriam said. 'During the day, I can ignore it, pretend it isn't really there. But I hear it calling sometimes, in the night. There have been times when I have tied myself to the bed to be sure I won't answer its call in my sleep. One summer night, some months after

**135**

Margaret had passed, I woke up, nearly naked, halfway across the Square and in sight of the house… the alleyway had opened, it had opened up its jaws for me.'

She took a quick, shaky sip from her cup.

'Ironically, it was a young homeless man who saved my life that night. He thought I'd had one too many and guided me home. I let him sleep on my sofa, and in the morning, before he left, I gave him quite a lot of money. I haven't seen him since, I'm pleased to say…'

Morgan swallowed some more of his brandy-laced tea.

'Just lately, it's been quiet,' Miriam went on. 'I'd begun to hope that it had died itself, because I had stopped it claiming any more victims. But I should have known better,' she added angrily. 'I should have known it had something like this up its sleeve!'

'Don't be so hard on yourself,' Morgan said. 'You saved me, didn't you? You saved me twice.'

She looked at him closely for a moment, but then looked away and avoided his eyes. Tired as he was, Morgan noticed it.

'What is it?' he asked.

Miriam shook her head forlornly. 'It was more than six months killing Margaret, but then I suppose she only got halfway up the stairs…'

Morgan remembered the other tracks he'd seen in the dust, the footsteps that he now believed the house had sought to hide. They had been made by this woman's sister.

But there was something else being implied here, something he was unable to put his thumb on.

'I don't understand what you're trying to say,' he said.

'Finish your drink.'

He automatically swallowed the rest of his tea, and grimaced. The bottom of it was grainy and bitter.

'Don't worry, Danny. That's just the painkillers. And some crushed up sleeping tablets. To make it easier.'

'To make *what* easier?'

Once again, Miriam wouldn't meet his eyes.

There was a thud and a breaking sound, and when he looked down he saw that his empty cup had fallen from his grasp and broken on the floor. He looked down at his shaking hands and was shocked. His hands were covered in wrinkled flesh dotted with liver spots, the knuckles twisted and arthritic.

A monstrous suspicion appeared fully-developed in Morgan's mind. He looked back at the photographs of the two sisters again, and remembered Miriam saying, '*It was more than six months killing Margaret...*'

Then he understood.

There were no photographs of the grandmother or great-grandmother here because there never *was* a grandmother or great-grandmother. There had only ever been Miriam's sister. Her *younger* sister, Margaret, summoned by the house as Morgan had been summoned, and then drained of all her youth.

He looked back at Miriam, who was crying again. For her this must have been like reliving the same nightmare all over again

'You said it took six months for your sister to die,' he said, his voice catching in his throat. 'So

**137**

she… she aged a little more each day, until she became…'

She nodded. 'The person you saw with me.'

Morgan closed his eyes and swallowed. 'Then I have only half a year to live....'

'No,' Miriam said softly. 'I'm so sorry, but no. Margaret was in the house less than ten minutes. You must have been in there for almost an *hour*. Maybe even longer.'

He looked down again at the grey cat hairs on the throw — there were more of them now. He raised his hands to his head, feeling his shoulders complain, and as he ran his fingers across his scalp a drift of hair fell into his lap, grey hair which this morning had all been brown.

'I'm so sorry, Danny. I'm so very sorry…'

Morgan's strengthless arms dropped into his lap. He could feel his remaining energy leaving him, feel his muscles wasting away, his body shrinking, his organs failing.

It didn't hurt exactly, Miriam's pills must have been powerful indeed, but the sense of loss was acute. Through his failing vision he could see that she was crying again, but he could no longer hear her.

Then something flitted into being behind Miriam, sitting on the back of a hard-backed chair. It was the bird, the small scarlet bird with its golden plumage, come back once more.

Morgan smiled, revealing his few remaining teeth, and he wondered what had really summoned him here today. Was it the house's terrible appetite, or had it been his own small family, who had waited too long for him to keep his promise?

*Writers are always being told to write about what they know, which makes sense, I suppose, as knowledge is widely regarded as preferable to ignorance. Unfortunately, what writers mostly know about is writers and writing, and very little else. Little wonder, then, that when an opportunity to indulge their vanity arises, they're usually unable to resist the temptation. Sadly, as the existence of this story about an aspiring young author so amply demonstrates, in this regard I am just as guilty as the rest of the scribblers.*

The first time Stevie saw Valerie, he was completely stark bollock naked. He was also thinking very seriously about taking out an option on a new name. Well, not so much a new name, he supposed, but more of what they call a *nom de plume,* or a *pseudonym* — a pen-name, in other words. This was something that had been on his mind for quite a while, ever since he'd had his *Really Big Idea.*

It was a gorgeous July day, around about noon, and the first things he saw when he woke up and opened his eyes were his tidy desk and the homemade shelves above it, with all his school textbooks regimentally aligned along with his neatly colour-coded revision files. He'd finished the last of his ten A-level examinations just over a week before, and had spent most of the time ever since just chilling.

Staying up late playing games with his online friends, binge-watching movies and box-sets, surfing the web, whacking off, and sleeping late, late, late. Just being a normal teenager, in other words.

As the days slowly passed, he'd been able to feel all the tensions and stresses of the last two years gradually leaving him, like a persistent migraine finally worn away by repeated doses of Excedrin. Now, lying naked on his bed in a pool of bright, warm sunlight, his single sheet kicked to the floor after a peculiarly humid, overheated night, he felt truly at peace. He was in the mood to speculate about the future, and what his particular place in it might turn out to be… if he was lucky, that was.

'Hi, I'm Marc Elstrom,' he thought aloud as he watched a revolving constellation of dust drift through the beams of sunlight coming in through the gap in his curtains.

That one wasn't *too* bad, he thought. Put it down as a possible.

Now that his exams were over and done with, and with university shimmering like a mirage on the horizon, he finally felt free to return to the *Really Big Idea*, which had come to him like a waking dream a few months ago, but which he had responsibly set aside while he finished his studies.

*Tried* to set aside, at any rate.

Stevie had only been about nine- or ten-years-old when one of his schoolmates — Tabitha Eldon, soon to become Stevie's very best friend and his greatest supporter — had first wised him up to the fact that he had the same name as a very rich and famous writer. Of course, Stevie was a '*v*' rather than a '*ph*' kinda guy, but that seemed like such a tiny, insignificant detail, and he had lost no time in heading to the local library to check out his namesake's books.

'*Salem's Lot* had been his very first taste of the prolific Mr King's output. Stevie had swallowed it whole without pausing once for breath, and the fact of the accidental similarity of their names had nothing whatsoever to do with it. Simply put, he had been completely and utterly enthralled, by the characters, the story, the atmosphere... by just about everything. So then he'd had to read every other book King had ever written, just as fast as he could get his hands on them.

Over the years he had even been inspired to write some short stories of his own in the same genre, although at first they were just a page or two long, and generally very closely (but quite clumsily) based on King's characters or storylines.

When he thought of these early efforts at creation, he viewed them as energetic but rather unambitious examples of fan flash-fiction, no more, no less. He'd written maybe two or three stories every year, purely for his own amusement, and only whenever the urge took him or he didn't have anything more important to do, which was mostly on long rainy afternoons, or instead of boring homework assignments.

However, over the last year or so, Stevie, without thinking about it too much or too deeply, had tentatively struck out on his own, writing half a dozen short stories featuring his own characters and his own plots, and he thought they'd turned out pretty well. Everyone who'd read them so far seemed to think they were good, anyway, and some people had suggested that maybe they were perhaps a little better than merely *good*, which Stevie had found both flattering and incredibly encouraging.

One of those people, of course, had been Tabby Eldon, who was the only person in the world to whom Stevie had confided the true extent of his ambitions and hopes for the future, and who, quite astonishingly, hadn't laughed in his face when she'd heard them, as Stevie had feared she might.

Even so, he'd mostly still thought of writing as just a hobby, a generally harmless, although increasingly diverting, pastime. But then, a month or two into the New Year, Stevie had his *Really Big Idea*, and that had changed absolutely everything.

He'd realised immediately that this was no mere short story-sized idea, it wasn't even a *novel*-sized idea — it was at least a *trilogy*-sized idea, and the more he thought about it the more he could see it stretching far beyond the original trilogy and becoming some kind of multi-volume saga, like *The Dark Tower* series.

Every time he'd closed his eyes, he found himself world-building at a frantic pace, and all the materials he needed seemed close at hand.

'Yes,' he grandly proclaimed to his bedroom ceiling, 'I *am* VG Panderholt…'

Okay, he thought, so maybe *that* one wasn't so hot. Toss it in the direction of the discard file, Tabby would have said if she were here. Rip it up and start again, Stevie.

After a careful study of the way the traditional publishing world seemed to be heading, Stevie was planning to e-publish his work on all the available digital platforms once it was ready for public consumption, and then offer paperback copies for sale through print-on-demand services.

As an experiment, he thought that maybe he'd try bundling all his original short stories together into a single, low-priced collection first, to test the market, before launching the *Really Big Idea* on an unsuspecting public.

Then he supposed the hope was that he'd eventually start making a big enough splash for the trad' publishers to notice him and come along waving their chequebooks, their enormous print runs, their access to the book clubs, the international marketplace, and the supermarket shelves... and then what?

Well, fame and fortune, *obviously*. Duh!

Stevie knew deep down that the whole thing was probably something of a pipe-dream, but he discovered he was more or less fine with that. He was young and had the advantage of a small, natural window to try chasing down his dreams, which he believed no one could begrudge him. After all, lots of young people took advantage of a gap year before they went off to university, although he guessed that these days the majority of them went travelling around the world.

Stevie meant to go them all one better, by travelling to *another* world, one entirely of his own creation.

Nor did he really mind being one of the millions of struggling self-publishers, because he had faith in himself, he had confidence in his work-ethic, and, above all else, he had an unquestioning belief in his *Really Big Idea*.

Of course, the biggest problem he faced when he started thinking about the moment that he would finally present the fruit of his labours to the world (not counting writing it as well as he knew it *could* and *should* be written) was simply the name he had been blessed with at birth.

The thing was, you couldn't just put your titles out there and start screaming for attention — not when your name was Steven King and you were writing in the horror/fantasy genre, you couldn't. Tabby had said that at the very best he'd simply confuse people, and at worst he'd piss off and alienate an awful lot of his potential readers, neither of which Stevie had the slightest intention of doing.

Hence the need for a suitable pseudonym.

'Harry Jacobson, Lawrence Aldrich, Peter Calloway... Gordon Chappell, David O'Brian, Kieran Patterson…'

Ah, he thought, what's in a name?

Stevie closed his eyes again, stretching luxuriously across his mattress, and then thought, hey, what about a *female* pseudonym? But then, on second thoughts, he guessed maybe he'd pass. He really didn't see himself being comfortable with becoming Betty Goldtinkle or Fanny Arbuckle — or even Stephanie King, for that matter — but the notion of taking a feminine identity did lead him to another, much more appealing idea.

Stevie's mother had died when he was around five-years-old and he had very few real memories of her, but the ones he did have, and those his father had shared with him over the years, had become the bedrock of Stevie's emotional existence, his life's touchstones.

His mother's maiden name had been *Aston*, and Stevie discovered that he really liked the sound of that, he liked the *feel* of the connection in his heart and mind. Then he thought that maybe he could use his own middle name, which was *Richard*, and then combine the two.

*Richard Aston*? Or what about if he made it *Richard Aston King*? That way there would be a little of them all in it, Dad included, and everyone would be represented.

Yes, he thought, it was plausible, it was a real possibility. It felt *genuine*, and somehow solid and dependable, a name you could trust.

Stevie really liked it, and he began to try the name out, rolling it off his tongue to hear how it sounded:

'Richard Aston King, the celebrated fantasy author, is in town today to sign books for his legion of adoring fans…. World-renowned writer and creator of the *Forbidden Land* Cycle, Richard Aston King, will be with us in the studio later this morning, folks, and the phone lines are already jammed with callers… In Los Angeles, California, today, the British fantasy author Richard Aston King has finally married his movie-star girlfriend, following the world premiere of her latest blockbuster, based on one of King's most acclaimed novels…'

It was an intoxicating daydream. But then something made the hair on the back of Stevie's head suddenly rise, and as he was pulled from his private fantasy world, he *knew* that someone was watching him. Knew it without a single shred of doubt.

He should have been entirely alone in the house, so his first thought was that it was an unlawful intruder, someone who'd broken in, a burglar or worse, and he sat up and twisted at the same time in a kind of corkscrew movement to face the doorway at the foot of his bed.

To his astonished surprise, a middle-aged woman was standing in the open doorway, staring at him, at his nakedness and at his involuntary wake-up hard-on, with something approaching horror.

So many different reactions to the sight of this woman went through his mind at the same time that it was difficult to peel them apart and examine them clearly. One of them, oddly pervasive even though he knew it couldn't be true, was that she was a ghost. Outside of fiction, ghosts didn't exist, of course, but the idea remained curiously difficult to shake.

The next idea was that he had accidentally left the front door downstairs unlocked last night (although he knew he hadn't), and that this strange woman, having probably escaped from a so-called 'secure' psychiatric unit earlier this morning, had tried the door handle speculatively, and then simply wandered in looking for somewhere soft and tender to plant her axe.

And that there *was* something strange about the woman was immediately apparent to Stevie without her even opening her mouth.

Apart from the emaciated body and the wide-eyed horror of her expression, which was so extreme that she looked like a caricature of someone reacting with horror, there were her clothes. They were as devoid of colour as the rest of her. Her dress was grey, as were her tights, as was the little cardigan so primly buttoned up to her neck, but all slightly different shades, and all mostly wrinkled and grubby. Her hair was grey and so was her face. The only points of colour in or on her at all were her eyes, which were of a cold, pale blue.

All this went through Stevie's head in a fraction of a second, but then his mind decided for him that it didn't matter who or what she was, he needed to react in some way to her presence.

He reached behind his back and snatched his pillow up to cover his shrinking genitals. As he did so, he also heard slow, heavy footsteps coming up the last of the stairs, and a thrill of anticipation shocked its way up his spine — what next?

The following moment, his father's head appeared around the doorframe, which was another surprise, as Stevie hadn't been expecting him back until late the next evening.

'Dad!'

'Hello, son,' his father replied without even a trace of his usual brightness.

Donald King was sombre, glum, and clearly exhausted, and Stevie had a momentary flashback to the afternoon thirteen years ago when his father had sat him down, a tiny little five-year-old boy who only wanted his mother to come home from the hospital, and told him that he had to be brave. He had to be very brave, because something had *happened*, something terrible

'Perhaps you could come downstairs, Stevie, when you're dressed. I'd like to talk to you. *We'd* like to talk to you.'

Stevie watched his father turn about and begin to stump his way tiredly back down the stairs. Every footfall sounded like it weighed a thousand pounds.

Despite the oddness of the situation and the vague sensation that he hadn't actually woken up yet and was involved in some weird fever-dream, Stevie discovered that instead of dispelling his apprehensions, as he might have expected, his father's appearance had only made them worse, and not only because he sounded so dreadfully tired and miserable.

Mostly, it was the way he *looked*…

After mum had died it had just been Stevie and his dad together for the next decade. They were the boys. The lads. The terrible twosome. Partners in crime. His father had committed himself to their relationship like a man clinging to a life-raft, and Stevie had done the same thing. It had been a case of mutual dependence, mutual survival. But as Stevie had grown older and begun to demand more independence and autonomy in his life, his father had carefully, and generously, taken a step back and allowed it to happen.

Later on, with his son's genuine blessing and encouragement, Donald had also started building a little social life for himself, joining several local clubs and societies, and making a few new friends along the way.

Then, about a month ago, through one of these clubs, he'd had a chance to join a group on a cruise ship touring the Azores and Madeira. It had sounded like a great opportunity, especially the heavily-discounted price due to the large numbers of people in the group. But at first Donald had turned it down because it meant he'd have to be absent for Stevie's final exam period.

'I won't be here to support you,' he'd worried. 'If you have a problem, I won't even be in the *country…*'

'*Go*,' Stevie told him for perhaps the two-hundredth time. 'You've supported me my whole life, Dad. You can't help me any more right now. The rest is down to me, and it's a good job, 'cos I'm the most organised student in the world…'

It was a claim which almost had to be true — all his dad had to do was look at that tidy desk and the colour-coded revision materials to see the proof.

Eventually, he'd managed to convince his father to go on the cruise, and privately he had to admit to himself that he'd found it a distinct relief not to have to cope with King the Elder's exam stresses on top of his own. But until now, Stevie hadn't realised how much he'd missed his dad while he was away, which he supposed was why seeing him in the flesh now evoked such worry.

After all, the man had been on a boat cruise around the North Atlantic for almost a fortnight, and Stevie had been expecting to see a substantial tan when he got back, or, at the very least, a badly peeling nose.

But God, there was hardly *any* colour in his face at all, unless dishwater-grey was an actual colour.

In fact, his complexion, usually fairly healthy, cruise or no cruise, actually bore a strong resemblance to that of the woman who was still standing in his doorway, now looking distastefully around Stevie's room, at the rock-band posters tacked all over the walls, and especially at the shelves of fantasy and horror novels that were Stevie's real passion in life.

Then, at last, he cottoned on to the substance of what his father had just said:

*I want to talk to you…* we'd *like to talk to you….*

What, Stevie wondered now, was all this *we* business?

He looked more closely at the woman, whose attention now seemed fixated on the top three shelves of his extensive book collection, which had been given over entirely to the works of Stephen King, including a couple of German-language editions Stevie had found in a charity shop one weekend and hadn't been able to resist buying for the sheer novelty value.

As she stared at the books, the woman's thin grey lips gradually curled into an ugly sneer that wouldn't have looked out of place on a rabid dog like *Cujo*.

*We?*

After considering this tiny word for a few more moments, Stevie swiftly passed 'worried' and rapidly began to approach 'extremely disturbed'.

Apart from allowing himself a little breathing space to study, the main object of the cruise he'd talked his dad into taking was that it would be a complete break from everything the man knew, giving him a chance to fully recharge his batteries for the first time in more than a dozen years, and to enjoy a safe little adventure with a group of friends his own age.

The *subtext* of the exercise was that his father might possibly meet someone, some nice, comfortable, smart little woman to have a twilight romance with, which was something that Stevie would have been more than happy to endorse.

But a terrible, terrible thought had now occurred to him — what if this grey, Puritan, book-burning, cold-eyed bitch *was* that someone?

He looked at her again and found her staring back at him with those pale blue eyes. There was a large jagged fleck of bright yellow in the iris of her left eye that Stevie hadn't noticed before, and it seemed to unbalance her gaze, making it creepily unnerving, especially as she had now pointed it so directly, and apparently judgementally, at him.

She didn't even seem to blink.

'I believe your dear father told you we'd like to see you downstairs,' she said, her voice a disconcertingly chill breeze in the warmth of the summer's day.

Then she leaned forward across the foot of Stevie's bed, angling her head so that she seemed to be viewing him only through the eye with the yellow fleck. Now that she was closer, Stevie saw that the fleck looked more like a scar, like a rip in the fabric of her blue iris.

This moment of mutual inspection seemed to last forever, and then she bared a jumbled mouthful of yellowing, grey-filmed teeth at him, in what he thought was meant to be a smile.

'So chop-chop, little man,' she said, 'chop-chop!'

Stevie watched her turn on her heel and leave his room. He waited until he had heard her descend the stairs before he even dared to move.

The scene that met him downstairs in the kitchen a few minutes later was somehow worse than he had ever anticipated it could be.

The pair of them were waiting for him in silence, having drawn chairs up to one side of the kitchen table and arranged another chair at the other side for him, as though he were there for an interview. Instinctively, he'd refused the chair, and stood instead by the fridge with his lower back resting against the edge of the worktop.

'Hello, son,' his father said, and again Stevie was struck by how unhealthy he looked, and how the greyness of his skin made him and this odd woman look so alike.

'Why are you back early?' Stevie asked.

His father blinked rapidly a few times, as though confused by the question, but then he cleared his throat, looking down into his lap as he spoke.

'Oh, there was a good deal of illness on the ship, unfortunately. A number of deaths, too, on the tenth night out, and the captain took the decision to return to port ahead of schedule.'

'Deaths? What was it, food-poisoning? Some kind of outbreak? Legionnaire's, or....' Stevie felt his alarm growing for his father's health.

That dull, strengthless tone of voice. That exhausted grey skin.

'They don't know, really. There's going to be some kind of inquiry, I believe.'

'Well, I should hope so. How many people died?'

'I believe it was seven.'

'Seven! All in *one* night?'

'I'm afraid so. Five women and two men, all in their sixties and seventies. All apparent heart attacks.' Stevie's father looked for the first time at the woman he had brought home with him. 'In fact, Valerie was a little under the weather that very same night, weren't you, my dear?'

'Yes, Donald, I was very poorly indeed. But with your help, and God's love, I managed to pull through.'

'I was so very worried.'

Stevie watched, appalled, as his father's and Valerie's hands entwined, and he saw with revulsion the way his father's great, rough fingers seemed to sink deep into her grey, doughy flesh. When he looked back up, he saw that his father was finally smiling at him, but it was the smile of a man who is in a great deal of pain and has absolutely no idea why. His lips were trembling and sweat was beading on his colourless brow.

'Dad, who is this woman?'

'This is Valerie,' his father replied. 'Valerie Hepton. We met on the second day of the cruise, and spent almost all our time together after that. We have become very fond of each other. She… she hasn't quite been herself since her illness, but she'll come around, I'm sure. I think the two of you will become great friends.'

'I really doubt that,' Stevie instantly snapped.

Valerie turned from Donald and stared up at Stevie, and he was struck again by that bright yellow scar marring the cold blue of her left eye, and the way her head swivelled from subject to subject as though the other eye was dead and blind. In fact, if not for the frightful, electric vitality of her one-eyed gaze, Stevie thought that she could easily have passed for dead herself, a corpse that could still walk and talk.

As soon as the idea popped into his head, he began to *smell* her, an odour of perfume splashed over a slab of rotting meat that was almost strong enough to make him gag.

'Really, Stevie,' his father protested mildly, 'I don't think there's any reason for you to be quite so rude to Valerie.'

'Don't upset yourself, Donald,' Valerie said brightly. 'The truth is always best, no matter how bad the taste. It's good that your son is speaking so openly. It only helps to further reveal the demon that has become lodged in his soul.'

'Say *what*?' After a moment of stunned, disbelieving silence, Stevie pushed himself away from the worktop. 'What did you say?'

'You heard me, demon,' Valerie said. 'You cannot hide from me. I can see how you have made your wretched nest in this good, Christian household, and how you are twisting this poor boy's mind to your foul master's corrupt ends…'

With a dramatic flourish, Valerie lifted something from her lap and help it aloft.

'And *this* is where the possession began!'

In her shaking hand, a grey talon, was Stevie's old paperback copy of '*Salem's Lot*, now read ragged and the cover repaired twice-over with clear tape gone yellow with age.

He realised Valerie must have swiped it from his shelves while he was distracted, perhaps when he'd been staring in dismay at his father's unhealthy pallor.

'That's *my* property,' he said, holding out his hand to take it.

'No, it may have been in your *keeping*,' Valerie relied, shaking her head, 'but it is *owned* by the devil! It is his tool for spreading his filthy ordure throughout God's clean world! This, and all the other works of evil in your keeping, are full of degradation, acts of obscenity, sodomy, licentiousness, and spiritual and physical corruption! They are the veritable bibles of sin!'

Stevie amazed himself by laughing out loud at this ridiculous tirade.

'Wow, are you sure it isn't Clive Barker you're really thinking of?' he asked. 'I've got an old copy of *Weaveworld* I could let you borrow if you like…'

A great, unexpected calm had suddenly descended upon him and he took a long step back, putting his hands in the pocket of his jeans.

'Look, Valerie, it's pretty obvious to me that you've never even *looked* inside one of Stephen King's books, much less read one. If you had, you'd know that they're just *stories*, not evil tracts or witch's spells… and what's more, they're mostly stories about decent, courageous people, usually with a very strong sense of moral responsibility, who just happen to have encountered evil, and who are struggling to overcome it, even in the face of appalling danger.'

'Oh yes, the devil *speaks*,' Valerie glimmered at him, 'and the tainted *listen*. Words are his power....' She pointed triumphantly to the strapline on the old book cover. 'See, it even admits it here — "*words are his power*"!'

'You're absolutely fucking crazy,' Stevie said, and almost laughed again, but now he was also growing angry.

He turned to his father.

'Dad, you have to know that everything she's saying is complete bullshit?'

But Donald wouldn't meet his son's eyes. 'Now, Stevie, you know I was always unhappy about you reading all those gruesome horror books.'

'You were worried that they'd give me nightmares, but when you saw that they didn't, you *stopped* worrying. Don't you remember this? They actually got me into reading, if you think back, and my English grades went up as a result... I even got *you* to read a couple, remember? You said you enjoyed them!'

'Nonsense,' Valerie snorted. 'Your dear father was strong enough to resist the evil, that's all. I suppose that's why I was drawn to him, to his moral strength, to his shining inner light.'

She fixed Stevie with that expression again, that toothy grimace he supposed was meant to be a kind and comforting smile, but which actually made the blood curdle in his veins.

'But *you*, my poor boy, you are *not* strong enough to resist. You have fallen by the wayside. Even worse, the evil inside you has now begun to begat more evil. God has told me all, God has seen through my eye, and God has whispered your secret truths into my ear. You have begun to create your own works of evil, have you not?'

At last, his father looked up at him. 'Stevie, is that true?'

'It's true I've started writing something, yes,' Stevie replied, even more startled by Valerie's knowledge of his *Really Big Idea* than he had been that she'd known the revelation of reading *'Salem's Lot* had been the genesis of his creative life. 'But it isn't evil, it's just—'

'Oh, you poor, poor boy,' Valerie crooned. 'If you do not accept the truth of your demonic perversity, if you do not allow us to help you, you will be damned for all eternity. Please, think of your late mother….'

Stevie reached his flashpoint faster than he ever dreamed possible. This foul, noxious woman trying to use the memory of his own mother against him was too much to bear.

'Don't you ever talk about my mother, you sick, twisted bitch!'

He dashed out of the kitchen and into the living room, and then returned brandishing the framed photograph of his mother and father on their wedding day which had sat on the mantelpiece his entire life. He thrust it in his father's face.

'Look! This was your wife! This is my mother! Everything you've ever told me about her, about everything she thought and believed… everything *you* believed in and taught *me* to believe… all of it, it's just…'

Stevie was practically choking on his own words, and he desperately tried to steady himself.

'Dad, you can't possibly think that this woman is a suitable replacement for Mum, you can't possibly agree with anything she says. It would be a complete betrayal of yourself, of our family, of everything we ever....'

He looked at Valerie again. She was glaring at him, her one good eye, the one she claimed her God had seen him through, both wild and delighted. A weird chuntering noise had begun to come out of her, like a steam train getting up to speed, which Stevie eventually realised was her version of laughter.

'Oh no,' she chuckled, 'the devil doesn't like it when you step on his tail, does he, Donald?'

'No, Valerie, he doesn't.'

Suddenly, the glass of the picture frame in Stevie's hand shattered explosively and he dropped it. He looked down at the blood dripping from a long cut across the palm of his hand and a wave of nausea and dizziness washed through him.

'Stevie,' Valerie said firmly, 'your mother is trying to send you a *message*. You must heed it. There is only one thing for you to do now, only one course of action by which your soul can be saved from the demon that has its coils so tightly wrapped around your heart and soul.'

She stood up in a cloud of sick, stale sweat, of powdered-over dirt, of some kind of bone-deep rot. Her weird left eye turned up to his face, the yellow

**159**

scar like a fissure in reality that opened into some other world.

'Valerie, my dear,' Stevie's father asked fervently, 'what can we do to help him?'

'Donald, we must heed the righteous word of the Lord. We must answer His call immediately…. and we must exorcise the Stephen King right out of your son!'

'Fuck you,' Stevie hissed at her. He held his bleeding hand to his chest, wrapping it in his t-shirt as he backed towards the door to the hallway. 'Fuck you both!'

He turned and he ran.


Stevie spent the rest of the day and most of the evening in the company of his best friend, Tabby Eldon.

After she'd disinfected and bandaged up his hand, Tabby got him a t-shirt from the chest of drawers in her bedroom to replace his blood-stained one. Stevie was surprised to see that the shirt was one of his own, one that he had long believed lost at one of the back-garden campouts they'd had with a gang of friends when they were younger. It still smelled of the deodorant he used. It still just about fit, too, although now it was stretched tight across his well-developed shoulders and chest.

Once she had him fixed up with a mug of sweet hot chocolate, Tabby sat quietly and attentively on the end of her bed as Stevie described his bizarre encounter with Valerie Hepton, not stinting on his description of her odour, her appearance, her apparent mania, and her general aura of unsettling weirdness, and including her crazy suggestion that demonic possession was the reason that he had begun to write his own stories — and that creepy yellow gash in her one good eye, of course, he couldn't forget that.

'What do you think?' he asked when he'd finished pouring out his tale of woe.

Tabby thought for a long moment, and then, at last, she suggested that the whole thing sounded rather like something that Stevie, or indeed his infinitely more famous namesake, might have written after a long night of cheese-fuelled nightmares.

'I don't know if you realise this, Stevie,' she said gently, 'but sometimes you do occasionally have a teeny-tiny tendency to *fictionalise* your life somewhat. I suppose that all writers must do the same thing. I mean, I've heard you describe a routine dental check-up as if you'd spent a year in the dungeons of the Spanish Inquisition.'

Stevie said that this time wasn't one of those times.

'Okay, fine,' Tabby said. 'Maybe it went down just the way you say it did, and maybe this Valerie woman is everything you say she is…'

'Which she is!'

'Fine. But try to think of it this way; there you were, off in your own little world, thinking about your stories, thinking about pen-names, all warm and comfortable, still half-asleep, completely relaxed — and maybe four or five minutes away from knocking one out, am I right?'

Stevie blushed in embarrassment, but then laughed along with her when she cracked up.

'Yeah, that's what I thought… but then, out of nowhere, this woman suddenly appears in your doorway and you get a massive shock to the system. Everything that happens *after* is coloured by that shock. Yeah, okay, so she sounds pretty damn weird, and is probably a religious maniac to boot, and that doesn't help, of course, but then you further realise that she's got her hooks into your *dad*, who's been the most important person in your whole life, like forever. You're crazy if you don't think there was at least a small element of jealousy on your part.'

Stevie shrugged, and Tabby put her hand on his shoulder.

'Stevie, you've got to face it, your dad's only human. This is probably the first bit of love-action he's had for several centuries — he's pussy-drunk, that's all….'

Stevie started making gagging noises and making the time-out sign.

'But I *know* your dad,' Tabby persisted in spite of her own laughter. 'He's a genuinely good bloke. Once he gets a bit of perspective on this woman, when sees her in his own home and not on a cruise ship, once he sees how she fits into his world, he'll start to see what she's really like, and then, *bang*, she'll be gone so fast you won't believe it.'

'But the way she knew about my writing, about my King books…'

'You think your Dad doesn't know you? You think he didn't tell her all about you on that cruise?'

It was a while before Stevie began to take on board his friend's sage advice, but eventually he was able to accept that it was at least *possible* that he himself might have over-reacted to the situation.

Then he began to feel guilty at the way he had stormed out of the house like a little kid having a temper tantrum, and even more so about the way he had spoken to his father at the end — he couldn't really think of another time that he had sworn directly at his dad, and the memory of doing so now made him feel incredibly ashamed.

When Tabby offered to put him up for the night in her mother's spare room, Stevie declined, thinking that if he went home tonight, he could apologise and clear the air before they all went to bed. Then they could make a fresh start the next day. Or, if Valerie and his dad had already turned in for the night, at least he would be there first thing in the morning to rectify his mistakes.

At the back of his mind, Stevie was clinging to Tabby's idea that the sooner his relationship with his father was back on track, the sooner his father would be able to see how weird Valerie really was.

Tabby stood at her front door and waved him off with a promise to call at the house sometime in the morning, not only to show her support, but also to get an eyeful of the wonderful Valerie — and maybe her familiar presence in the house would become another hint to Stevie's dad of what 'normal' actually looked like.

Then, just as he reached the end of the drive, he heard Tabby's footsteps lightly running up behind him.

When Stevie turned about to face her, she placed her hands on his shoulders and planted a long, lingering kiss on his lips. Eventually she drew back, and he stared at her in astonishment. Her beautiful brown eyes seemed huge and luminescent in the darkness.

'What was that?' he asked breathlessly.

'Just something I've been waiting to do for about… oh, I'm going to say, nine or so years?' She shrugged, smiling. 'It suddenly seemed like exactly the right time.'

They stared at each other in complete silence for what seemed like several hours.

'You know your visit tomorrow morning?' Stevie eventually asked.

'Yes?'

'Make it *early*…'

'Okay,' Tabby laughed.

Stevie slowly wandered home in a far, far better frame of mind than he had left, and for the first time since she'd popped up in his bedroom like a Halloween spook, Valerie wasn't anywhere in his thoughts. All he could think about was Tabby, his best friend, his closest confidante.

He thought about Tabby's calmness in the face of his hysteria when he'd turned up on her doorstep with his hand dripping blood, and the way she had instantly analysed the situation, made some kind of rational sense of it, and presented it back to him transformed into a more positive, less schlocky-horror form. Of the two of them, he thought it was Tabby that should probably have been the writer, because she always seemed so clever and wise.

He also thought about how she'd kept his 'lost' t-shirt carefully preserved in her drawer for about three years like a secret treasure. He thought about how she'd apparently wanted to kiss him since the day they'd met in the school playground almost a decade ago, but had waited and waited until the timing was right.

He thought back to all the days, all the years, they had spent so happily in each other's company, and wondered why it had never occurred to him that the reason they were best friends was because they loved each other.

When Stevie got home, he discovered that the house was in darkness.

Of course, he thought, fumbling to get his key into the door, they've just come back from a less than relaxing holiday, they're probably stressed-out and exhausted... but as he began to climb the stairs, he found that it had been something other than exhaustion had driven them to the privacy of his father's bedroom.

He paused as he reached the landing and just stared at the closed door, shocked by the sounds he could hear from the room beyond. Stevie had little personal experience of real sex, but like any other teenage boy, he had seen a fair amount of stuff online. As far as he was concerned, a lot of it looked so ridiculous it was actually funny.

But there was nothing funny about the noises his father and Valerie were making.

Nothing at all.

There were noises that sounded like they were wrestling, noises that were like animals grunting and growling, and making high-pitched squeals, sounds of pain. Then something fell over and smashed, the bedside lamp, maybe, and that roused Stevie from the trance into which he had fallen.

He turned to escape into his own room, but before he could shut his door, he heard another loud cry of passion or pain, and then Valerie's voice, low, but penetrating and venomous:

'Fuck me! Fuck me hard, you useless cunt! Fuck me now!'

Stevie closed the door and all but collapsed on his bed, completely sickened and dismayed.

All his earlier optimism had entirely faded. He couldn't imagine what was going on in that room, or what kind of relationship had developed so quickly between his father and this awful woman, and he didn't *want* to know. Right now, all he wanted was to escape. In the morning, Tabby would come, and then he'd have some welcome back-up, which he now suspected he would need more than ever.

The noise from the other room suddenly became even louder, with a series of cries that were almost screams, and sounded, Stevie thought with increasing dismay, like his father's voice, like his father begging Valerie to stop.

He dragged his duvet over him, slipped on his headphones, and cranked up the volume.

Eventually, he slept.

Stevie woke up the following morning to find a hand touching him, and actually not so much touching as *caressing*.

The hand was stroking lightly over his chest, fingertips tightening slightly as they dallied at his nipples, then down over his flat stomach, and then

**166**

further down, where his penis was already rising in anticipation.

His mind immediately leapt to the memory of Tabby's glowing brown eyes as she kissed him on the lips, and to her promised morning visit, and also to the fact that she knew which rock in the garden the King family hid their emergency key under.

The hand enfolded him, gripped him tight, and then began to squeeze, first hard, then harder, and then *too* hard.

Stevie cried out in pain and opened his eyes, fully conscious now and fully conscious that things had just got a lot worse a lot quicker than he could ever have believed.

He realised that he was naked, and that he was actually tied to his bed with what looked like the washing line from the back garden, and realised also that the hand which had first tantalised his nerves and then doused them with passion-killing pain belonged to Valerie Hepton.

She sat on the side of his bed, looking down at her hand as it worked on him. She was also naked. Her skin seemed even more grey and lifeless than it had been the day before, with a kind of muddy discolouring under the surface that reminded Stevie of the flesh of rotting fruit. In addition, her body, from her flat, drooping breasts to her shapeless, withered thighs, was covered with a patchy film of drying blood in which small, dark clots were suspended like crushed fruit in gelatine. She smelled like death.

Then all Stevie's thought-processes dissolved into mush as he saw the long knife Valerie had resting across her discoloured thighs.

It looked like one of the knives from the set in the kitchen, a boning knife that had hardly ever been used from one year to the next, but now seemed to have been sharpened and honed obsessively until it was almost as thin as a needle.

He saw the drying blood on her body, he saw the insanely sharpened knife, and he instantly thought of his father.

'My dad,' he croaked. 'What have you done to my dad?'

'Fucked him half to death, I think,' Valerie cackled.

When she quietened and looked up at his face, Stevie saw the way both her eyes had now dulled to an opaque blankness, as though they had developed cataracts, except for that one sliver of yellow in the left eye, that crack through which something else was staring at him.

He finally realised that she was not human.

'What are you?' he asked.

Valerie dragged her claw-like nails up and down the length of him, back and forth, the pleasure and the pain almost indistinguishable now.

'I'm an old thing,' she said at last, and suddenly she *sounded* old.

More than old, ancient. Ageless.

'An old, old and lonely thing. The last time I saw this world was on a sailing ship in the year 1872… the *Mary Celeste*… only ten miles from shore, only ten miles from freedom, when I was betrayed... The captain gathered his men. They caught me, bound me in silver chains. They sailed far away from land, and they drowned me again, the fools. I took them down with me, drowned them as they drowned me, but it was no consolation, my chance had gone...'

Her hand ceased to move, but her one good eye moved restlessly. Her voice was ragged and bitter.

'One hundred and forty years, and not a single vessel came close enough for me to reach. All I heard were distant voices, voices, calling, teasing... and then finally the iron ship sailed directly over me, and I *leapt…*'

She began to laugh, a grating, crow-like sound.

'Barely any strength left, I leapt into the first soul I found. But the body was too old and worn out to contain my spirit, and its heart exploded, split in two…. I leapt to another, and the very same thing happened, and then the same *again*, and again, and again! A gigantic vessel, filled with old, frail bodies!'

She shook her head, as if in disbelief.

'Finally, I found this one. Its heart faltered as I entered, but it managed to survive, barely...'

She laughed again, so harshly that a moment later she had to spit a mouthful of dark, clotted blood on to the floor.

'How could I have known until it was too late that while the heart was still strong, every other organ in the body was failing, diseased. Shortly after I entered, it fell into a coma. It would still be in a coma now, were it not for the power of my will.'

Her hands found the knife in her lap, and she raised it.

'Please,' Stevie said. 'Please don't…'

Valerie gently placed the tip of the blade on to Stevie's chest and began to trace archaic patterns over his body, but she didn't draw blood. Not yet. Stevie helplessly watched the knife's progress, while Valerie cackled at his terror.

'What's wrong, boy,' she said. 'Don't you want that demon exorcised from your body?'

Stevie had to tear his eyes away from the knife, but he managed it, and stared into her frightful eye. '*You're* the demon,' he said.

'Valerie…?'

Stevie's head whipped in the direction of the doorway, in which his father now appeared, shambling like an old man, and he gasped in shock.

'Daddy!'

Donald King was as naked as Valerie, and he was also smeared with blood and other substances Stevie couldn't even begin to put a name to. He looked like he'd been savagely attacked and then dragged through a pit lined with decaying corpses. Stevie saw that underneath the blood, his father was speckled with deep bite-marks, most of them centred around his genitals.

'Daddy, help me!'

Donald slowly turned his head toward his son, shuddering with effort. 'I… I *can't*,' he sobbed. 'I can't, she won't let me!'

'Then run, get away!'

Instead his father almost collapsed, but clung to the doorframe to hold himself up. His sobbing grew heavier.

'Weak,' Valerie whispered to herself. 'This one has no value…'

'Valerie, please,' Donald begged, 'just let Stevie go. You can do anything you want to me, but please, he's my son…'

'He *was* yours, now he's mine, mine, mine.'

Valerie turned back to Stevie and held up the knife before his eyes.

'This is the moment…'

Stevie could only stare at the yellow gash in Valerie's blue iris, unable to respond in any other way.

'No!' Stevie's father shouted.

Until this moment he had been incapable of resistance, but now he had somehow summoned up from deep within himself the strength to defy the creature that held him under its spell.

'*No-no-no-no…*'

Donald King abruptly launched himself across the room — but not at Valerie. Instead, he ran headfirst into the opposite wall so hard that his head rebounded like a ball. Without the smallest delay, he turned and ran back the way he'd come until he collided heavily with the solid wooden doorframe, and something inside his head loudly cracked. Then he staggered back, and spun to face the bed.

Valerie began to laugh. Stevie began to scream in horror. His father's face had almost been broken in two, his nose crushed, his forehead split and spurting blood. His eyes appeared to be looking in two opposite directions.

One of his roving eyes settled on Valerie and instantly steadied. He was like her now, Stevie saw, one-eyed, but all vestige of the trance she had put him in seemed to have vanished from that single focused eye. He was there, he was present in the moment, and he knew what had happened to him and what was about to happen to his son.

While Valerie was still chuckling, Donald threw himself at her. The attack was so unexpected that he was able to seize hold of the hand that held the knife and to wrap his other arm firmly around her scrawny, sagging neck.

'He's not yours, you bitch,' he panted into her ear, and began to drag her away.

'Kill her, Dad!' Stevie shouted. Then he filled his lungs and screamed, 'Help! Help us! Help!'

Valerie moved. Stevie could never have described exactly how. Only that Valerie moved in some way that defied all human understanding of movement.

One moment she was being wrenched from the bed with all of his father's weight bearing down upon her, but in the next she stood beside the bed having somehow thrown Donald King from her. Then she struck Stevie's father with overwhelming force and he flew across the room and crashed through the bedroom window, taking most of the frame with him.

The screaming from outside began almost at once, screaming and shouting, and voices raised in cries of alarm. Stevie imagined — he hoped — that the appalling noises they had been making must have gathered a substantial audience from among their neighbours.

Among the many voices he heard, one very familiar voice seemed distinct from the rest.

'Tabby!' Stevie shouted at the top of his voice. 'Tabby, help, call the police!'

Valerie's deadweight sagged onto the bed once again, cutting off Stevie's view of the demolished window. She was looking down at the grey arm with which she had dealt Donald King such a devastating blow. To Stevie, the arm appeared to have broken in two or more places.

'These bodies are so frail,' she muttered, and then began to clamber across him, straddling Stevie's body with the knife in her good hand.

From below in the hallway, Stevie heard voices calling through the letterbox, and fists pounding on the door. The police were on their way, the voices claimed. An ambulance had been dispatched. Then he heard Tabby's voice again.

'Get out of the way, I have a key!'

He heard the key Tabby had retrieved from under its rock chattering around the lock, and dared to look into Valerie's triumphant face, even though he knew his would-be rescuers would arrive too late. She raised the knife again and grinned at his terror.

'Oh, don't worry, boy. This blade isn't for you. It was *never* for you. I won't harm an inch of your precious body.'

'Then what—'

'It's for *me*… This stinking sack of flesh must die before I can leap again. I meant to take your father, the very instant we reached land, but then I saw the images of you he carries in his little magic box...'

Stevie realized she meant the photos on his dad's mobile phone.

'Younger, stronger. So many years of use, so many years of pleasure ahead.... I knew you would be mine…'

Footsteps on the stairs, so light, but so fast. Many heavier feet following on behind, lumbering in comparison.

'Stevie!' Tabby stood framed in the doorway, but only for a fraction of a second, and then she jumped at Valerie.

Without even seeming to look, Valerie batted her away with her broken arm, and Tabby crashed into the wall and lay for a moment, stunned. Valerie gave Stevie one final grey-yellow smile and then began to plunge the long sharp knife into her own chest and abdomen over and over again.

Dark blood, blood like black ink, began to pour out of her wounds, splashing down over Stevie's body and upturned face, coating him in the creature's filth.

'Oh Jesus! Jesus Christ!'

Stevie became aware of the raised voices of men, and of a clump of bodies jammed in the small doorway, frozen by the scene they had stumbled into.

Still dazed by the blow she had received, Tabby swayed to her feet and screamed at the men to get Valerie off him, and one of them, braver than the others, stepped forward and kicked the old woman high on the shoulder, throwing her off the bed. She fell into the corner where Tabby had been seconds before, where she continued to roll and thrash around, hacking and slicing at her body, until eventually all movement ceased.

The world began to fade to darkness.

Stevie could hear Tabby's voice commanding the others to untie him from the bed, to let her wipe the blood off him so they could see how badly he was hurt. He felt hands tugging at his bonds.

In the distance he could hear the sound of sirens coming closer, shrieking, warbling. He wondered if his father was still alive. He wondered if he would ever see him again.

Then it was gone, the world was gone.

He woke up in the ambulance. A young man with a very kind face leaned over him and smiled.

'You're okay, Stevie,' the young paramedic said. 'There's nothing to worry about, you're just fine. You weren't stabbed or hurt in any way that we can see right now. My name's Owen. We're just taking you to hospital to get you checked over properly, and maybe keep you in overnight. You've had a bit of a shock.'

Panic surged into Stevie's heart as he remembered what Valerie had claimed she meant to do by killing the body she was in… but when he searched his thoughts, he felt entirely like himself. He didn't feel as though anything, anyone, was in his brain, directing his actions or controlling his thoughts.

His mind was his own.

Maybe, he thought, whatever demon had inhabited Valerie's body had misjudged its powers of possession. Either that or it had badly misjudged *Stevie's* own power to resist such an attack — after all, he was a strong, healthy young man at the very peak of his physical and mental powers, not a diseased old woman who had been slowly ticking off the few remaining boxes on her pedestrian bucket-list.

On the other hand, Stevie thought suddenly, maybe there never *was* a demon at all, just a crazy old bitch with delusions of grandeur, some addle-brained lunatic who had somehow managed to infect Stevie, just like his father before him, with her own peculiarly grey-shaded brand of madness.

And really, didn't that rather more mundane explanation of events sound just a little more likely than anything else? Now that the worst of the ordeal was over, he believed that it did.

Stevie glanced around the interior of the ambulance. Apart from the paramedic, he was the only occupant. There was no siren.

'Where's my dad? Is he… is he okay?'

The paramedic smiled again, but slightly differently. He placed a comforting hand on Stevie's shoulder.

'He's alive. He was taken in the first ambulance. I won't lie, he's in bad shape, Stevie, but there's always hope. Put it this way, I've seen people come back from far worse.'

'And Valerie?'

'Who's that?'

'The woman with the…' Stevie made a stabbing gesture.

'Oh, yes. *Her…*'

Now the paramedic frowned and new creases appeared on his forehead.

'She was in some kind of state, let me tell you. Not just those self-inflicted wounds, either, but her whole body was in…it was almost as if she had…'

He ran out of words and just shook his head.

'I dunno, really. I just wish I could be there for the post mortem. That'd be a real eye-opener, I reckon.'

'And what about Tabby?'

'Tabby…?'

'Tabitha Eldon, my friend… my girlfriend. She was there, too.'

'I'm not sure, hang on…' Owen looked away towards the front of the moving vehicle and shouted to his colleague, who was driving. 'Joe, did you see Stevie's girlfriend back there?'

Something was shouted back, and Owen asked Stevie what Tabby looked like.

Stevie told him.

'Young, slim, tall and blonde,' Owen echoed in Joe's direction.

More shouted response.

Owen nodded, then leaned closer to Stevie and said, 'Joe says is she the girl with the sectoral heterochromia?'

Stevie shrugged in confusion. 'What's the hell's that?'

'Part of one of her eyes is a different colour. You know, the iris?'

More muffled shouting from the driver's seat, and Owen nodded again.

'Yeah, Joe says the girl he saw had massive brown eyes with a huge chunk of yellow in one of them. That your girlfriend?'

His heart seized in a cold, claw-like grip, Stevie minutely nodded.

'Joe says he saw her running out of the house soon after we arrived. Says she was moving like a bat out of hell.'

Smiling, Owen took Stevie's hand and squeezed it comfortingly.

'Don't worry, she's probably on her way over to the hospital to see you right now...'

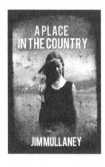

*I suppose this story could be loosely defined as my version of a zombie story, although it doesn't take place in a post-apocalyptic future landscape, as so many examples of the genre seem to. Nor does any character express or demonstrate an appetite for consuming brains — or any other body-part, for that matter. So perhaps in the end this is really just a story about the betrayal of youth and innocence, and the terrible consequences for the guilty when the raddled hand of justice reaches out from the grave. I can live with that.*

Rachael lived in the ground now, below several layers of topsoil and compacted leaf mulch, at the centre of a small copse of trees isolated in the middle of farmland, like a desert isle in a vast ocean of grain. She used to live elsewhere, of course, among the truly living, a person in her own right, a vibrant young woman… but she couldn't remember much else about that time anymore, not even when that time might have been.

Village or town, single or married, happy or sad, it was all mostly gone.

Grandparents, parents, siblings, all unknown.

The trouble was that every time it rained the water would seep through the shallow grave in which she had been buried and wash another tiny little bit of her away, a fractional amount of her poor mind along

**179**

with the rest of her decaying body, and it seemed to rain a lot these days.

Rachael sometimes felt that her memory was like a small pebble on the seashore, slowly but surely being eroded by the highs and lows of the relentless tides, and when the last convolutions and folds of her brain had finally been smoothed out by this steady, incremental process, she would completely forget that she had ever existed at all, forget even her very own name.

She sometimes wondered if perhaps this might be a blessing in disguise.

She wondered if it would be better to know absolutely nothing, rather than the little she did.

In all honesty, she really didn't mind the rain, with its slow but almost certain promise of eternal peace, but she liked best of all those glorious summer days when the sunlight forced its way through the foliage of the trees and warmed the earth over what remained of her face.

That blissful, welcome heat, muted though it was, could still be a surprisingly nourishing and energising experience.

She imagined that the person she had once been had loved the summertime above all other seasons, that it had been her special time of the year.

In all likelihood, she thought, she had been a child born in the summer, a girl who had flourished every year when summer rolled around again, and who had eventually blossomed into full womanhood during the course of one particular summer, the warmer temperatures almost forcing the changes in her body and her mind, as if she'd been a tulip or daffodil flourishing in a greenhouse.

Every so often, she *also* imagined that sweetly blossoming girl walking quickly, so quickly that she was almost running, through an enormous field of ripening wheat to get to the small copse in which her bodily remains now lay.

She imagined the golden summer sun smouldering in the girl's long blonde hair and the dry wheat tickling and chaffing at her long bare legs, so smooth and slim, as they flashed beneath her skirt.

She imagined the girl's heart beating so hard and fast in her chest that, even as young and healthy as she was, she could hardly catch her breath.

Rachael suspected that these vivid images and the accompanying memories of powerful sensation were not mere flights of imagination at all, but fragments of things that had really happened, things that she had actually done and experienced when she had been a living creature.

Pieces of the puzzle, clues that might help unravel the secret of her personal mystery.

But the memories, unconnected and almost abstract, went no farther than this, and she was left with only questions:

Why would a girl like her have been all the way out here, in the middle of this agricultural vastness, entirely without company and so far from shelter?

Why might she have been approaching this small, insignificant clump of trees at such a frantic pace, and with so much apparent excitement racing in her heart?

Why had getting to this place been so very important to her?

Once she had probably known the answers to these simple questions, she realised, but she doubted that she ever would again.

Rachael wasn't entirely alone out here, of course. She wasn't starved for company, for Mother Nature was her constant companion.

There were always the insects, naturally, along with the worms and snails and caterpillars, although in truth they had very little to offer in terms of entertainment. But the birds always sang for her, which at least separated the days from the nights, lifting her spirits each morning and at twilight, and the larger animals which passed through, the hedgehogs, the rabbits, the squirrels, badgers, foxes, and deer, were even better.

Actually, these higher creatures were *far* better, largely because Rachael had discovered that whenever they came close enough, and if they lingered long enough, she was sometimes able to enter their minds for a very brief while. She was able to see through their eyes, to run with them, to smell the world as they did, and taste as they tasted.

The experience never lasted for very long, only a matter of seconds, typically, but when it happened it was truly marvellous, and she was always watchful for another opportunity.

Once a stray mongrel bitch had paused in its ramblings to sleep uneasily in the copse for a whole night, curled up nose-to-tail directly on top of Rachael's secret, unmarked grave, and the following morning, she had found she was able to travel with the dog for quite some distance — almost halfway through the broad wheat field, in fact, and within actual sight of the narrow farm-track which bordered it.

Furthermore, and purely by the force of her will, she had even been able to make the dog turn and look back at her present home from that unaccustomed perspective.

The copse was much larger than it had been in the beginning, that was what struck her first and most forcefully at the time. The trees, a pleasing mixture of oak, birch, and hawthorn crowded together on a natural rise in the land, seemed to have far outgrown Rachael's patchy memories of them.

It became clear to her then, for the very first time, that actual *years* must have passed by while she'd been mouldering away in the ground. But exactly how many?

How long had she been dead, she wondered? Five years? Ten?

*More*?

Something which perhaps gave her some small clue as to how long she may have been lost to the world had arrived in the form of two young people, a courting couple, who had come to escape from the day's heat by picnicking in the copse's cool green depths.

The pair had spread their tartan blanket above her, curiously like people making up a bed, and then laid out their sandwiches, pickles, cakes, and a flask of tea, and proceeded to speak at length of their recent engagement and the life they planned to have together after they were married.

Only a few short moments into their unknowing intrusion, Rachael had been pulled from one of her long periods of dormancy, those deep and dreamless sleeps that were like the dark ocean covering her head, and abruptly she found herself thrust into the molten core of the woman's mind.

After the first initial shock of her awakening, Rachael had been completely enthralled.

Seeing though the eyes of animals was a dull pleasure indeed compared to seeing through human eyes again. The colours they saw were nothing short of stunning, the taste of their food and drink was amazingly rich, and the woman's fiancé was so handsome that Rachael could hardly keep her eyes off him for more than a few seconds at a time.

The sound of their voices and the expression of the language they used were like a wonderful music after the limited vocabularies of the animals' minds, and she almost fell into a trance listening to the couple's easy conversation, of friends and family, of colour schemes and soft furnishings, of honeymoon destinations and baby names.

And after a while, she had also been able to feel the woman's *other* hunger, the one that lay beneath the quickly diminishing appetite for food and the steadily growing craving for the future, for a home and children of her own... she could feel the *special* hunger, for physical satisfaction, growing more and more powerful until it dominated her whole being, mind, body, and soul, and Rachael was inside her like a passenger.

Even before they had properly finished eating, by unspoken consent the couple quickly began to clear away the remains of their picnic, throwing all the paraphernalia of food and drink back in the basket in their sudden eagerness to touch one another.

The young man stood up and glanced through the gaps between the trees, presumably to ensure that they were in no danger of being spied upon. Then, satisfied that they would be undisturbed, he leant over the woman as she knelt on the blanket at his feet and he kissed her deeply, putting his tongue into her mouth and taking her tongue into his.

Rachael could taste the sweetness of the tea they had drunk, the still-sharp aftertaste of mustard from their sandwiches and the grains of salt on their lips, and she could smell the man's tangy aftershave, feel the heat of his breath in her mouth, and the beginnings of rough afternoon stubble on his dimpled chin.

When the kiss ended, the man knelt down beside the woman and casually peeled the summer dress from her body, simply pulled it up over her head and set it aside.

Rachael was absolutely astonished.

Far from resisting him, as she had fully expected, the woman actually *helped* the man to do it, by obligingly raising her arms as it was whisked away. What's more, beneath her dress the woman was almost entirely naked, and wore only a pair of translucent black briefs so small that they seemed barely worth wearing at all, and through the front panel of which an unnaturally small tuft of dark pubic hair was clearly visible.

The man immediately began to fondle the woman's large breasts, dipping his head to suck and tug at each engorged nipple in turn. While he did this, she brazenly rubbed the swelling mound at the front of his trousers, and then she opened his flies and eased out his stiffening penis.

The man smiled at her so lovingly, tenderly stroking the hair back from her face all the while, and then she lowered her head and took his erect penis into her mouth just as readily and pleasurably as she had earlier taken his tongue.

Overwhelmed, shocked, and saturated with intense sensation, Rachael had swiftly withdrawn from the woman's mind, and then seemed to fall a long way back into the safe and comforting darkness of her underground existence.

What exactly had she just experienced?

She felt sure that women had never been such openly sexual creatures when she had been alive. Had the women of her day even gone about in public without wearing a brassiere? Or wore such shamelessly revealing underwear, at any time? *Decent* women? Had they ever touched their men's bodies with such confidence, knowledge, and lack of inhibition, even in the secret darkness of the marital bedroom?

She didn't know, couldn't remember, but surely the way her mind had recoiled from the sheer boldness of the couple's sexual intimacy told her something?

Maybe it told her that a great many years had passed while she had been gone — *not* just five or ten — but perhaps so many years that some great social

**186**

upheaval had occurred in the interim, some sexual revolution that had managed to change the world.

There was no way of knowing. It was confusing, and it was frightening.

For a long while after this all too vivid encounter, Rachael no longer dared to allow her mind to roam so freely. Animals large and small continued to pass through the copse on a regular basis, as before, but she felt no great desire to sample their senses.

A kind of weary despair had begun to wind its tenacious roots all through her mind, just like the tree roots that had begun to wind their way through her ribcage and pelvis and which she knew would very soon begin to pull her apart.

She simply did not understand why she should still possess this unsettling level of consciousness. After all, she was *dead*, wasn't she? She should have passed on by now, gone on to either Heaven or hell, which was surely the natural order of things. And if neither of those places really existed, then there should have been nothing at all, not even blackness and silence, because even blackness and silence were *something*.

She didn't understand why she had been condemned to this ghastly, eternal form of solitary confinement, to suffer everything that had once been hers being slowly eroded away, day by day, month by month, year by year.

Could she possibly have been so bad in her short lifetime that this agonising torment, this purgatory, was her allotted punishment?

The next time the dark waters of sleep beckoned her, Rachael welcomed them like old, dear friends, and hoped that this time she would sink faster and deeper than ever before, and never, ever rise again.

But, of course, she did rise.

She was *powerless* not to.

She awoke once again to the unmistakable odours of glorious high summer in the countryside, always familiar, and always so beautiful to her. But was it the *same* summer or the next, or the summer a dozen years hence?

She could not know, although she immediately understood that once again she had been drawn forth from the darkness to enter into the mind of another young woman. Another woman who was approaching this small, remote copse of trees in the company of a man.

But that was where the similarity ended.

Even though it had been unfamiliar and uncomfortable for Rachel at the time, all the strong emotions she had drawn from the first woman had at least been positive and life-affirming, all speaking of love and companionship and excitement and desire.

But everything she was getting from this new woman, this woman who she realised was in many ways still just a girl, was exactly the opposite. And Rachael was so completely inside this girl, and the fit was so perfect, that she knew they had far more in common with each other than she had with the first woman, who had been both older and much more experienced in the ways of life.

She understood that this new girl was roughly the same age she had been herself when she had died, and that she was interpreting the girl's feelings and fears so well because she had experienced exactly the same range of unsettling emotions in the last few desperate moments before her death. Before her *murder*.

Rachael opened her eyes. Opened the other girl's eyes, too.

She saw *herself* in the past.

She was moving towards the small copse through the enormous wheat field. The sun caught in her hair was making her head heavy, making her thoughts slow and lethargic, just when she most needed them to be sharp and alert. Her heart was pounding, and she wasn't *almost* running, she *was* running, and just as fast as she possibly could.

The dry wheat was scratching at her bare legs like a forest of thorns, and she could feel the presence of another person behind her, a personality whose snarling presence was driving her on like a mad dog trying to drive a stray ewe to exhaustion.

She had not been alone, after all.

The person behind her, the person *chasing* her, was the man who had charmed her and brought her to this distant place, far from prying eyes, far from curious ears. The man who had brought her a great many miles in his car, over roads she had never seen in her life before, making the prospect of finding her own way home seem all but impossible.

The man whose charm had vanished, layer by layer, the further they had journeyed from Rachael's safe and familiar world.

Each new discovery gave Rachael another shock of recognition.

She now realised that in her earlier memories of running through the wheat field, she had never been rushing out of excitement, but out of anxiety and fear. Out of sheer *terror*. She remembered that the man had begun to alarm her even before he had stopped the car on the little rutted farm-track by the side of the isolated field. *Long* before then.

But then he had tried to kiss her, first putting his hand underneath her skirt, and then trying to make Rachael put her hand on him, and the alarm in her mind had become deafening.

Rachael had told him that she had changed her mind, that she wanted to go home, she *needed* to go home.

Her father was a powerful man, she said, he knew people, important people. Her mother would be worried about her, she said. She had a doctor's appointment later that afternoon. She was meeting friends, and had to wash and set her hair. She had to collect her little niece from school. She had to be at her aunt's house in time for tea.

She was a girl, she said, who would quickly be missed, a girl people would soon come looking for.

She said, she said, she said.

*Take me home, please*, she had finally asked the man, begged him, and then watched with dismay his already shadowed eyes darken as he slowly shook his head.

*No*, he had replied.

In response to the answer that she had known all along in her heart of hearts he would finally give,

Rachael had flung open the car door and begun to run away – not toward the copse, at all, she now understood, but just away from the car and the track it was parked upon, and the man who had driven it there.

Away, in a blinding, thoughtless panic.

He had caught her quickly enough, of course, caught her when she was less than thirty uncoordinated strides across the field. He was lithe and quick and strong, a wild animal without mercy, cruel as nature.

He had grabbed her by the hair and swung her around by it until she faced him again, and then he had punched her hard in the chest, robbing her of breath. He had slapped her hard across her face, splitting her lower lip, and then struck her once again, this time high on her temple.

Then he had gathered her up in his arms before she could collapse to the ground, and slung her limp body over his shoulder like a side of beef to be carried into a butcher's shop.

Dazed, and nearly unconscious, Rachael had watched helplessly as a long, drooling gobbet of blood fell in surreal slow-motion from her broken mouth and landed on one of the ears of wheat a thousand or so miles below her dangling head, unevenly spotting it.

One spurt of blood, one ear of wheat, this was all she had time to focus upon, and then he was running for the copse of trees, heading for cover, and her upside-down world became a shaking, jumbled blur of darkness and light, darkness and light.

Back out of her own memory and into the new girl's body, Rachael entered the cool shade of the trees on her own two sandaled feet and looked at the beautiful sunlight dappling the thick eiderdown of leaves over her grave.

The man's heavy hand settled upon her shoulder.

*See*, he whispered softly, *I told you it was beautiful in here. And private. This is a secret place*, he said, *our secret, yours and mine. Whatever we do here is up to us, and only we will ever know about it*.

All of these words seemed as familiar to Rachael as the natural perfumes of summer, and she remembered hearing something almost identical being breathed into her own ear after her killer had carried her into the trees and roughly laid her down on a bed of last year's leaves, holding a hand across her bloody mouth and trying to silence her screams before they truly started.

*Nothing bad is going to happen*, he had falsely promised. *Nothing will happen that you don't want to happen. We'll just go slowly, and gently, and you'll like it. You'll like it so much that you'll never want me to stop*.

He had been panting with exertion and excitement, and his breath was foul, the breath of a hyena, a scavenger of carrion, a predator of the weak and the lame.

Rachael found that she was now unable to decide whether the words she had just heard were the words of *now* or the words of *then*, but she understood that this distinction was almost entirely without relevance.

The words and the exact circumstances might have differed in minor details, and her life and this

**192**

new girl's life might have been generations apart, but essentially their stories were exactly the same.

An older man, a younger woman, and murder.

She made the girl turn and face the man who had brought her to this lonely, lovely place in the country in order to rape and kill her, and that was the greatest shock of all. Because it was the *same* man. The very same man, but maybe thirty years older.

*Teddy*, she thought suddenly. His name is *Teddy*.

Rachael immediately began to catch more flashes from the past, fragmentary memories of the younger Teddy playing his little tricks on the innocent young woman she had been, paying his little compliments, bestowing his little smiles, and getting bolder and bolder every day.

A kind word here, a cheeky pat on the bottom there, playing her, drawing her, fascinating her.

*You call me Teddy, my little darling, 'cos from now on I'm going to be your favourite Teddy Bear...*

She discovered that the girl she was now inside had an actual name for this aggregate process of subtle coercion. She thought of it as 'grooming', an unfamiliar word to Rachael in this context, which nevertheless made complete sense to her.

But simply having a handy nomenclature to hang the evil, scheming process upon didn't appear to have protected the girl from its effects one little bit.

Even though Teddy was so much older, and both softer and heavier into the bargain, Rachel saw that he was still a handsome man, still strong and vital, with thick, lustrous hair only now just beginning to silver at the temples, an effect which didn't seem to age him, only served to make his saturnine good-looks even more striking.

His eyes, his dark eyes, were still hypnotising pools of challenging mockery and forbidden suggestion, calculated to make young, inexperienced girls want to dangle their feet in the waters of his regard, unaware of the lethal predator that lurked beneath the surface glamour.

Oh but Rachael was aware, all right. Yes, she knew the awful truth.

The girl was beginning to panic now, her strong young heart like a wild animal caught in a poacher's snare. Rachael could feel it racing in the girl's breast and the blood beating drum-like in her pulses, but she knew that panicking would be a terrible mistake. Panicking would only make Teddy feel that he needed to rush the job, to make the ordeal short and violent with no chance to fight back, no space to think to outwit him, to defeat him.

That was how it had been for Rachael, a short and violent attack to smother her panic, and then the bruising, tearing invasion of her body, and then the strangling, and then the two actually together, as though for this strange man, this terrible human hyena, one savage pleasure was no good without the other.

But Rachael didn't want the same fate for this young girl. She was determined that this atrocity was not going to happen again, not while she was here. And then it came to her that perhaps this was *exactly* why she was here, still here after all these years, in this strange no-man's land between the worlds of the living and the dead. Maybe she hadn't passed on for this very reason.

Some force, some intelligence, a higher power beyond her knowledge and comprehension, had known that one day her killer would return to the scene of his crime with another innocent victim in tow, and had somehow preserved her here for one purpose alone.

To stop him.

Until now she had been a mere passenger inside the girl's body and mind, the way she had been with the other woman as she made love to her fiancé, but now Rachael reached out, stretched, expanded, and asserted dominance with a strength she had never suspected she possessed.

Not even when she had managed to make the dog she was travelling with stop and look back at the copse had she felt so in control of another creature's actions.

She felt her hands slip inside the girl's hands as though they were gloves, felt the girl's face cover hers like a mask. For a second or two, Rachael felt that there were two tongues in her mouth, as though she and the girl were French kissing, the way the courting couple had, but then the sensation faded and there was only one tongue.

And it was Rachael's.

Teddy had a tight hold of her right forearm, so tight that the girl's wrist and hand were almost numb. With his free hand he had been fumbling at the buttons of her blouse, but the tiny pearlescent buttons were tricky and his excitement had made his large hands clumsy and his patience short.

Rachael could tell that Teddy was getting ready to rip and tear, that he only needed an excuse to begin, just the smallest excuse.

*Wait*, she said abruptly. *You're all fingers and thumbs, you silly man. Here, let me do it...*

She had thought it would take powerful machinery to make him release his grip on the girl's arm, but his hand fell away almost the moment she had begun to speak, and he was staring at her intently.

*He knows*, Rachael thought. *Somehow he recognises me*.

But it wasn't that at all, of course. It was just that the situation had somehow changed in a blink of an eye, and Teddy had picked up on it, the way Rachael imagined a hyena would instinctively pick up on the signs of weakness given off by a young antelope trailing at the back of the herd.

Except this was a change that had happened almost in reverse. A second before the girl had been purely a victim in his eyes. Now, by pretending to cooperate with his desires, she had become what? Some kind of unwitting collaborator in her own doom, which was quite probably this man's greatest fantasy?

Rachael made the girl smile and raised her hands, allowing her fingers' easy familiarity with the buttons to do their work. For everything else, she called upon the few things she had learned from being inside the first woman, her sensual confidence and the powerful awareness of herself as a sexual being.

She watched Teddy's eyes following her hands, greedy for a sight of what lay beneath the blouse, which turned out to be a plain white brassiere similar to the sort that Rachael herself had worn over the few short years that she had needed to wear one at all.

Oh, it was all coming back now.

It was almost funny, she thought, how Teddy was so much older now, and yet his intended victims had stayed around the same age and maturity, and she wondered how fragile his ego and confidence had to be, if they could only be fed and nurtured by the seduction and destruction of young women not long past childhood.

Once the last button had tumbled open, Teddy reached for her again, but she took a single step backwards and told him to wait, and his avid eyes snapped back to hers, darkened still further by a storm-cloud of violent anger she now recalled all too well.

*Wait*, she said again, as she kicked off the girl's sandals, the leaves a soft carpet under her bare feet. *Just watch….*

She slowly eased the blouse back over the girl's narrow, delicate shoulders and then removed it altogether. She tossed it away behind her, where it landed neatly on a bed of bracken, as though deliberately hung there. Then she reached around her back to unhook the virginal white brassiere.

Teddy had all but stopped breathing in anticipation, but when Rachael finally slipped the garment off, revealing the girl's beautiful small breasts with their tiny pink nipples, he actually gasped. She gave him another few seconds to stare and drool, and then she cast the brassiere away too, high over her head, and which flew even farther than the blouse had.

Then, before he could think to move, before he simply *had* to reach out and touch her no matter what she said or with how much authority she said it, Rachael hooked her thumbs under the waistbands of the light summer skirt the girl wore and her underwear at the same time, quickly pushed both garments down below her knees, and then stepped out of them in one flowing movement.

She immediately threw the skirt back over her shoulder to join her blouse, but she held on to the underwear for a few more moments, coyly posing with them for Teddy's benefit. Like the brassiere before them, the plain cotton briefs were white and innocent, the underwear of a girl whose mind was not yet ready to be a woman's, no matter what her body's biological development believed.

After teasing him just a little more, she used the elastic in the waistband to catapult the briefs at Teddy, who caught them awkwardly with hands which seemed satisfyingly shaky.

He raised them to his nose and inhaled deeply before tucking them away in his jacket pocket, a trophy he intended to gloat over at some later date, Rachael presumed.

*Sit down there, on the ground*, she said, slowly beginning to stroke the girl's hands over her slim torso, as though applying a rich lotion to her skin, first over her ribs and her chest, and then further down, circling over her flat belly and the button of her navel, and then over the fine angles of her hips and down on to her thighs.

Now it was her turn to play, to draw, to fascinate... and her intentions were no less deadly than his.

*Sit down*, she repeated.

This time Teddy did as she had commanded him, lowering himself to the ground and settling cross-legged among the leaves.

Rachael saw that the light of mockery, which had seemed ever-present in this man's eyes, the look that reminded her so much of a cat toying with a mouse, had now temporarily vanished. The show she was putting on for him, using the enticement of the young woman's body, the mature sexuality of the older women she had briefly inhabited in some other summer, and her very own sense of determined purpose, had totally derailed him from his method, hypnotising him, if only for a brief window of time.

It was a window Rachael intended to use to its utmost.

Very much aware that she was revealing herself in every detail to the older man's greedy, crawling eyes, Rachael slowly stepped forward, exaggerating the swing of her narrow hips, only stopping when his face was bare inches from the girl's scant dusting of golden pubic hair. She knew that she could no longer avoid him touching her, and in fact, she didn't want to avoid it, however unpleasant it might be.

It was a necessary evil, a means to an end.

She even widened her stance slightly, in a kind of invitation, and then closed her eyes as his hand slipped between her legs and his dry, blunt fingers began to probe.

*You've been here before*, she said, forcing herself not to cry out. *Out here in the country, in these trees…* A single large tear ran down her right cheek

*Only once, a long, long time ago*, he replied. Intent upon his explorations, Teddy did not notice the tear, and wouldn't have cared if he had. *But as soon as I laid eyes on you, I knew that it was time to come back again. You remind me so much of a girl I used to know back then…*

Carefully maintaining her balance by winding the fingers of both hands into his thick, sweaty hair, Rachael slowly raised her right leg and gently settled the sole of her foot on Teddy's left shoulder.

Teddy grunted in surprise and pleasure. He probably imagined that the grip the girl had taken on his hair was the result of a passion he had awoken in her, and that she had opened her legs this way to allow him even greater access to the most intimate part of her body. He instantly responded by probing even more aggressively and more deeply than before, and then a little blood began to flow from her, which excited him beyond all measure.

This time when Rachael opened her eyes there was a thinness to the girl's vision that she at first mistook for the haze of tears, tears of pain and humiliation and shame. But then she realised that the lack of clarity was down to something elsc entirely.

It was because her mind had now split in two. Part of her consciousness was still in the girl's body, while another part of it had drained away, seeped into the ground like the rainwater did, and then leeched back into the rotten sponge of her brain. And a part of the girl's energy and lifeforce had gone into Rachael, too.

Into her body.

She raised her head to look beyond Teddy's darkly intense face as he rooted around inside the girl, seeing just how far he could go before she began to protest, before pain overrode what he assumed was pleasure, and she saw a small section of the leaf-cover behind his back begin to bulge upwards in exactly the place she had hoped.

A few seconds later, something emerged from the leaves, something that had been pushed up from the ground below. It was a sharp-edged rock about the size of a cooking apple, and she already knew how it would feel in the girl's hand.

Rachael gathered herself, both in the girl's mind and body and in her own, and then she screamed out:

*NOW!*

She used all the strength in the girl's young legs and every single ounce of her small bodyweight to kick down, her right foot driving Teddy backwards with such sudden ferocity that she was left with bloody strands of hair wrapped in her clenched fists.

Caught completely unawares, Teddy's back crashed down onto the bed of leaves, and his lolling head struck the unearthed rock so hard that he cried out loud, barely noticing the hair that had been torn out of his scalp at the roots.

But unprepared for the attack or not, he recovered quickly, his eyes swiftly clearing of the pain. And then such a look of wildness came into them, such *savagery*.

It was the killing look.

Lust was forgotten. It would come back later, after the girl was dead, of that Rachael had no doubt, but for now all Teddy wanted was to kill her, and with as much pain as he could manage.

She saw his shoulders twitch as he began to swing himself upright... but then the ground either side of his torso erupted in a shower of leaf-mulch and topsoil, and two grey skeletal arms burst out into the shadowed air and immediately wrapped themselves around Teddy's body, one across his chest and the other locked tight around his throat, and he started to scream.

As soon as he began to struggle, shaking pieces of her rotten flesh loose like lumps of clay, Rachael understood that her body was now too fragile to restrain Teddy for even a short length of time.

Although the three decades that had passed since she had last pitted her strength against his may have weakened him slightly, they had been a great deal more unkind to her. If he didn't simply twist free of her clutches in the next few seconds, she realised that he might actually manage to tear her arms from her shoulders entirely, like the wings twisted from the carcass of an overcooked chicken.

Concentrating fiercely to control both of her bodies at the same time, she made the girl step forward again to stand over Teddy's twisting, bucking figure, and then, abruptly, to drop down on to it with all of her weight. Her knees landed on his pot belly and sank in, driving all the air out of him in one great gust of foul breath, and for a moment or two his screaming and shouting ceased.

In this brief pocket of silence, Rachael made the girl lean forward, so that her small naked breasts were close enough for Teddy to kiss, if he had still been in a kissing mood, and then made her snatch up the rock she had unearthed for just this moment.

As she had expected, the rock was as perfect a fit for the girl's hand as it had been for her own under the ground, roughly seamed with ridges that allowed a firm, steady grip.

*Remember me?* Rachael made the girl ask.

Then in her own voice, from the fibrous remains of her own rotting vocal cords and filtering up through the earth and the leaves and into her killer's ear, she croaked:

*Don't you know who I am, Teddy Bear?*

Then she brought the rock down on Teddy's head and face a dozen times or more, utilising the girl's young muscles and eye for accuracy.

Blood flowed freely from the three deep gashes she put in his forehead, half in and half out of his handsome hairline, and literally spurted from the divot she dug out of his brow with one particularly forceful cross-swing. The eye below this wound was already closing and visibly swelling as she paused a moment later to examine her handiwork, breathing hard. In addition, she saw that she had broken his nose, and fractured his cheekbones. Some of his teeth were also shattered, but she didn't know how many.

Teddy was completely unconscious now, but that was okay, Rachael thought, that was quite all right. It would make the next part of the plan far easier to accomplish, and much less stressful for her host.

She got the girl up and moving once more, making her swing the rock again and again, relentlessly hammering away at selected portions of Teddy's anatomy until bones broke and splintered, cartilage and ligaments were severed or snapped, and the joints became separated.

First she destroyed both his knees, then his ankles, before moving on to his elbows, wrists, and finally his shoulders, pounding and pounding and pounding until there was no way he would be able to even *move* once he regained consciousness, let alone fight back.


Finally, it was all done, and it was time to turn her attention to the girl. There were things Rachael needed to do for her, because she would not be able to do them for herself without a little help.

All the while Rachael had been inside her body and mind, she had been able to feel the girl's spirit or soul somewhere far away in the background of her consciousness, although mercifully asleep in some way, like a bird with its head folded beneath its wing.

Soon it would be time to awaken her from her slumbers, but not just yet.

Rachael brought the girl back to her feet and made her collect her scattered clothing item by item, including her briefs still tucked away in Teddy's jacket pocket. Before Rachael dressed her, she first had to use handfuls of dried leaves to wipe the many spots and streaks of Teddy's blood from her smooth, pale skin – incriminating blood that would have saturated the girl's clothing, if Rachael hadn't had the presence of mind to first remove them and then to throw them clear.

Then, without looking back at either Teddy's unconscious, broken and blood-stained body or the skeletal arms and hands that still held tight to it, she walked the girl out of the copse of trees and into the sweet, sweet sunlight.

As they began to cross the field of wheat in the direction of the distant farm-track, Rachel was pleased to discover, through a gentle examination of her mind, that the girl was a good deal more knowledgeable of the world than she had been at the same age. To begin with, she actually knew approximately where they were, and remembered most of the roads Teddy had followed to bring them here.

Even better, although she had no licence as yet, it seemed the girl had been taking lessons for several months and was fully capable of driving Teddy's car back to her home in perfect safety.

As the farm-track grew closer and closer, Rachael quietly began to speak to the girl, communicating directly with her subconscious mind.

While she was doing this, she thought of a film she must once have seen at some long-ago cinema, sitting in the darkened theatre while a black-and-white Hollywood melodrama unfolded in front of her, as a doctor of the mind spoke to a patient he had put into a trance to cure her of a mental disorder.

In this case, Rachael was the doctor, and the disorder she wished to cure was called *memory*.

The girl was to carefully drive Teddy's car to a place she knew, but a place where *she* was not known.

She would find a quiet street or alleyway to abandon the vehicle unobserved, but before she left it with the windows open and the keys still in the ignition, she was to use the hem of her skirt to erase the many fingerprints she was bound to have left on the car's interior, on the steering wheel and gearstick, on the dashboard surfaces, the radio knobs, and the door-handles.

Then, and only then, was she to get out of the car and walk away, and never look back, never *think* back. She was to forget.

Rachael watched as the girl's feet operated the car's clutch, brake, and accelerator pedals, and her capable little hands changed gears and steered as she took the car through a neat, perfectly executed three-point turn on the narrow farm-track.

Once she had the car turned around and slowly heading back the way it had come, she began to speak to the girl of what she must do when she finally got home.

*Run a deep, hot bath for yourself*, she told her, *and while it is running, put your clothes in to soak with plenty of detergent. If you find a little blood in your underwear, it will be of no concern, it's just spotting from an early period, and any physical discomfort you may feel down there is merely another symptom. Try not to worry, in a short time it will pass...*

The girl nodded, and nodded, and nodded, wondrously responsive to Rachael's powers of suggestion.

*You will soak yourself in the tub for as long as you are able, and as you soak and relax you will continue to forget everything about this day, about all its pain and its filth and its terror, about where you have been and who you were with, and about everything you have seen and done. This day will be a blank page in the book of your life*, she told the girl, *but at least now you will have the opportunity to fill up all the other pages, and complete your own story.*

And suddenly, as she was speaking, and as the part of her that was still a part of the girl was making the girl listen and take heed, a series of images appeared before her, superimposed on the view of the farm-track rolling away beneath the car she saw through the girl's eyes.

Rachael saw a small cottage, the last in a short row, its garden filled with a profusion of summer flowers, and she knew that this was her home. Not the girl's home — which was in some kind of rectangular building so tall that Rachael couldn't understand how it had been built in the first place, let alone how it managed to remain standing with so many people living in it — but *her* home, the house she had grown up in.

She saw two middle-aged people working companionably in the garden, a married couple, weeding and pruning and trimming, and she knew that they were her parents.

She found herself speculating if one or both of them could still be alive after the thirty or more years she had been gone, and if they *were* alive, she wondered if that lovely little cottage was still the place they called home? And if it *was*, were they still waiting there for their long-lost daughter to come back to them?

*I could find them…*

The moment the idea occurred to her, she understood that it was a real possibility. Her bond with the girl, and her possession of the girl's body and mind, was of an entirely different order to anything she had previously experienced. Rachael sensed that she could remain inside the girl for a long, long time, quite probably for as long as she needed or wanted to.

But then she thought, *what would be the point*?

How likely was it that she would be able to convince her parents that their beloved lost daughter was living as a guest inside this girl's mind? Wasn't it more likely that they would assume she was a poor deranged orphan, quite possibly an escapee from some kind of local institution, and call the police?

And even if she was able to make them believe her extraordinary story, what would be the result? Did she really imagine that it would ease her parents' minds to know the terrible manner of her death, or the decades of misery she had known in the ground? Wouldn't she simply be opening up fresh new wounds in among the old scar tissue, and blighting whatever remained of their own lives?

In the end, though, all her questions paled before the central fact, which was that any reunion with her parents, either bitter or sweet, could in any case only last but the shortest length of time. Then she would be

**208**

gone once more, this time never to return. Even if it were possible for her to stay inside the girl indefinitely, which for all she knew it very well might be, Rachael's conscience would not allow it.

The girl had her own life to lead, and if Rachael were to deny her that, if she were to steal any more of her life away, she would be no better than Teddy was.

*Ah, Teddy...*

For a moment she had forgotten Teddy, and that wouldn't do. Teddy was unfinished business.

The car finally trundled to a dusty halt at the end of the long farm-track, which formed a crooked T-junction with a narrow country lane lined either side with trees and hedges. There was no other traffic within sight, no sound but the sound of a breeze moving through the trees. The girl just sat there silently, awaiting her instructions, ready to do as she was bid without question.

Rachel sensed that a right-turn at this point would take the car in the direction she most wanted to go, toward that little cottage and perhaps the chance to see her parents one last time. But the left-hand turn was the way back to the girl's life, and it was therefore the direction that she *had* to turn.

Really, she had no choice.

*Turn left*, she told the girl, and then as soon as the car began to move again, Rachel let go, came untethered from her host's body and mind, and was immediately drawn back along the rutted farm-track and dragged through the field of wheat at a speed that would have taken her breath away, had she had breath to take.

Then, with thump she imagined but did not feel, she was suddenly back inside herself, in her own intimate darkness, living within her own liquefying mind.

And yet she was not dismayed that the freedom the girl had bestowed upon her was gone forever, for now she was totally convinced that there had been a purpose to all her suffering, and equally sure that her time in purgatory was very nearly at its end.

She believed that the higher power which had preserved her for so long still had plans for her, and she thought — she thought, she hoped, she prayed — that she knew what they were.

Soon she would move on to another plain of existence.

Time was almost at an end.

Very gradually, Rachael began to be aware that only a matter of inches above her, Teddy was beginning to regain consciousness.

She felt first the stirring in his mind, and then, even before he woke, he began to moan as his nerves came alive to the massive trauma his body had undergone at the girl's hands. Soon Teddy's moans and groans took on a more coherent form as they began to be interspaced with words.

Many of those words were ugly words, and still more were directed at God or Jesus, beseeching our Lord and Saviour to take away the agony of his injuries, to restore him, to make him whole again.

Rachael was filled with real wonder that Teddy actually believed he had the right to ask for these blessings.

He had forgotten all about her, of course. His many pains and agonies had numbed him to the lesser pressure of her arms about his body, and perhaps temporarily driven her from his memory. But it was time now to remind him that she was still here.

Rachel slowly tightened her grip around his neck and her hold on his chest, but so slowly that for a few moments he did not notice.

And then she spoke:

*Teddy*, she whispered, her voice a chill breeze from an unknown world. *Teddy, it's time now. Time for me to move on. Time for you to take my place.*

Then, with the last remaining vestiges of her strength and at the absolute extremes of her body's integrity, she began to drag Teddy down.

Down under the leaf-cover, down into the rich mulch, and then down under the topsoil, one painful, agonising half-inch after another, with Teddy screaming as much from terror as from the pain in his shattered joints, screaming all the way, screaming as he begged for forgiveness, bellowing his rage and fear and agony, screaming until topsoil, clay, and stones were forced into his open mouth and down his throat, gagging, choking, and finally silencing him.

He fought her all the way, Rachael gave him that much credit. He fought her as much as he possibly could, fought as she herself had fought as he first pinned her down and then thrust himself inside her, fought for breath as she had fought for it while he choked the life out of her, his fingers burying themselves deep into her throat, crushing her windpipe.

But finally, inevitably, he succumbed, as had she.

She felt his living mind fade away like an echo...

...and then felt it return only moments later in the form of a dead, dark cloud of confusion, doubt, and fear.

Rachael knew that she could speak to him now, if she chose to, she could explain that this was the prison to which he had condemned her for the last thirty years. But she decided that she actually preferred to leave him to discover the sheer horror of what lay in store for him in his own time.

Besides, it was time to go.

This was his place now, not hers. Her trials were over, his just beginning. Her time had lasted three decades, and she had been a complete innocent. How long might Teddy's black soul endure in this place?

Then she felt her hold on this level of existence begin to slip, her sense of herself as a personality begin to fade. Suddenly there was no more copse of trees, no more fields of wheat, no more Teddy at his day of reckoning, and no more Rachael, either in body or in spirit.

For a moment or two she had the sensations of vertigo, of loss, of emptying out, and of an immense black void opening up before her, a void filled with an all-encompassing darkness that made the one she had known for thirty years seem like the darkness a child made as it hid from the morning light under its bed-sheets.

But in the next instant all her fear had gone, and she threw back the sheets to her new world, and there was light, such *gorgeous* light, and the smells all about her were the epitome of summer.

She turned around and around, bare feet dancing on the gorgeous nap of a well-kept lawn. Beds of beautiful flowers surrounded her.

Here was the garden. Here was the cottage.

And here *they* were…

*This is one of those stories that appear as a complete bolt from the blue. One moment it didn't exist in any way, shape, or form, but then my mind wandered off on its own, as it occasionally does, and in the very next moment the story not only existed, it existed down to the very last detail. This was a wonderful, totally unexpected surprise. However, judging from how this story pans out, I can see that I'll have to have a very long talk with my mind about the kind of places it wanders when I'm not paying attention.*

'Twas was the night before Christmas, when all through the Manor House Veterinary Clinic not a creature was stirring, not even Little Daisy, the King Charles spaniel bitch that had been spayed late that afternoon as the last procedure of the day.

Of course, in addition to currently being the surgery's only overnight guest, Little Daisy was still fairly heavily sedated, and so would hopefully remain unstirring until after the morning shift-change. This would leave Paul Coburn to enjoy his Christmas Eve in absolute peace, which this year meant sitting on his arse in a comfy chair, half-listening to a festive chart on TV, and cultivating a semi by perusing voyeur-porn on his mobile phone.

As this was pretty much the same way he imagined he would have spent the evening anyway,

Coburn believed that the double-time he was earning for doing absolutely sod all amply made up for the fact that he couldn't enjoy a festive tipple or two to while the hours away. He was also quick to remind himself that after tonight he had five days off in a row, which he felt would give him more than enough time to give his liver a decent seasonal workout.

Coburn had been a qualified veterinary nurse for almost a year now, a couple of months more than he'd been a singleton. He'd still been settling into the job when his long-time girlfriend, Judy, had dumped him for some new guy with a big flash car and a big flash salary to go with it. This was a bit of a kick in the teeth, all things considered, as Judy had always professed to be unmoved by material things such as status symbols and fat wallets, although clearly she *could* be moved when it suited her.

But you lived and you learned, Coburn reckoned, and since then he'd been busy relearning how to live his life and enjoy his pleasures as a single man. He figured spending Christmas alone would just about complete his studies on the subject. As for other people, he'd just about given up on them entirely. Animals were better company.

He glanced up at the wall-mounted TV as the over-familiar songs on the Christmas compilation show suddenly started to break up into loud, grating white-noise, and he saw that the picture was undergoing the same degeneration as the sound, the images rapidly dissolving into a snowstorm of electronic fuzz and static.

'Oh, for fuck's s—'

The final word of his sentence was cut off as the TV emitted a sharp snapping sound and abruptly went completely dead. At the very same moment, his mobile began to vibrate in his hand. When he looked down at it, he saw the images of the amateur lesbian romp he'd been enjoying first freeze, then rapidly degrade, and then disappear altogether as the screen went black. Suddenly his phone was just as dead as the TV.

At the other side of the room, still unconscious with her head cradled in the cone of shame, Little Daisy began to whimper, all her legs beginning to twitch and kick in distress.

Coburn jumped up immediately, the TV and his phone temporarily forgotten, all his concern centred on the dog. He was halfway to the recovery cage when every ceiling light in the large treatment/recovery room went off, leaving him in total blackness. The lights reappeared again only a few seconds later, but only at about half their usual brightness — the emergency lighting had obviously cut in. But the TV hadn't come back on, and neither had the electric fan heater he'd been using.

Somewhere, he thought, something electrical must be severely fucked.

In her cage, Daisy continued to kick and whimper, and Coburn ran his fingers through his hair in irritation. This was absolutely fucking typical, he thought bitterly. This was just about his fucking luck. He couldn't get a break, not even at Christmas. Anything that *could* go wrong for him *did* go wrong. It had been the same ever since Judy had run out on him for that rich little prick, as if she had been the charm that made his life run halfway sweetly, and her unexpected departure was the final straw. Without her, things just weren't the same, and now if there was any bad luck going, he was sure to get a basinful of it. A *big* basinful. It was practically carved in stone.

Well, tonight he decided that he wasn't going to eat it all himself. Not this time, he wasn't. Maybe it was the season, but tonight he was in the kind of mood to *share…*

He crossed the room to the desk and picked up the receiver for the landline. He didn't imagine that the Practice Manager was going to thank him for calling her at midnight on Christmas Eve, but as he and Ms-fucking-Mary-fucking-Thomas were never going to be bosom-buddies, he found that he really didn't give much of a shit. After all, she was one of the main reasons he had given up on people.

Besides, hadn't she told him time and time again over the months, whenever she'd decided to find fault with him — which had been often, by the way — that she was responsible for absolutely everything about the running of this surgery? The authority came with the title, she always said, and the title came with a large salary.

Okay, he thought now, fine, so let her take responsibility for the fucking electric going down, let her earn her money.

Coburn had already tapped in the first couple of numbers before he realised that the landline, just like his mobile phone and the TV, was also dead. There was no dialling tone, no irritating beep-beep-beep signal, not even a *hum* on the fucking line. Behind him, Little Daisy now began to chunter and growl, as though in whatever doggy fever-dream she might be having, she was becoming more and more distressed and was getting ready to bark, maybe even to howl.

'Oh what the fuck *is* this shit?' Coburn demanded, slamming down the phone in frustration and anger… but then a much calmer, more composed, and reflective part of his mind admitted to a certain confusion; it had questions, plenty of them, and it required answers.

Okay, this other part of him said, so maybe the power supply has failed, either for the surgery or for the local area — that's fine as far as it goes — but how could *that* have killed my mobile?

Coburn didn't have a clue. He'd fully charged his phone less than an hour ago, and the battery wasn't prone to dying on him unexpectedly, so it was hardly likely to be a coincidence. And what about the landline? Even in electrical power cuts, the phones were still supposed to work. The wires carried their own power, didn't they? So how could the landline also be dead?

His stomach suddenly dropped and he spun on his heels as Little Daisy began not to bark, not to yelp, or even howl, but actually to *scream*, as a human being might scream, in an absolute frenzy of pain and terror. Despite all his experience, Coburn had never heard an animal scream, or ever known that they *could*, and it scared the living shit out of him. He rushed to the cage and dropped to his knees to open the gate, his hands shaking as he fumbled with the latch.

Despite the awful noise she was making, Little Daisy appeared to be still deeply unconscious, but her whole body was now in spasm, the plastic cone frantically scraping across the steel bars and churning up the layers of newspaper lining the cage. Her paws were clenching and unclenching, and a thick white foam of spittle was forming around her soft muzzle.

Oh my God, Coburn thought, maybe it's a bad reaction to the anaesthetics.

He tried to remember everything she'd been given — everything *he'd* given her. Pentothal to make getting the endotracheal tube down the dog's throat a little easier for himself and less stressful for her, Seroflurane prior to administering the gas, and then the gas anaesthesia itself… Maybe this was some kind of delayed anaphylactic shock, or maybe Dr Nichols, the miserable old lawsuit-dodging bastard, had somehow fucked up what should have been a very routine procedure, maybe left his car keys or his fucking wristwatch in there or something, or slipped with his scalpel and nicked something vital, or maybe...

Maybe you should stop panicking, the calmer side of Coburn suggested. Remember your training…

Okay, okay, Coburn thought, trying to pull himself together, I can do this. I can do this!

Little Daisy might be bleeding internally or not, or her colon might be trying to process Dr Nichol's second-best pair of cufflinks or not, and in a way it didn't matter *what* it was, but Coburn knew that if she continued to thrash around like this all her outer stitches were going to come open, and that wouldn't help the situation one tiny bit.

He leaned into the cage to try to restrain and calm the poor animal, but the very second he laid his hands on her, she went still again. Absolutely still and absolutely stiff. In her last extremity, her eyes had opened wide and were now stuck that way, the pupils blind and fixed. Her bowels had opened and her bladder had voided and the smell of her shit and piss was so thick and heavy in the air he could taste it. She was dead.

'No fucking way,' he moaned, 'this *can't* be fucking happening…'

Coburn searched frantically for any sign of life in the dog, a pulse, a breath, a heartbeat, but all without success, just as he'd known even before he started the pointless exercise. He'd seen a lot of dead dogs during his time here at the Manor House, and this one had to be about one of the deadest.

He thought briefly of ransacking the drug cabinet and maybe trying to inject adrenaline into Daisy's heart, which was exactly what his calmer side was busily urging him to do. Adrenaline would concentrate blood around the heart by peripheral vasoconstriction, strengthening any remaining cardiac contraction, however small, and maybe, if he was lucky, stimulating the heart back into meaningful action.

But Coburn's argument against taking this course of action was that even if he tried it and managed to bring Little Daisy back to some semblance of life, he still wouldn't really know what was wrong with her. He wouldn't what had caused her so much agony that it had actually *killed* her, so how could he be sure that he wasn't just delaying the inevitable and actually increasing the poor dog's suffering? He'd got into this business primarily because he loved animals, and the idea of actually tormenting one to no good end was abhorrent to him.

Instead of rushing to the drugs cabinet, he sat back on his haunches and stoked the dead dog's pretty face and used a clean tissue from his pocket to wipe the froth from its jaws.

'It's okay, girl,' he whispered softly, 'it's all over now…'

He began to think about how he would report this in the morning at shift-change, always assuming that the power didn't come back on in the next hour or so and he could go ahead with his plan to ruin the Practice Manager's Christmas Eve. He just *knew* that they'd make him call Daisy's adoring owners to break the awful news before he left, and what a joyful experience that would be on Christmas morning.

Moreover, due to Ms-fucking-Mary-fucking-Thomas's frequent lectures on the matter, he understood his role in the scheme of things perfectly well — Coburn knew that somehow he would be made to cop the blame for *everything*. If Daisy's death was a reaction to the anaesthesia, it'd be his fault for sure, or if Dr Nichols had dropped his false teeth into Daisy's body cavity before he sewed her up, it would be Coburn's fault by default, for not double-checking everything the old coot did. The blame game wouldn't stop at the dog's death, either, it would also stretch to cover whatever had fucked up the power in the surgery, too.

Ridiculous but true, but that was the way the world worked, it seemed to Coburn. At least, for people like him it was.

If you lost your lucky charm, if you put yourself in the firing line, people shot you down, and the bitch of a Practice Manager would be only too happy to take aim and pull the trigger on him. He had been hired by one of the senior vets while Ms-fucking-Mary-fucking-Thomas was on holiday in Florida, and when she'd returned she'd taken an instant dislike to him and had simply never changed her mind. He imagined she would be absolutely delighted for a fresh opportunity to rip his nuts off.

Well, happy fucking Christmas, he thought. Happy f—

Coburn jumped when the emergency lights suddenly cut out, plunging him into absolute darkness once again. This time they didn't come back on, even at half-power. Then he jumped yet again when he heard a frantic banging noise from somewhere else in the building. A second later he identified the sound for what it was. It was somebody hammering on the plate glass door of the front entrance.

Somebody strong.

Under his hand, poor Little Daisy's soft fur seemed to be growing drier and coarser as the heat continued to leave her body. It wasn't a particularly pleasant sensation, but he found himself suddenly reluctant to leave her. The darkness and the violent banging at the door had chilled his blood. Then he shook his head, and berated himself for being an idiot — he was chilled for exactly the same reason Daisy's body was growing cold far quicker than it otherwise might have; it was December and the heating had gone off at the same time as everything else when the electricity failed… how long ago, half an hour?

He glanced at the luminous hands of his wristwatch, which, maybe because it was an old wind-up model with no electrical component, still seemed to be working fine. It was midnight exactly.

A little late for carol-singers, he thought, with a nervous little giggle.

He carefully stood up and began to cross the blacked-out room, heading in the general direction of where he thought the door might be. He shuffled with his hands held out before him, desperately trying to avoid tripping over anything — something like the fan heater or its power cable, for example — and ending this perfect night by bashing his head open on the corner of the desk.

Halfway across, he remembered that he had seen an old torch rolling around in the desk's bottom drawer a few weeks ago, and he changed direction again. He found the desk and edged his way around to the other side, already aware that this would be a waste of his time. Even if by some miracle the torch was still there, the batteries were sure to be as dead as Daisy the dog, and then he'd be back to square one.

Meanwhile the hammering at the front door continued, loud and relentless.

'Wait!' he shouted. 'Just wait a minute, I'm coming!'

Fucking *wait*, he added to himself silently, opening the bottom drawer and beginning to root around. He even thought he knew who it was out there, too — it was Ms-fucking-Mary-fucking-

Thomas, of course, the fucking remorseless bitch, who else?

Obviously she'd tried to phone the surgery to check up on him, got no reply, then tried his mobile, and again got no reply, and then probably assumed that he was somehow in dereliction of his duty — like maybe he'd sodded off down the pub for a few quick ones while no-one was looking. Now she was here in person, hoping to catch him out and then tear him a new one large enough to get her jackboot into.

His fingers found the torch at the back of the drawer and he lifted it out. He fumbled for the switch, already knowing that it wouldn't work, and was therefore surprised when it instantly snapped into life. For once, something had gone right, although he didn't think it would put much of a dent in the list of everything that had gone wrong tonight. He cast the beam of light around the room, running it over all the empty recovery cages, with Daisy's body at the bottom of the nearest, looking shrunken, somehow diminished by the absence of life.

At the front door, the hammering grew even louder and even more frantic.

'All right, I'm coming!' he yelled.

Jesus Christ, he thought, the bitch is going to smash the fucking glass if she keeps that up.

Using the torch, Coburn negotiated the various obstacles in the room and exited through the door into the corridor. Off the corridor, open doorways led into half a dozen Consultation Rooms, not a scrap of light coming from any one of them, although there should at least have been the yellow spill from nearby streetlamps.

The power must be down all over the area, he thought, which made at least one thing the bitch wouldn't be able to pin on him.

The person at the front door must have seen his torchlight wavering ahead of him, because the hammering suddenly ramped up another step or two, and Coburn experienced his first moment of doubt as to this person's identity.

First, he doubted that Ms-fucking-Mary-fucking-Thomas, even pissed off and hopped up on crazy female hormones, speeding on critical-mass stockpiles of Oestrogen, and in the wake of the worst PMT fallout the world had ever seen, would risk damaging company property by what amounted to an assault on the plate glass of the front door. Second, Ms-fucking-Mary-fucking-Thomas had her own set of keys to the place. The door wasn't bolted or double-locked, so why wouldn't she just let herself in?

Coburn finally made it to the lobby area and his torch immediately illuminated the person at the door, who stopped hammering when she saw him. He stared back at her in astonishment.

It wasn't Ms-fucking-Mary-fucking-Thomas, that was for sure. It was a young woman he'd never seen before, her breath a cloud of vapour in the frigid air. She had left one delicate hand on the glass, as though to plead for his help. The other was pressed to the huge swollen mound of her belly. She was very heavily pregnant, and the front of her plain, too-thin-for-the-weather dress, at just about crotch-level, was soaked through with blood. The insides of her legs and her bare feet were spattered with blood. There was blood between her small toes and under her nails. There was a *lot* of blood.

Coburn shuffled forward, unable to stop staring at this apparition. Where had she come from? How did she get here in her bare feet? It was cold enough inside without the heating, what was she doing out in the sub-zero temperatures in that rag of a dress?

Although a busy duel-carriageway passed by only a hundred yards away, the surgery could only be reached down a long gravel drive. The nearest private dwellings were probably the best part of a mile away. He could see no vehicle parked behind her, so she *must* have walked. But that begged the question, why had she come here at all?

He moved closer to the door. The girl's face was a picture of agony and terror. Her huge dark eyes were streaming tears and she had chewed her lips until they bled. Now that she had stopped hammering at the door, he could finally hear her voice, although it was still muted by the thick glass. She wasn't speaking English. It was some kind of Eastern European language, he guessed, and he didn't recognise a single word, but what she actually wanted wasn't in doubt.

She wanted to come in, and she wanted his help to deliver her baby.

'I'm sorry, this isn't a hospital,' he said through the glass door, but at the same time he was turning for the lock, opening the door. 'This isn't a hospital for people,' he clarified as the girl almost fell into the lobby. He closed the door again. 'This is a hospital for animals. Dogs, cats…' He waved his hand at the posters on the wall, advertisements for flea treatments and dietary preparations. The girl only stared at him, her huge, terrified eyes fixed unwaveringly upon his.

She muttered something else, a mouthful of Eastern European gobbledegook that could have meant anything at all. But then she said, in hesitant, thickly-accented English, 'It comes, it comes…'

Coburn nodded and tentatively offered the girl his hand. She took it instantly, squeezing it so tightly that he grimaced in pain.

'It comes, please. It comes…'

'I know, I get it,' he replied. 'Come with me, let's try to get you more comfortable…'

He slowly began to lead her into the nearest Consultation Room, trying to guide her safely in with the torch. Her dark, wounded eyes stayed on his face as he manoeuvred her in and gingerly helped her up on to the examination table. He snatched a couple of towels folded on a low shelf and rolled them into a makeshift pillow, and then placed it behind the girl's head as she lay back with a small cry of pain.

All the while, Coburn spoke to her in as calm and gentle a voice as he could manage, explaining yet again that this wasn't a hospital, it was a veterinary surgery, and he wasn't a doctor. He told her that she needed a hospital, but he couldn't phone for an ambulance because something had happened to all the power, the landline didn't work and neither did his mobile.

The girl seemed half crazy with pain and terror. One hand constantly massaged her hugely swollen belly, and the other clung to his like a clamp.

'It comes, it comes…'

She's like a broken fucking record, Coburn thought wildly, but then he couldn't blame her. She was alone, clearly in agony, fearful for her own life and her baby's life, in a foreign country, unable to speak anything but a handful of words in the local language, and now she was in the dubious care of a veterinary nurse who felt like he was having some kind of mental breakdown.

And all that blood…why was there so much blood?

Suddenly he closed his eyes and invited back that calmer side of himself, and he told the guy it was time for them to get back in harness together, because they finally had work to do. Throughout all his training and during his time here, he must have seen a hundred animals being born, from cats to cattle and most things in between, and for the most part all the vets did was stand back and let the animals get on with it. Instinct told them what to do and when to do it, and he assumed that the same generally held true for human beings. After all, women had been having babies for countless millennia before there ever were such things as doctors and midwives.

Coburn opened his eyes again and smiled at the girl, attempting to radiate a professional confidence. A little twitch of a smile in response was his reward, and he saw how pretty the girl would be under normal circumstances. More than pretty, in fact. Beautiful. Even in this state, she made his ex, Judy, look like the ugly friend. He wondered how she had come to this country, and who had gotten her pregnant, and where they were now... but he realised that those were all questions for later, and probably it would be the police asking them.

He smiled warmly once more at the girl, and he told her again all the things he had already said. That this wasn't a hospital and that at the moment he hadn't the means to get her to one. That he wasn't a doctor, but he had some medical training and had assisted in births of many animals, and believed he would be able to help her if anything went wrong. He could offer her anaesthesia and pain-relief if she needed it — he thought briefly of Daisy as he said this, but quickly pushed the memory away; he knew in his heart that he hadn't fucked up there, because he was always so careful when it came to the animals in his care. It must have been something else.

The girl clutched his hand even tighter, then threw back her head and screamed. Her scream was unnervingly like Daisy's. Suddenly a flood of blood and amniotic fluid gushed out of her and swept across the examination table upon which she lay and ran over the edges in torrents.

Coburn almost gagged, not at the sight of the blood, but because of the powerful odour that rose up off the fluid like steam from a thermal spring. The smell was awful, septic and rotten, and bad enough to make him swipe at his stinging eyes.

In the shaking torchlight, the girl's face was drawn into a rictus of agony.

'It comes! It comes!'

Now far beyond any notion of civility and decorum, he pushed the girl's ruined, soaked dress up over her thighs and above her waist, and without wishing to, was forcibly reminded of the last time he had done anything like this to a woman, which had been with Judy, in a copse of trees during a country picnic a couple of months before she ditched him. The memory was momentarily distracting, but then he was brought back to the present with a vengeance.

The girl was naked beneath her dress, and as her shapely thighs parted, he made a sound of horrified disgust and had to stifle another gag as everything he had eaten that day tried to make the return journey.

Between the girl's blood-spattered inner thighs, her dilated vagina was raw and inflamed with infection, ringed with a brown crust of scabs. A steady stream of dark, almost black blood leaked from her and showed no signs of stopping, and he wondered what on earth he was going to do, because he had never seen anything like this before in his entire life.

*...ohmygodohmygodohmygod*, he thought, and his formerly calmer self was saying it right beside him, both voices raised in some kind of terrible harmony, a screaming, full-blooded duet straight out of hell, *ohmygodohmygodohmygodohmygod...*

Then the consultation room abruptly seemed to be filled with light.

He stepped back in what was almost shock as another five people suddenly entered the room at speed, all of them wearing medical gowns, caps, and masks, as though they had all just stepped out of an operating room. The light came from a lamp fixed atop a professional-looking video camera one of the gowned figures carried on his shoulder as he filmed the proceedings like a news cameraman.

The girl screamed even louder and tried to get off the examination table, but two of the new people, both men, rushed to restrain her, each holding one of her arms and pushing her back. The other two newcomers, both women, began to examine the area between the girl's legs, holding open her thighs and muttering quietly to each other behind their surgical masks in a language that seemed to be much like the girl's, in that Coburn found every word utterly incomprehensible.

They poked and probed at the sobbing, screaming, struggling girl's infected vagina while the cameraman bobbed up and down, making sure that he recorded everything.

Coburn finally found his voice again and began to ask these people questions.

Who were they, where had they come from, how come they seemed so well prepared, why were they filming this birth, what was wrong with the girl's body, what kind of infection did she have, all these things and more besides, but for the most part his words were lost amongst the girl's screams and the quiet, professional conversation of the medical team, who paid him not the slightest scrap of attention.

'Hey, tell me what's going on?' he persisted. 'Who are you? Who is she?'

He reached out and touched the shoulder of one of the women peering between the girl's legs, and she turned toward him.

A pair of fine blue, clearly intelligent female eyes, heavy with black eyeliner, studied him momentarily. She said something in her language to the others. The camera swung briefly in his direction and then went back to the girl. Then the nurse or doctor, or whatever she was, took Coburn's arm and tried to move him backwards and out of the room.

'Is okay, believe me, is okay,' she said, sounding just like the girl with her broken English. 'It comes, all will be well, it comes. You come away now, come please...'

The girl's screaming suddenly escalated and Coburn raised his head and saw that she was looking directly at him, her eyes full of the same plea he had first seen at the door. She was begging him for help. She was trying to reach out for him, but the two male doctors were holding her down ever more forcefully.

When she struggled to rise once more, one of them wrapped a large hand around her slender throat and slammed her back down.

'Just wait a fucking minute!' Coburn shouted angrily. 'You can't do that!'

The female doctor tried to push him back again, but this time he resisted. What they were doing was completely unacceptable, utterly reprehensible, and he wanted them to know he meant to put a stop to it.

Then he saw the second female doctor bend over between the pregnant girl's legs and produce a scalpel from somewhere in her gown, and before he could do more than open his mouth to protest, she had swooped down and sliced deep into the girl's perineum, opening up the wall of tissue between her vagina and her anal canal. Fresh blood jetted out as if from a hose and the girl shrieked in agony.

'No!' Coburn was now completely incensed. This was brutality beyond belief. He had never seen an animal treated this badly, let alone a human being.

He began to fight his way back to the table, shrugging off the woman's efforts to push him back. Then he heard a collective sigh from the people around the girl. The female doctor between the girl's thighs drew back to allow the camera a clearer view. Against his will, Coburn found his eyes drawn back to the blood-soaked pit of the girl's mangled sex just as a leg emerged from her forcibly enlarged vagina.

The leg was long and thin, and covered with coarse, wire-like black hair that glistened with blood. It ended in a cloven hoof.

Coburn felt darkness like rain-soaked leaves falling over his eyes as he threatened to faint dead away. He actually felt his eyes rolling up into his head, and he slapped himself in the face as hard as he could, and then a second time. He gaped, his mind recling. The leg was still there, and now it was *kicking*, rapping against the examination table.

This time when the female doctor tried to move him, he had no strength to resist. As he was backed toward the door, the doctor almost crooned to him.

'…is okay, is okay, is okay…'

Just before he was shunted out into the corridor, he saw the other woman doctor go to work with her scalpel again, this time opening the screaming girl up all the way from her vagina to her belly button.

'…is okay, is okay…'

Stunned, shocked, disbelieving, he found himself manoeuvred all the way back down the corridor as far as the supply closet. The door was opened and then he was gently pushed inside.

'…is okay now, is quite okay…'

The woman paused briefly to administer a short series of rapid, almost strengthless blows to his stomach and lower abdomen, and then gently closed the door on him.

The darkness in the closet was not total, and Coburn realised that he was still holding the torch. Feeling numb and washed out and exhausted, he used the torch to look down at himself. The woman who had brought him here must have had a scalpel of her own, because blood was pouring out of the long, deep wounds she had painlessly driven into him.

'Fuck…'

Coburn felt all his strength run out of him and he fell down. The floor beneath was already slick with a pool of his blood. His breathing became fast and shallow. From the distant Consultation Room, the girl's screams peaked to an unearthly crescendo and then simply stopped dead. A moment later, another kind of screaming began. The scream of a new-born baby.

A human child, with the legs and the cloven hooves of a goat.

A Christmas baby.

Coburn rolled over onto his back. His hair was full of blood. His ears were full of a roaring sound, as though he were falling at a great rate through the air, as though he were skydiving. The light of the torch, still clutched in his numb fingers, shone up on the supply closet ceiling, where he saw that a spider had spun a large, complex web. He looked at this faultless construction for a moment or two, and then turned the torch off.

In the comfortable darkness, he patiently waited for the end to come, and listened to the distant foreign voices he could now hear being raised in some kind of song or hymn, a dark prayer, of thanks.

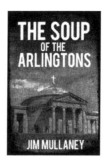

*This is both a monster story and a period-piece, set toward the end of the interval between the two world wars, at that moment in history when one kind of society was slowly coming to an end and another was on the horizon. In terms of style and content, it's something of a mash-up between PG Wodehouse and HP Lovecraft, with perhaps just a touch of Sir Arthur Conan Doyle thrown in for good — or bad — luck. Probably my own favourite story of this collection.*

Charlie Arlington had spent a perfectly wonderful New Year's Eve out on the town, drinking, dancing, smoking Cuban cigars, singing the popular tunes of the day in his dreadful off-key tenor and generally carousing with some of his new American chums, with the night finally culminating in an orgy of seasonal revelry at The Stork Club, on New York City's East 53rd Street. Balloons, streamers, the works.

Charlie had eventually taken his leave of that splendid establishment at a little after two o'clock in the morning, high as the proverbial kite, and declaring to anyone who would listen that he was about to fulfil his first resolution for the brand new year of 1937, which was to walk back to Fifth Avenue and climb the Empire State Building, just like that King Kong chap a few years back.

Old Goodtime Charlie, as his American pals liked to call him — or, to give him his full and proper title, the Honourable Charles Arthur Gawain Frederick Arlington, only son of Lancelot, the 15th Earl of Claverley, and former resident of Arlington Hall, in the county of Shropshire, England — probably didn't make it as far as the top of the Empire State.

In fact, he probably didn't even make it as far as the ground-floor of that amazing structure.

As drunk as the Lord he would actually one day be, Charlie hadn't too clear an idea of any one of the exotic and interesting locations his Manhattan Odyssey had taken him to after leaving The Stork Club, only that it had eventually concluded with a yellow taxicab abruptly depositing him on the kerb outside his Park Avenue hotel, the Waldorf-Astoria, bare moments before dawn, and in possession of the single worst headache of his entire twenty-eight years of life.

The one thing he was completely sure of, however, was that he must have had one hell of an eventful night in the Big Apple, and not just because of the epic qualities of his embryonic hangover. It was also because when he reached for his notecase to pay the exorbitant fare being demanded by the grim-faced chariot driver, he found that his pockets were chock full of unexpected treasure.

In this instance, the treasure took the form as a baker's dozen of champagne corks strung on a long golden chain like a bizarre necklace, a vast roll of one hundred dollar bills he certainly hadn't begun the evening with, a fragrant pair of French knickers (not unpleasantly soiled), and a silver-plated single-shot Derringer pistol with a Mother of Pearl inlaid handle.

This combination of dubious windfalls suggested a number of scenarios Charlie wasn't sure he had much interest in remembering in any great detail, even if it were possible for him to do so.

In fact, at that very moment, the only thing on the alcohol-induced fallen soufflé that had much earlier in the evening been his Oxford-educated mind was collapsing into bed and sleeping the clock around, before rising with the moon the following evening and starting the party rolling all over again.

For the past seven or so months, ever since he had departed the Old World for the New World, *every* eve seemed to have been New Year's Eve for Charlie, and if he could have had his way in the matter this was a pattern that would have continued indefinitely.

These days he was a young man with a thirst for life, with the accent very much on the word *thirst*.

However, after he had negotiated the challenging puzzle offered by the Waldorf-Astoria's revolving door and then staggered across the hotel's enormous lobby to the reception desk in order to collect his key, he found that there was an urgent message from home waiting for him there.

The crisp, efficient chap behind the desk handed him a telegram, and Charlie, suddenly fearing the worst, tore it open where he stood.

The unexpected missive was from Elms, Arlington Hall's venerable butler, whose family's loyalty and distinguished history of service to the successive Earls of Claverley was both long and unashamedly feudal.

The content of the telegram told Charlie that the party, *his* party, was finally over, and the sheer weight of all the other things it implied was almost enough to shock him sober on the spot.

It read:

**MASTER CHARLIE. COME HOME IMMEDIATELY. HIS LORDSHIP GRAVELY ILL. SPOKE GIVES HIM ONLY A WEEK AT MOST. TIME IS OF THE ESSENCE. REMEMBER YOUR DUTY. PASCERE EST FAMILIA.**

'Oh my God,' Charlie said, and then leaned forward and vomited copiously over the reception desk and the shirtfront of the crisp, efficient chap behind it, and then, by way of variety, vomited upon the Italian marble foyer floor and his own patent leather dress shoes.

He also vomited in the elevator on his way up to the thirteenth floor, and then vomited on the elevator operator himself, and then twice vomited in the corridors on the way to his suite of rooms, and finally vomited in his own bathroom before turning on the shower-bath and climbing into the tub while still wearing full evening dress.

Three minutes later, once fully lathered, he remembered to remove his top hat. Then he vomited into it.

It was three whole days before Charlie finally managed to secure an emergency berth on the otherwise fully-booked Queen Mary, which departed New York harbour on Friday morning and was due to dock in Southampton on the following Tuesday, some five days hence.

The wait for this voyage to begin was almost unbearable, especially as each new day brought fresh messages from Elms warning him, in the kind of plain, clipped language enforced by the telegraphic medium, that time was quickly running out, and that his father's health was visibly deteriorating on an hourly basis.

It was Lord Claverley's heart, it seemed, that had weakened critically over the last few months of Charlie's absence, and this weakness which in turn had precipitated the systematic and highly alarming breakdown in his general health.

Dr Spoke, the family physician, had temporarily taken up residence at Arlington Hall itself and was now in constant attendance, but even that egotistical old goat had privately admitted to the butler that he could do nothing other than make his Lordship as comfortable as possible during his final confinement.

Reading between the lines of this series of communications as he restlessly poured over them again and again, Charlie divined in Elms' words a kind of repressed hysteria that he understood very well indeed, perhaps because it so closely mirrored his own.

He could not, of course, speak for the butler who had known and watched over him since birth, but underneath his own repressed hysteria was a black horror Charlie did not wish under any circumstance to acknowledge, a sense of absolute dread which he realised had the power to completely unman him.

Early on the Friday morning, shortly before Charlie was due to leave the Waldorf-Astoria for the harbour with his cargo of bespoke leather luggage occupying a second taxicab, a final telegram arrived with the terrible news that his dear father had finally succumbed to the inevitable, passing away quietly in his sleep overnight.

The Earl is dead, Charlie thought miserably. Long live the Earl.

Elms further informed him that the funeral was to be held as soon as it could be arranged, and he trusted that Charlie understood the necessity of getting the body underground quickly, with a haste which might, to the uninitiated, appear to be almost indecent.

He also hoped Charlie appreciated that the need for him to return home as quickly as was humanly possible was just as important now as it had been while the Earl still lived, if not even more so.

But the butler need not have worried on either of these points — Charlie understood, all right, although he sincerely wished that he did not.

The new Lord Claverley's pokey little crew cabin aboard the Queen Mary was rather less than palatial, being located well below the waterline and certainly nothing like as magnificent as the immense rooms he'd occupied on the way over — and actually so far below his present station in life as to be laughable.

But it scarcely mattered, as Charlie spent most of his nights wandering the ship's deserted gangways in a state of pallid, drunken stupor and all his days laying in his miserable excuse for a bed in much the same state, listening to the throb of the ship's engines monotonously vibrating through the steel hull to which his bunk seemed to be bolted.

He saw virtually nothing of his fellow passengers in the evenings, nor of the glorious oceanic views the voyage afforded throughout the daylight hours.

His mind was filled with a terrible fog of panic and terror that the endless succession of gin and tonics, whisky sours, and champagne cocktails were unable disperse, and which only grew murkier as the near certainty of a sixth day and night on the ship loomed, as the Queen Mary diverted further south into warmer waters to avoid the threat posed by icebergs.

On most nights, generally around two or three o'clock in the morning, Charlie would find himself loitering in the otherwise deserted cabin-class dining room, where there was a large scale map depicting the Queen Mary's summer and winter routes across the Atlantic.

A tiny clockwork model of the vessel itself moved across this map, clearly illustrating the progress its larger counterpart was making, and it was always while staring at this that Charlie's bone-deep fears sharpened into actual soul-crippling despair.

All he could see before him was the vast, vast ocean, and the ship, so very, very small in comparison, moving so very, very slowly.

Too slowly...

Elms' last telegram, just like all those before it, had culminated with the Latin phrase PASCERE EST FAMILIA, which was the Arlington family motto, and appeared on a scroll which played a prominent part in their ancient heraldic coat of arms.

Loosely translated, it meant '*to feed the family*', words which until not so long ago Charlie had always taken to mean that the head of the family — in other words, the incumbent Earl — should be constantly vigilant to preserve and nourish the entire family tree, every part of it, from the largest branches of one's nearest and dearest to the deep underground roots of the distant cousins, many times removed.

This would even include those relations one saw maybe once or twice every decade, the ones with abnormally large heads, the odd extra finger or toe, or a set of ears like those of an African elephant.

Once upon a time, this Latin phrase had given the far younger Charlie a powerful sense of the greatness of his distinguished lineage and the proud obligations of his privileged birthright.

Now all it gave him was a severely unpleasant chill in his nether regions, and the distinct impression that a nest of undernourished rats, freshly released from the strictures of one of those new-fangled dietary regimes which had become so popular in America in recent years, had just set up home in his belly and were busily gnawing at his entrails as if trying to make up for lost time.

And Charlie recalled only too clearly the night he had lost his innocence and learned the truth that lay behind the Arlington family motto, not least because it had been the night following his mother's funeral.

He had woken with a start in the early hours to find Elms standing by his bedside, holding an oil lamp aloft as though the Hall's electrical system had failed. The butler's normally composed features were almost wild, and Charlie wondered shakily what could have happened.

The only thing he could imagine flapping the unflappable Elms would be another sudden death, perhaps that of the Earl himself, following on so soon after his beloved wife. His tongue refused to work to ask the question he least wished to ask, so it was a relief when Elms broke the silence for him.

'Master Charlie, your father would like you to join him.'

'What's wrong? Has there been an accident?'

'Easier if you just follow me, sir. Your father is waiting. You should wear a robe, and shoes, sir. The temperature outside has dropped considerably.'

'Outside? Why are we going outside? Where *is* father?'

'He's in the family crypt, sir.'

'In the crypt?'

'Yes, sir.'

Charlie just couldn't get his head around it. 'The *crypt*, you say?'

'Yes, sir. *In* it.'

'Oh my God.'

'Yes, sir.'

Confused and beginning to be a little nervous of what the immediate future might hold, Charlie had tied the belt on his dressing gown and slipped his bare feet into the shoes he had worn to the ceremony in the family chapel that very morning.

He followed Elms through the otherwise slumbering house, past the many closed doors behind which slept several generations of his hugely extended family, all here to pay their respects to his late mother's memory.

The butler took him out of the house through his own small pantry, cosy with the banked coals of his evening fire, then through the variously fragranced darkness of the kitchen garden, and then along the long moss-carpeted lane of yew trees in the direction of the chapel and the large underground crypt beneath.

A thick ground mist ran like a stream around their legs as they walked, and shadowy creatures of the night flitted about in the darkness above their heads, hunting.

As Elms once more held aloft the lantern he had brought from the house and began to lead the way down the crypt steps, Charlie had been uncomfortably reminded of a film he'd seen in the West End only a few months before — Boris Karloff in *The Bride of Frankenstein*.

He remembered enjoying the cosily entertaining chills of the Hollywood charnel house as he sat in the balcony with his arm around a pretty little minx of a dancer he'd started seeing from a new musical revue show over at The Criterion, Piccadilly Circus.

But the chills he was experiencing at that very moment were anything but enjoyable and cosy, and became even less so as they reached the bottom of the stone stairway and Charlie found himself face to face with his father, the Earl of Claverley himself, standing beside the open casket containing his dead wife, the Countess.

His Lordship looked haggard indeed at this advanced hour, and seemed to have aged a good ten years since the service only that morning.

'Ah, Charles, m'boy, you're here at last.'

Elms hung the lantern on a hook situated high on the stone-built wall. 'My Lord, is it time?'

'Yes, Elms, it is time. Please take your position, old friend.'

Still in a daze from realising that his mother's coffin had been reopened, Charlie saw Elms cross the chamber and open a small panel in the wall, inside which was a rusted windlass.

Mystified, he watched the butler begin to turn the iron wheel counter-clockwise, and then he spun around as the chamber was filled with the sound of stone grating against stone, and all the tales of terror he had read so avidly as a boy, and every cinematic horror he'd witnessed over the last couple of years, courtesy of Universal Pictures, suddenly came alive in his mind.

The grey stone walls with their bays of dusty caskets seemed to be closing in upon him. His always vivid imagination insisted upon showing him skeletal hands slipping out from beneath silk-lined coffin lids and clutching desperately in his direction, and he felt that at any moment he might scream and take to his heels.

But then he felt his father's strong hand settle on his arm, steadying him.

'Father,' he said, breathlessly, 'what's happening?'

'What *must* happen,' the old man replied. 'Look...'

Together they watched as a vast stone panel built into the crypt floor continued to slowly grate open in response to Elms and his windlass, revealing a perfect square of blackness beneath. Finally, the butler, seemingly exhausted by his efforts, stopped turning the wheel, and all was silent again.

The three men stared at the dark pit at their feet.

'What is it that you keep in there?' Charlie asked, his voice trembling.

'The family curse,' his father replied quietly. 'But also, our family's greatest blessing.'

'I don't understand.'

'Elms, would you please show my son what it means to be a member of this great family?'

The Earl turned away and Elms gestured for Charlie to join him at the side of the pit. He saw that the butler had now lit a second lantern which had been tied to a long length of grubby rope, and which he now proceeded to lower into the pit, coil by coil by coil.

Charlie cautiously leant over the edge and saw the lamplight playing over ancient stonework as it sank lower and lower.

'Is it some kind of dungeon, Elms?' he asked.

'No, sir. It is a lair.'

'A *lair*? The lair of what?'

'The source of your family's good fortune and power, sir. It is my personal belief that many of the older families may have such secrets in their keeping.'

'I still don't quite...'

'It's quite simple, m'boy,' Charlie's father called from the shadows.

He was standing before his wife's coffin again and staring down at her shrouded features — still deep in mourning, Charlie imagined.

'Great families like ours do not become great purely by accident. They are *made* great, frequently by the patronage of beasts such as the one we keep here in this pit, a creature which exudes a miasma of influence over all in its midst, shaping their destinies and desires into one.'

His father's words were causing Charlie's hair to stand on end. Meanwhile, Elms continued to play out the rope and the lantern sank ever lower, revealing only the strata of increasingly aged masonry. But now a very distinct odour from the pit had begun to announce itself, rising up from whatever entity skulked in the darkness below.

It was the stench of corruption and rot, and it quickly grew so sickening that Charlie had to use the sleeve of his robe to cover his nose.

'This beast, this creature… is it evil?' he whispered to the butler, trying not to inhale.

'I don't believe so, sir. I believe it to be a natural creature simply beyond our understanding, although perhaps not entirely of this earth.'

'It is not *evil*,' his father affirmed. 'But neither is it *good*. It is... *indifferent*... and it is always, always hungry.'

Charlie, still staring down the pit as Elms eased the lamp lower and lower still, sensed his father's approach, his steps even heavier and more laboured than usual. He glanced over his shoulder, saw at once the burden Lord Claverley was carrying, and recoiled with a terrible scream that rang around the chamber and echoed in the deeper, darker vaults beyond.

If Elms had not reached out a hand to steady him at that moment, he might well have fallen to his death in the pit.

'Oh my God!' he cried, backing away in horror. 'What are you doing, father? What are you *doing*?'

'I am performing the same rites that the heads of our family have performed for many generations past, making the traditional funeral offering, and thereby ensuring the continuing good fortune of our family...'

Lancelot, the 15th Earl of Claverley, held in his arms the naked, lolling body of his dead wife.

'This is the final truth of our family motto, my son,' he said softly. '*Pascere est familia*. To feed the family... to feed the dead of our family line to the beast, and so remain in its goodwill.'

He took one more step toward the edge of the pit, his face streaked with tears. He lowered his head for a moment to kiss the waxy brow of the Countess, and then he dropped her body into the pit.

Charlie saw it fall in silhouette against the thin lamplight, careening from side to side and breaking limbs against the walls as it went, and then saw it flash by the lantern swinging far below. He was biting the knuckles of his right hand in horror and revulsion, but he could not turn away.

For the lantern light had at last revealed something else down there... something that moved of its own volition.

Elms let the lamp drop another yard, and then stopped it with a jerk.

Just below the lantern, Charlie finally saw the beast complete.

It was a thick, glutinous, many-hued mass, neither solid nor liquid, and yet filling the bottom of the pit like water at the bottom of a well… but it was *alive*, alive with a shuddering, undulating surface that pulsed and surged against the stone walls of its prison like a miniature ocean.

In its depths floated a hideous flotsam and jetsam of human remains, of long bones and thick seams of yellow fat, and skulls and ribcages rank with decay, of limbs brutally dismembered and soft tissue partially dissolved.

The freshest, least digested part, the broken remains of his poor mother's body, was the epicentre of a bubbling, smoking turmoil that soon carried it away beneath the greasy, mottled surface.

A beast…that was what his father had called this grotesque abhorrence, while Elms had referred to it as a creature, a lifeform perhaps from another dimension and beyond human understanding. But to Charlie, staring down in speechless horror, it resembled nothing more than a sickening living stew, a gigantic, unspeakable soup made from the deceased members of his own noble family.

'Has it grown, Elms?' the Earl asked his butler.

'Yes, I believe it has, your Lordship. It seems to have grown a great deal. I had to use five yards less rope than the last time.'

'Only to be expected, I suppose. It's had a good few years out of us recently. So many of us have fallen...'

And Charlie recalled that there had been a great deal of mortality in the old bloodline in recent years, aunts and uncles and cousins twice removed... All of them had been buried here in this vault, in accordance with long established family tradition, and he now presumed that afterwards every single one of them had gone in the pit, more ingredients for this foul and loathsome soup.

He watched, all his senses numbed, as Elms began to haul the lantern back up again. As soon as it was out of the pit, Elms returned immediately to the windlass and began to seal the trapdoor again, the stone grinding as before, until finally, with a hollow booming sound, it was closed. Only then did Charlie's father seem to relax a little.

He placed a hand on his son's arm once again with a grip which, now that the deed was over and done, felt weak and grasping.

'Come back to the house now, Charlie. It's high time you finally understood the responsibilities of your position as heir to the title...'

Back in the calm, comforting sanity of the library, curled up in a pair of leather wingback chairs pulled up before a roaring fire, father and son faced each other over the enormously large whiskies dispensed by Elms, and Lord Claverley began to speak.

It was by far the longest speech Charlie could ever recall his father making in his presence, and it was dawn by the time he had finished his tale. Outside in the grounds, the birds were singing their usual morning chorus, just as if it were another ordinary day and the world had not entirely changed, and Charlie had learned far more than he had ever wanted to know about both his family's past and his own probable future.

The beast's origins, the Earl believed, lay somewhere in the Holy Lands, for it was his opinion that their ancestors, members of the Knights Templar, had brought it back with them from the Fourth Crusade at the beginning of the 13th century, shortly after the sacking of Constantinople.

Whether the immense fortune in gems and precious metals they had amassed out there was in any way due to the influence of the beast, or simply to the more general Christian practices of raping, slaughtering, and pillaging, no-one knew. But it wasn't long after their return to England that the family first purchased large tracts of land from the crown and began to build a permanent home upon their new estate, beginning with the chapel and the crypt beneath it... and beneath the crypt, of course, the pit...

The great house, Arlington Hall, came much later, almost as an afterthought.

Lord Claverley, like his father, grandfather, and great-grandfather before him, had absolutely no idea what the beast really was, where it had originated, how it was supposed to achieve its miraculous effects, or even how the terms of this bizarre bargain between man and beast might have been struck in the first place.

All he knew for sure was that it was a solemn and binding pact that had sustained and benefitted their family through almost eight hundred years of occasionally volatile history, and might continue to do so for many more centuries to come.

As the Earl had briefly explained down in the crypt, the pact was a simple case of reciprocal trade.

The beast would continue to aid their good fortune in return for its chosen tithe, which was that the dead of the Arlington family were to be given over willingly as its meat and drink, and that it was the solemn duty of the current Earl, and his duty alone, to make each offering.

It was also a requirement that the offering be made as soon as possible after each individual death, for the beast, they had learned, liked its food fresh.

'Have you never wondered why every single member of the family, of every single branch, no matter how distant, are brought to be interred in our crypt immediately after death? Have you never wondered why this became the tradition? It *knows*, you see. The beast knows when one of us dies, and then it waits... impatiently... in agitation, in hunger, in expectation...'

Charlie had grown a little green about the gills, wondering whether he would have been able to strip his own mother's body and toss her down the pit, as his father had done so readily. He found it absolutely intolerable that one dark night in the not-so distant future, he might be required to do exactly the same thing to his beloved father.

'Couldn't someone else do the actual... feeding?' he asked, glancing toward the closed library door, through which Elms had vanished after pouring their drinks.

The butler, he knew, had a fine, strapping son of his own who was currently working as a footman at the Hall, but who was generally expected to one day succeed his father as butler, just as Charlie himself would succeed his father as the Earl.

'Couldn't one simply give the command to a trusted servant?'

'No, Charlie, I'm afraid not. It must be the head of the family, always the head.'

'And if no offering at all were made?'

'Ruin, my son,' the Earl said, simply. 'Ruin. At best, the beast would merely abandon us, and its influence would be forever lost. At worst… at worst, I think it would seek to destroy us. All of us, from the youngest to the oldest. I believe this is how several great families in the past have met their ends, and I would not have the proud Arlington line suffer the same ignominious fate.'

'But what could it actually do?' Charlie asked. 'How *could* it hurt us? Don't you see, father, it's imprisoned in the pit, and if we were to keep it sealed up...'

'The pit is not a prison,' the Earl said, shaking his head sadly. 'The beast *chooses* to stay there, m'boy, the pit is its home — its lair, just as Elms told you. Make no mistake, should it ever choose otherwise… then there is nothing capable of holding it captive. Nothing.'

Charlie was pondering the bleakness of the future when his father abruptly seemed to change the subject of their conversation.

'Tell me, what's the name of that second cousin of yours, Charlie? You know, the pretty little dark-haired girl? She was sitting directly behind us during the services yesterday.'

The girl Lord Claverley was referring to was Stephanie Pirbright, the eldest daughter of one of the late Countess's younger cousins.

Charlie and the girl had been seeing rather a lot of each other in recent months, now that she had come of age. He blushed when his father began to ask him the frankest of questions regarding the depth of their present relationship and the direction of its possible future, and struggled to answer with equal frankness.

He admitted that he liked the girl, he liked her very much indeed, and confessed that the girlhood crush she had once held on him seemed to have deepened over the years into a genuine fondness and admiration.

'I *have* thought about marriage, father, but truthfully, I don't believe I'm quite ready to settle down, not just yet...'

Charlie tried to explain that he felt he had at least one more adventure ahead of him before his youth was spent, and perhaps a few remaining streaks of wildness which would first need to be tamed.

'Very well,' the Earl said, after some considerable thought. 'I'll allow you a year, m'boy. One year. You can take yourself away — somewhere overseas, if you like — and you may sow your wild oats as far and as wide as you please, and in whatever fields might take your fancy. But Charlie, you *will* put an engagement ring on that girl's finger before you leave these shores, and you'll send her love-letters and such like, to keep her sweet while you're away. Understand?'

'Yes, sir.'

'When the year is up, back you come. You will marry the girl and immediately begin breeding a new generation of Arlingtons. And I may as well warn you now, I'll want a great many grandchildren at my knee before it's my turn for the pit.'

Charlie felt uncomfortable when his father began to speak of his death this way, and said so, but his father was pragmatic on the subject.

'Death is inevitable, Charlie. Sad, of course, for those left behind, but inevitable and entirely natural. And don't worry about what must be done afterwards. I'll be beyond any kind of pain by that time, and at least I will have passed on with the satisfaction of knowing that the family's future is safe in your hands…'

An obedient son, if nothing else, Charlie had subsequently followed his father's instructions to the letter. He became engaged to young, besotted Stephanie Pirbright within a month of his mother's passing, and shortly thereafter left England for an entirely fictional one-year contract at a company that traded in commodities on the New York stock exchange.

He dutifully sent his new fiancée a love-letter a week, most of them composed in nightclubs and theatres, usually between acts, or else in the bed chambers of liberal or professional young women, usually between acts of a very different kind.

Not one of these frequent sexual liaisons, however, no matter how passionate or erotically charged, meant that he didn't care deeply for Stephanie, and have every intention of soon becoming the very best husband he was capable of being. The simple truth was that his continual philandering was a direct parallel to his other new love-affair — with the bottle.

In the seven months that Charlie had been a guest on the island of Manhattan, it was unlikely that he had passed more than two or three consecutive days without being thoroughly intoxicated.

Indulgence had become a way of briefly escaping his recent, nightmarish memories, and a method of taking the edge off his worst imaginings of what his life might become after this single year of liberty was over.

Numbed by the constant flow of alcohol, and fitfully distracted by the pleasures of the flesh, Charlie had begun to believe that he had managed to sort everything out in his mind, and finally resigned himself to the inevitability of his fate.

But then the first shocking telegram from Elms had arrived, and he realised that he had been fooling himself all the time.

He was not resigned to his fate. He was terrified by it.

Charlie was among the first passengers to disembark after the Queen Mary docked in Southampton, at shortly after ten o'clock on Wednesday evening.

Much earlier in the day he had taken the unusually proactive step of slipping the ship's First Officer a small purse of gold to arrange for all his luggage and other effects to be sent on to Arlington Hall the following morning by private car. This additional freedom of movement enabled Charlie to dash down the gangplank without pause or hindrance and rush to his faithful old jalopy, which the ever-thoughtful Elms — no slouch on the proactive front, himself — had organised to have waiting at the harbour, already freshly refuelled and ready to go.

When he reached his car, he found that there was yet another telegram waiting along with it, in which Elms informed him that his father's funeral had taken place that very morning, with the whole of the extended Arlington family in attendance.

This would have been at just around the same time that Charlie had been standing at the ship's prow, taking frequent nips from his hipflask against the frigid cold, and waiting in vain for the English coastline to materialise upon the horizon. The butler went on to say that he believed all was now in readiness for Charlie's keenly anticipated return to Arlington Hall — to the Hall, and thence to the crypt.

Now it all came down to how quickly he could get there.

Charlie was saddened almost beyond words to have missed his father's official send-off.

He imagined that it would have been pleasant, in later years, to hold on to the memories of a dignified, civilised service, with epitaphs, eulogies, hymns, and whatnot, and to be able to take comfort from them, instead of dreading the quite different memories that he suspected would really be haunting his dreams for decades to come.

No doubt there had been a few of the more militant members of his immediate family who were offended by the autocratic manner in which Elms must have taken charge of the funeral arrangements, unilaterally making the decision that the ceremony must go ahead as planned, even though the Earl's son and heir was so conspicuously absent, still in transit from the United States.

If it had been up to them, Charlie was quite sure they would have waited for his return. But as he recalled the butler mentioning in one of his earlier telegrams, these people, blood-relatives or not, were the uninitiated, and could not be expected to have any appreciation of what was really at stake here.

Elms' telegram finished by expressing the true gravity of the situation in the clearest terms yet.

There was no more needless repetition of the family motto, and nor was there the slightest attempt at restraint in the sense of desperate urgency the butler wished to convey.

The message simply ended:

**HURRY SIR. OR ALL IS LOST.**
**HURRY. HURRY. HURRY.**

Charlie's old jalopy, as he liked to call it, had actually been bought new only the previous year, for the princely sum of £395 sterling.

It was a superb two-seater sports car, an SS Jaguar roadster, with an eye-catching cherry-red livery. It had a chassis wheelbase of 8ft 8 inches, and 18 inch wire wheels, and its 2.5 litre, 100bhp engine had twin carburettors bolted directly to the cylinder head. It went from 0-60mph in 13.5 seconds, and with the windscreen lowered it had a maximum speed of 95mph.

But of course, in all probability those kind of performance statistics had been recorded on a series of test tracks under ideal conditions, and certainly not facing the kind of obstacles with which Charlie now found himself about to encounter.

The drive from Southampton to Claverley, in Shropshire, was a distance of approximately one-hundred-and-sixty miles, and it was a further five miles to the gates of the Arlington Hall estate itself, which lay to the east of the small market town of Bridgnorth, on the River Severn.

The greater part of this long, winding journey had to be made on road surfaces that were often no better than country lanes, and which were frequently hardly wider than the car itself.

Add to this the multiple difficulties of driving at night, under a sky clogged with opaque black clouds that obliterated both moonlight and starlight, and then add fierce little flurries of snow and the occasional gale of sleet, add stubborn drifts of old hard-packed snow and treacherous patches of black ice, and then further add clouds of freezing fog that loomed up out of the blackness with the suddenness of vengeful wraiths… and then the theoretical top-speed of the sports car, recalibrated for the present conditions, dropped by almost two-thirds.

All in all, the nightmare journey home took slightly less than five hours, with Charlie sometimes driving through periods of near blindness at speeds which, for the conditions, were all but suicidal. However, the danger he was risking on the roads was just about the last thing on his mind.

The funeral he had missed was not for just any old Arlington, after all, but for the Earl himself, and Charlie could easily imagine the beast's infernal hunger building and sharpening as it impatiently waited to dine on the tastiest titbit on the menu.

And what, he wondered, would be the result if the beast tired of waiting for the new head of the family to return and make the expected offering?

Charlie's father had now been dead for eight whole days, and if it was true that the beast liked, if the beast *demanded*, its meals fresh… Charlie refused to speculate any further on what might happen if the beast's patience were to dwindle before he arrived, but only pressed harder on the Jaguar's accelerator. It was all he could do.

When at long last he turned in through the estate's gateposts and began to accelerate up the mile-long length of Arlington Hall's gravel drive, it was a few minutes past three o'clock in the morning.

The arduous drive had exhausted him in body and mind, but he found that he was also strangely exhilarated, and hopefully ready to face the first and most important duty of his tenure as the 16th Earl of Claverley.

As he had driven through the darkness, Charlie had even pictured the coming moments in his mind, imagining the likely sequence of events and trying to prepare himself to meet and overcome each challenge, no matter how distasteful or shocking.

He had seen himself motoring up to the dark, silent house and braking to a halt in a subdued spray of gravel before the tall portico. He had then imagined the faithful and resourceful Elms emerging from the shadows, lamp in hand, before once more leading him along the lane of yew trees towards the chapel, and then down into the crypt, where everything had been prepared for their dark task.

But sadly, as Charlie was slowly beginning to learn, things seldom worked out the way one imagined them.

What he actually saw as he rounded the last turn of the drive and the house came into view was Arlington Hall lit up as though for a grand summer ball, not the aftermath of a solemn winter funeral.

Despite the extremely late hour, electric lights showed at every window on every floor, without exception, and the great carved oaken doors beneath the Hall's portico were flung wide open to the night, an invitation to one and all to come and go as they pleased. And yet there were no people to be seen anywhere.

No mourners, no servants.

Not a single one.

Charlie stopped the Jaguar in front of the portico and leaped out, intending to run up the steps and into the house and make straight for Elms' pantry, where he meant to briefly help himself to a medicinal glass or three of the butler's excellent port before he got around to asking for explanations.

But he only made it up half of the dozen front steps before his impetus was halted by an incredibly unpleasant discovery.

At first he thought it was some kind of rubber mask, some novelty item discarded by one of the family children at a much earlier hour, or perhaps thrown out of a window from one of the upper floors as a prank. But it was not a prank and it was not a mask.

It was a face. A human face, which bore more than a passing resemblance to the goatee-sporting Dr

Spoke, perhaps because it *was* Dr Spoke — or at least, it was a very small part of him, which had been messily torn free from the rest.

Shaking his head slowly, as though a simple denial of what he was seeing might somehow make it less real, less believable, Charlie climbed the rest of the steps like a sleepwalker.

At the top, he paused again, both appalled and mesmerised, having discovered that the threshold of the broad doorway had become the shoreline of a small inland lake of blood that extended almost halfway into the deep entrance hall, glistening darkly as the breeze blowing in through the open door sent a series of shallow ripples skimming across its crimson surface.

A second or two later, when he was able to drag his eyes away from the spectacle, he realised that there were a good many other signs of mayhem and murder in the further reaches of the great raftered hall, including items of antique furniture that had either been overturned or smashed to pieces like so much balsawood, and heavy doors wrenched off their brass hinges like the wings of butterflies pulled off by cruel children.

So much for the mayhem.

As for the murder…

Everywhere his shocked eyes wandered they seemed to find long trails or gouts of blood spattered extensively across the stone floors and the rugs and up the broad staircase, and even some that stretched to unfeasible heights up the walls, paintings, and tapestries, wildly arrayed in great arterial sprays that were very like some of the new modern art Charlie had seen in the fashionable Manhattan galleries.

It all came home to him then.

Against all his hopes and his secret inner belief that all would be well — that everything would work out in the Arlingtons' favour, just as it always had in the past, that the family luck would hold — Charlie was too late.

The wait for the Queen Mary to sail had been too long, the seasonally extended journey across the Atlantic had been too slow, and despite his very best efforts, the difficult and hazardous drive home had turned out to be a challenge too far. Clearly, the beast had assumed that it had been cheated of its tithe, and the pact therefore broken, and it had decided to exact a terrible, terrible revenge upon his family, all of whom had been conveniently close at hand to suffer the horrific consequences.

He became aware that his right hand had crept into his pocket and fastened upon the silver-plated Derringer pistol he had mysteriously acquired on what had been his very last night of genuine freedom, and which had been in his overcoat ever since, knocking about like a piece of loose change.

The toy-like palm pistol seemed somewhat rather less than adequate for the perilous situation in which he now found himself, although he could not deny that the simple feel of having any kind of weapon in his hand still imparted some small measure of comfort.

Charlie realised that, if he wished, he could easily lay his hands on something far larger and more dangerous from his father's well-stocked gun cabinet, which was situated in the boot-room toward the rear of the Hall... but re-arming himself in this fashion would entail actually *entering* the house, and he found that he was unable to make himself do that just yet.

At that exact moment, as he stood hesitant and undecided and afraid on the threshold of his own home, something caught the corner of Charlie's eye, a small clump of solidity in the centre of a puddle of blood at the foot of the staircase, and after he had numbly stared at this object for some few seconds, he finally managed to identify it.

It was a hand, a delicate female hand, and upon one of the slender fingers was a diamond engagement ring he recognised — which was not so terribly surprising, as he had placed it there himself only seven months before, while down on bended knee.

It was sweet little Stephanie Pirbright's left hand down there, he realised, the fingers loosely curling in towards the palm as it rested in a slowly coagulating pool of blood. Her poor hand torn from her arm, and then cast inconsequentially aside like litter, like the scraps from a glutton's table.

Charlie felt his eyes fill with tears.

Even though he had been in his cups almost every single day during his life in New York, he still recalled the many wonderful, heartfelt letters she had sent in reply to his own poor, distracted efforts — bright, witty, moving letters that were so full of affection and hope for their conjoined futures that he had read and reread them many times over.

He had kept each and every one safely among his personal effects, wrapped in a silken handkerchief which Stephanie had perfumed with her own favourite scent and given to him on the day he sailed to America. Love letters written by the same gentle, savagely detached hand he was looking at now.

But where was the rest of her, he suddenly wondered?

Was it possible that his fiancée had somehow survived the Arlington beast's brutal attack and was still alive somewhere in the house — badly injured but, crucially, alive — perhaps desperately holed up in a closet, hiding, barricaded, praying that someone would come to rescue her?

The thought seemed to wake Charlie from the trance he had fallen into, unlocking the paralysis that had shackled his limbs, and galvanising him into action. He cuffed the tears out of his eyes, then pulled out the small silver pistol from his coat pocket and stalked into the house, shouting for all he was worth, and never mind that the Derringer carried only a single shot.

He moved as quickly as he could through the entire Hall, climbing every staircase, searching each and every nook and cranny, including the servants' quarters, the kitchens, the bathrooms, and every single bedroom.

At first he was only calling out Stephanie's name, but eventually, as he began to despair of ever finding her, he also began to shout the names of all the people he knew had attended his father's funeral, and whose possessions he saw littering the bedrooms, scattered around now like so much garbage.

And the blood. Oh Lord, all the *blood*…

Everywhere he went the pattern was exactly the same, a pattern of gore, gore, and more gore, as though his defenceless relatives' bodies had been ripped into until they literally burst like balloons, before being dragged into that hideously animate soup and absorbed. The only trace of the people the beast had taken were the small fragments it had discarded along the way, as it greedily pursued yet more terrified victims. Fragments like Dr Spoke's face, and Stephanie's hand.

Charlie saw half a man's leg perched atop a wardrobe.

He saw a woman's scalp and long blonde hair dangling from a chandelier.

He saw a child's foot still in its buckled shoe.

He saw an entire set of internal organs piled in a bathtub like the display in a butcher's offal cabinet.

But of the remainder of poor Stephanie there was no sight at all. The beastly soup, that satanic broth, had feasted well this night.

And what, Charlie suddenly thought, did any creature do when it had finally eaten its fill? Well, it returned to its lair, of course, *that* was what it did, and he had no doubt that the beast had now gone to ground to rest while it began to digest the spoils of its gluttonous rampage.

'This ends right now,' he said aloud.

His voice hardly sounded like his own lazy, privileged drawl, and was full of cold fury and iron resolution.

'One way or another, it all ends tonight...'

Less than fifteen minutes later, Charlie was hurrying along the mossy lane of yew trees on his way to the crypt, having picked up a few necessities before he set out, the first of which was a significant upgrade from the tiny Derringer. He now carried his late father's favourite firearm, a massive Purdey under-and-over 12-bore double-barrelled shotgun, which was loaded but broken over his right arm for safety.

The second necessity, swinging from the other hand, was a jerry can full of petrol he had brought from the Hall's garages. In addition, the pockets of his overcoat were stuffed to overflowing with fresh shotgun cartridges that slapped and rattled against his thighs as he strode on resolutely, and he had tucked a huge stag-handled hunting knife into the belt of his trousers.

He had retained the silver Derringer, too, and now had it tucked away in his coat's inner pocket, although less as a weapon of offence than as a kind of good luck charm, a tangible link with a time when everything had seemed to fall into his hands like magic, and nothing harmful could befall him.

Now that the beastly soup had withdrawn its favour from the Arlington family, he certainly needed *some* kind of luck on his side, and wasn't silver meant to have some kind of power over evil? He was not entirely convinced this was correct, but he most fervently hoped that it was.

He remembered that the last time he'd walked this route, in the dead of night and in the company of Elms, he had been merely nervous. This time around he was almost petrified with terror, and so afraid that he was amazed he was still capable of forward movement and rational thought. But he recognised that it was anger which motivated him now — anger, and a brand new appetite, a new thirst, for revenge.

His ancestors' valiant blood had risen in his own veins, and for the moment he felt capable of anything.

As he emerged from the cover of the trees, the rising wind found him and immediately sliced through the heavy material of his winter overcoat like a fish-knife. Icy though the wind was, Charlie actually welcomed it, as it seemed to sharpen his already keen senses and focus his desire.

The family chapel came into view first. Candles had been left burning inside following his father's funeral, and now the warm, trembling glow clearly illuminated the designs of the large stained-glass windows, and for an instant, Charlie was transported back to his childhood.

He recalled sitting in the chapel during the long, rambling weekly sermons given by a succession of aging Anglican priests, all of them growing old and fat on hand-outs from the family purse.

He remembered that while the other members of the family, his father among them, only knelt and prayed with their heads bowed low, his own eyes always seemed to be drifting to the stained-glass windows to follow the story the images told, a story where courageous Knights Templar of old — Arlington ancestors one and all, naturally — were engaged in a glorious quest that involved righteous battles in foreign lands, and the discovery of an awesome treasure buried in some kind of ancient underground temple.

He remembered that his excited schoolboy fantasies of the actual nature of the quest had varied wildly from week to week and month to month, but as adventurous and exotic as those fantasies had been, never had they come even *close* to what he now understood to be the truth.

After he had nervously circled the chapel, moving carefully through the shadowed darkness, and finally reached the head of the stone stairway leading down into the crypt, he paused for several moments, staring down as he steadied himself. The iron door at the bottom had been left both unlocked and ajar, and he could see the waxing and waning glow of an oil lantern on the dusty flagstones beyond it.

He snapped the shotgun closed, slipped off the safety, and then slowly began to descend, one careful step at a time, attempting to make as little noise as he could.

Charlie had a plan of sorts in mind, but it was a plan which depended rather heavily for its success upon the element of surprise.

If he were to find the beast resting in its pit, as he hoped, he meant to slowly dribble the entire jerry can of petrol down the side of the wall, hoping that the gorged, sleeping creature would not notice, until it was far too late to escape unscathed. Then he intended to throw down an oil lamp to ignite the fuel, and then simply blast away with the Purdey until either the beast was done or he ran out of ammunition, whichever came first.

When he reached the bottom of the stone steps and gently edged in through the doorway, he discovered that the beast had been just as destructive here in the crypt as it had been over at the Hall.

The lantern was in the same place Elms had hung it before, dangling from a hook high on the wall, and by its yellow glow he saw that all the ancient caskets had been wrenched from their bays and torn to pieces, as though the beast had been desperately searching for more sustenance.

But its search would have been in vain. The caskets had long been empty, of course, their previous inhabitants already offered and already consumed, many of them several generations before.

Beyond a pile of splintered timber, Charlie saw that the small panel in the wall was open, revealing the windlass apparatus, and that the stone seal to the pit had been drawn back again, leaving the gaping hole in the floor. He swallowed nervously, then took a single step toward the square of darkness… but then a loud crash away to his right almost made him jump out of his skin, and the jerry can fell from his grasp and clanged heavily to the flagstones.

Then, from one of the crypt's deeper chambers, something lurched out of the shadows into the lamplight, and Charlie almost let it have both barrels before he realised that it wasn't the beast.

It was a human figure, a man, but a man who had been through a terrifying, traumatic attack.

Something in the Arlington soup, something impossibly corrosive, like a powerful kind of stomach acid, perhaps, had eaten away at his flesh and clothes alike, melting the material into his flesh and melting some of his flesh down to the bone, and his own mother would have been unable to recognise his ruined face.

He had lost his left arm and most of his shoulder to the beast's appetite, but the enormous wound seemed to have been almost cauterised by the acid. One of his eyes was milky and blind, but the other rolled, madly, trying to look in all directions at once.

Then the rolling eye settled upon Charlie, and the poor soul began to babble.

He tried to approach Charlie, but suddenly he fell, and Charlie saw that his foot must have been dangling by a strap of ligament and skin which had now snapped entirely. The man struggled not to scream, but as his body hit the stone floor, the rest of his skin seemed to burst open, splitting like the skin of a sausage in a hot pan, and his screams were unearthly, the screams of the damned in hell.

Charlie was rooted to the spot, appalled and horrified, until the poor wretch settled into an uneasy, quivering silence. He hoped the man was dead, or was about to die. No human being was meant to endure so much agony. Then the man began to whisper something, inaudible at first, but slowly rising until Charlie was finally able to make out the words. And as soon as he was able to understand what the man was saying, he knew for certain who the man was.

It was Elms.

He rushed to the butler's side, and knelt beside him, but didn't dare touch him. His flesh was now smoking in the chill, dank air, and he seemed to be melting into the ground. But still he tried to speak.

'I'm so sorry, sir…so sorry…heard the creature trying to get out…getting wilder, angrier…you were gone too long…thought if I made the offering it might be appeased…but it knew I wasn't the one…the bargain was broken…'

Charlie tried to comfort him, but it was impossible. Every few seconds a fresh spasm of agony ran through the diminishing pile of flesh that was his body like an electric current, and then his screaming was unbearable, forcing Charlie to clamp his hands over his ears.

At a rare moment of relative calm, he leant over and glanced down into the pit. The lantern dangled at the end of its rope, revealing the depths of chamber, which were empty. The beast had not yet returned.

'…it means to end the family, sir…I'm so sorry…I failed…forgive me…'

Charlie turned back to the butler and had to stifle a scream of his own. Elms was now almost a puddle of liquid flesh, his bones also liquefying and turning into a substance that Charlie realised resembled the soup itself far too much for his peace of mind.

For the first time, he really began to wonder about the beast's origins. Had it actually once been human itself? Some innocent, ordinary human that had come into contact with something unnatural and evil? Something not so much cursed as *infected*?

Elms inhaled massively, for the final time. His skull had now almost collapsed, and his jawbone, as he struggled to speak, was like rubber.

'…can't fight it…have to run, sir…go far…far away…run…now…'

Elms was dead, and was, in fact, no longer precisely Elms. Only his right hand had been untouched by the soup, just like Stephanie's. The rest him was molten flesh and a kind of translucent jelly. Charlie could not seem to take his eyes off the butler's remains, but then he noticed something even more awful.

The mush which was all that was left of Elms was still moving. Slowly, almost imperceptibly, it was crawling over the stone floor toward the pit, as though consciously seeking shelter.

Charlie stood up on shaky, uncertain legs, and he knew that whatever courage had brought him all the way across the Atlantic and down into the crypt, whatever sense of moral outrage had been fuelling him so far, it was now spent and utterly gone.

He decided that Elms' final words had been perfectly correct. The only sensible thing to do now was to run far, far away, and for once in his life, he was going to do the sensible thing. He began to back away from the terrible sight of the new portion of soup making its way to the pit. Now it seemed that the butler really *was* a part of the old family, or very shortly would be.

'Goodbye, Elms,' he whispered. 'I'm so sorry I was late…'

Now, you get yourself back to the old jalopy, Charlie-boy, he thought to himself, trying to regroup his thoughts as quickly as he could. Take the jerry can with you and empty it straight into the Jaguar's tank, and then simply drive away. Don't look back. Drive back to Southampton as quickly as you came, drive like the devil, and let's see that damned soup try to follow you there. Climb straight back on the Queen Mary, if you can, and sail back to New York with the morning tide.

Let's see that infernal muck try to swim the Atlantic Ocean!

He picked up the jerry can from where it had fallen, and then turned and planted his foot on the first step... and then he saw it.

The soup was now absolutely huge.

It had gathered in an enormous throbbing mass at the top of the crypt steps, and although it was faceless and therefore eyeless, it nevertheless seemed to be staring directly at him, looking into him, and recognising him for who and what he really was. Then it began to move slowly forward, oozing down over the first riser, and then the second, and then the third, with what seemed like a playful but very deadly intent.

Charlie tried to match its murderous progress in reverse, with a series of clumsy little backward steps that made him feel off-balance and unbearably vulnerable. In the soup's cloudy, gelatinous depths he could see so many terrible new ingredients shifting around and around, as though in motion with a digestive current.

An arm here, a head there, and a long purple and grey thread of intestine, as though it had unwound some poor soul like a ball of twine.

It was at this precise moment that Charlie really began to accept that his life was quite probably at an end. He didn't believe that any single man could fight and defeat a creature like this, however he might be armed, and he felt that whatever he did now —

whatever lengths he might go to, whatever tactic he might try — it would make no real difference to the eventual outcome.

The soup would take him as it had taken the rest of his family, it would tear him to pieces, and then it would begin to digest him while he was still alive and in absolute agony.

Even the *thought* of experiencing the horrors of Elms' hideous death at first hand almost amounted to a kind of torture in itself, and he had no intention of subjecting himself to the stark reality. Not when he had the means of deliverance from such a terrible demise in his own hands, not when he already possessed the tools he would need to escape into peaceful oblivion.

'You'll not have me, vile monster!' Charlie cried with sudden decision, and then tossed the jerry can to the foot of the crypt steps.

Almost as though it knew what he meant to do, the soup began to pour down the stone staircase like a flash flood.

Charlie raised the Purdey, calmly settled the leather-covered stock into the hollow of his shoulder, and very deliberately sighted down the length of the barrels.

One good shot, one direct hit on the petrol-filled jerry can — that was all he really needed. The resultant blast and fireball may or may not injure the beast in any way shape or form, but Charlie was reasonably confident that even if he didn't manage to kill *himself* outright, he would at least be able to knock himself unconscious, which would probably be just as good under the circumstances.

Meanwhile, the soup came on faster and faster, and almost seemed to be rolling down the steps now, in a virtual tsunami of greed and rage. But Charlie knew that it would not be able to reach him in time. He was supremely confident on this point.

Luck had nothing to do with it.

'Too late, you infernal soup!'

Just as the beast was about to engulf the jerry can with its bulk, Charlie began to tighten his finger on the Purdey's double triggers and widen his stance to steady himself for the inevitable recoil... but, as he stepped back, his foot landed in what was left of his butler and slipped out from under him as if he had trodden on a slick bar of soap.

The shotgun went spinning off into the darkness of the crypt, unfired, and Charlie tumbled backwards into the pit.

The long drop seemed to last no time at all. One second he was slipping, the next he had hit bottom and broken what felt like every bone in his body. The pain was colossal, immense, unthinkable. It was all too much for his mind and body to process, and he blacked out for a few moments.

When the world came back into being, he could feel something soft and spongy cushioning his head when he tried to move it, and he knew that it was probably blood and brain matter, because his skull must have shattered like the shell of a soft-boiled egg dropped on the kitchen floor.

Also, there was a long spur of burning pain that began in his lower back and then seemed to lance up through his guts, and he thought despairingly of the stag-handled knife he had stuck in his belt earlier.

A few moments later, he noticed that Elms' remains had continued to liquefy and were now descending into the pit one drop at a time. As he watched, something a little larger dropped and bounced to a halt directly in front of his face. It was the butler's single surviving feature, his unclouded eye, which seemed to regard Charlie with a terrible sense of awareness before it, too, began to dissolve into goo.

With the last reserves of his strength, Charlie turned his head again, and peered to see beyond the dangling lamp's luminance — to see the soup come to claim its prize.

He didn't have to wait very long.

First he saw it as a shadow looming large and blocking the high distant square of light at the pit's entrance, and then, in much more detail than he cared to see, as it approached the lamp. Then it dropped even lower, easing down the walls, briefly enveloping the lamp and then releasing it.

Finally, it hung suspended only a matter of inches above Charlie's broken body, and the lamp light from above highlighted the depths of its translucence. Far back, beyond the other limbs and body parts, he saw his father's detached head slowly revolving in some internal digestive vortex. His father's dead eyes were either open or the lids had been eaten away, and the irises were bleached white.

Charlie knew that he was staring at his own terrible fate. But he wasn't beaten yet.

Not just yet, he wasn't.

His right arm seemed to have escaped the very worst of the injuries he had received in the fall, and he managed to get his right hand into his inner coat pocket and brought out the Derringer. Of course, possessing only the single shot it still wasn't much of a weapon, but then it really didn't need to be — because it wasn't for the beast at all, it was for Charlie himself.

Without the slightest hesitation, because he knew how little time he had to save himself from a torturous death, he brought the tiny pistol up to his head and stuck it in his mouth.

Then, with a last flourish of bravado, he tried to tell the soup that it could go to hell, but it came out wrong, it came out sounding like he had a hot potato in his mouth, or, perhaps, a silver spoon.

Nevertheless, the beast seemed to draw back suddenly, as though it might have changed its mind. But Charlie knew that there was to be no last minute reprieve, and he was not fooled for a single second. Instead, he silently commended his soul to God, and then pulled the Derringer's trigger…

…and a small compartment built into the top of the pistol sprang open and a tiny yellow flame appeared from it.

Charlie, all but cross-eyed trying to hold the flame in focus, stared in disbelief and horror.

The Derringer wasn't a real weapon, after all. It was simply a novelty cigarette lighter… and the soup had *known*, he was sure of it. It had known all along, and it had actually waited to see if he would try to use it, waited and watched, for its own perverse amusement.

Charlie had time enough to cast the useless trinket aside with a rough curse, and time enough to open his mouth to beg for mercy, but that was all.

Then the soup dropped on him and drowned him, flowed into his mouth and ears and eyes, and slowly began to digest him, one screaming layer of nerve cells at a time.

For the Arlington family, it was the end of the line.

# (Excerpt)

*This is a very brief taste of Comeback, my first ever published horror novel, which is about Sam Parker, a writer whose fictional city, the hellish City of Eldritch, and some of its more fearsome citizens, are beginning to make bloody inroads into the real world.*

Far sooner than he had ever expected, Sam found himself in his attic office with the night pressing at the windows like a giant moth. He was a little chilly even though he'd exchanged his wet clothes for dry ones, but like everything else the chill didn't register in his mind, because his mind was already full to bursting.

Sam blinked and he was sitting before his computer, which had been fired up. He had no memory of moving there, or of turning on the power.

He opened a new file with the format he always used for his novels. It was time to be honest, he thought. When you were looking at a blank screen that was the only thing to be if you wanted to write something worthwhile. He had told the audience at the convention that he'd just taken a holiday from

Eldritch. That's what he'd told everyone, including his agent and his friends.

But really, it was more like he'd run away from the city.

For some reason he didn't understand, the idea of writing the thirteenth Eldritch novel had begun to fill Sam with absolute dread the very moment he had finished the twelfth. The more so because he knew exactly what it would be about, what it *had* to be about. It had a pre-ordained quality he didn't like, but couldn't trust himself to resist.

Hence the distraction of the *Deep Water* novel. By looking at unfamiliar skies he had felt that he was striking a blow for self-preservation, and it had worked for a while. But holidays end, and someday everyone has to come home. As Sam was home now. He was wary of his fear and apprehension, but he still wanted to write the book. He wasn't sure he even had a choice.

One of his office walls was dominated by a large, framed Eldritch promotional poster. In heavy Gothic type against a blood-red background, it featured the three-word epigram that prefaced every Eldritch novel, and which had given the Eldritch fan club its name.

*Stories Never End.*

Sam had always believed that. He believed it now.

Unconsciously, he had allowed his hands to creep into the home position on his keyboard, and now he consciously pulled them back. Intellectually, he knew that he couldn't start this book. He hadn't planned anything. He had no synopsis, no outline, no notes. But tonight his intellect was asleep and his gut feeling was in control, and this told him that the story would write itself.

Even the title was a foregone conclusion, referring as it did not only to the ultimate ambition of the book's protagonist, a former Eldritch crime-boss who was dead and didn't want to be, but also to Sam's own return to the city.

No plan, no synopsis, no outline, but Sam knew exactly how it would begin, and where. Still filled with that strange combination of fear and excitement, he let his hands go back where they wanted to be. The keyboard, like his house, felt like home.

It was time to tell the world what really haunted Sly Jack Road.

He began to type...

# 10

## *COMEBACK*
### *Part One*
## *THE BEGINNING*

### *CHAPTER ONE*

*Smooth Harry Flanagan, talented seducer of Eldritch's young women, had parked under the trees less than ten minutes ago with a pretty little seventeen-year-old called Rena White. Rena was a bright girl who knew her own mind, or thought she did. "Take me* somewhere spooky, Harry," she'd demanded, so he'd driven her to the spookiest place he knew, Sly Jack Road.

Smooth Harry had opened the windows and lit Rena a cigarette even though he didn't smoke himself, because he was smooth enough to realise how sophisticated the cigarette made Rena feel. She was bright but she was still young enough to deceive herself that easily.

Perhaps it was thinking of her as a child that encouraged Smooth Harry, more than twenty years her senior, to tell Rena a few stories about dirty old Sly Jack Road. About the number of bodies reputed to have been buried here over the years, in shallow graves, and about the unquiet spirits that walked here after dark.

Tonight the night was dark indeed, and at this hour very few cars passed along the country lane. Even if there had been a traffic jam, however, the cars' occupants would not have seen Smooth Harry's ride. The old Honda Accord was black, and Smooth Harry had parked it deep under cover of the trees on the eastern side of the road. It was a good spot for intimacies, explorations, and fledgling understandings. He had used it before.

The ghost stories were going down very well, which was precisely what Smooth Harry was hoping young Rena would do after he'd loosened her up a little. Rena had lovely white skin, and when aroused or excited her face and arms turned bright pink, as though she'd just stepped out of a hot bath. Smooth Harry was desperate to see if the rest of her body reacted the same way.

Rena was staring at him with those big, big eyes as he spoke and the cool night air slipped into the car through the open windows. Without interrupting the flow of the story he was telling her - and making up as he went along, as it happened - Smooth Harry casually leaned across to take off Rena's safety belt. As he eased the belt across, he let the back of his hand graze over her breasts and felt that her nipples were already hard, like little knuckles under her blouse. Her colour rose and her eyes seemed to shimmer and dilate at his touch, but Smooth Harry never let on that he had noticed, because that wouldn't have been smooth.

He wanted to be so careful, so gentle with this one. He was gentle with most of his conquests, those who needed it to be gentle, but this one was special. He didn't understand why, but this one was very special.

*Smooth Harry's mouth, spinning tales, seemed to be working independently of his brain, which was making up its own story. He imagined Rena's mini-skirt rucked up high around her waist, little black panties twisted into a glistening cord dividing her labia, her white thighs spread wide and burning like radiators. So gentle. Her sweet succulence oiling his fingers. The provocation of her nipples to bite, bite, bite. But so gently. He saw the image of his large tanned hands roving over her small white body, roving everywhere, before they settled on her throat, her white throat.*

*Her throat.*

*Wind soughed in the dark, giant trees, and the night that entered the car also entered Harry. There were whispers, snaking through and around the girl's heartbeat, skipping like stones over the incoming tide of his own pumping blood, and he reached for her. He wanted to be gentle, and he thought he was being gentle. Even after it was all over, he still believed that he'd been gentle.*

*It was only when Sly Jack Road stopped speaking to him that he realised its voice had ever been there at all. But by then, of course, it was too late. The evil had been set in motion, and it had attained its first claw-hold in the long struggle.*

*To come back.*

*The next thing Smooth Harry knew, his car was moving again, cruising through the neon wasteland of Eldritch's strip. Then he saw a blue light flashing in the Honda Accord's rear-view mirror…*

Sam's fingers lifted from the keyboard and he felt the flow of power halted, as though an electrical circuit had been broken. He frowned at the screen, now filled with words, and wondered what had broken his concentration. Then he heard Jo softly calling his name. Before he had begun to write, the unexpected voice would probably have made him jump like a kangaroo. Now, simply because he had written something, all his fear and nervousness had evaporated, and it evoked nothing but mild surprise.

He swivelled around in his captain's chair. Jo was on the stairs, her head barely appearing above floor-level. She looked sheepish. There were a few tears in her eyes, and she was trying to smile. She looked human again.

'I've come to apologise.'

Sam nodded. She wouldn't have come back otherwise. 'Why don't you come up?'

She glanced at the monitor behind him. 'Are you working?'

'Yes. It's Eldritch time again.' Sam was amazed that he could announce this so calmly.

'Then I won't come up. But I'd like it if you came down. I mean, if you can, if you're not too busy...'

To show Jo there were no hard feelings, Sam put on a brief pantomime of frantically saving his work, as if he couldn't wait to join her. He heard her laugh a little, and thought that everything between them would be all right.

She waited for him on the stairs until he came, and then took him by the hand to lead him down to the first floor and into the bedroom where she had lit two aromatic candles, one either side of the bed. She swung the door shut behind them and grabbed Sam in a fierce embrace, which he responded to passionately. Her hand snaked around to the front of his jeans. They kissed almost hard enough to bruise.

'We could have been doing this all night,' Sam breathed into her mouth.

'Yes, but then you wouldn't have started the new book.'

Eventually, Jo sat him down on the end of the bed. 'We can't make love,' she said.

'No?'

'No. It's my time. That's why I've been in such a terrible mood, I suppose.'

'I would have been happy if we were just together,' Sam said. 'All that stuff earlier was just−'

'I know, I know. But shush now. *Shush'*

Jo let down her hair, which seemed to have regained its life, and it cascaded over her shoulders in rich, glossy waves. She knelt between Sam's thighs and gently pushed him onto his back.

'Just lie down.'

Sam closed his eyes as she began to fondle and stroke him through his jeans. After a few moments of divine pressure, she unbuckled his belt one-handed and then pulled down his pants. Her soft hand continued to stroke and roll, pull and tug, but then withdrew.

Sam opened his eyes to see what she was doing.

'Shush,' she said again. She lifted her sweater over her head and dropped it to the floor. Underneath, she was naked, her body magnificently heated. 'I'm going to take care of you now.'

Jo leaned forward between Sam's thighs, her heavy breasts mashing against his balls, and then bent her head to take him into her mouth.

Sam gasped. He reached out to hold her hair back so that he could see her face, and then abandoned himself to image locked to pure sensation, to a world where words didn't matter.

## *Other Works*

## <u>Crime</u>
(writing as PJ Shann)
The Queen of Hearts
Perfect Day
Perfect Peace
The Hunted Man 1: Old Dog New Trick
The Hunted Man 2: Identity Crisis
The Crime Short Story Collection

## <u>Horror</u>
(writing as Jim Mullaney)
Comeback – a novel
The 1st Horror Short Story Collection
The 2nd Horror Short Story Collection


Please visit me at:
**storiesneverend1.wordpress.com**
or my **Amazon Authors Page**
or contact me at:
**crimemysterysuspense@gmail.com**

*Thanks for Reading*

37529621R00168

Printed in Poland
by Amazon Fulfillment
Poland Sp. z o.o., Wrocław